RIVAL DEMONS

THE SHADOW DEMONS SAGA, BOOK 5

SARRA CANNON

DEAD RIVER BOOKS

To Kris.
For all the bedtime stories told to your little sister in the dark.
You taught me how to imagine.

A WHOLE NEW LIFE

I lifted my eyes to a foreign sun, inhaling the fresh scent of flowers as warmth seeped into my skin. I wanted to throw my tired arms into the air and twirl around like a little child.

I'm alive!

Jackson's warm hand entwined with mine, and I smiled. He had come for me. Standing there in the ritual room, I had believed I was dead. But the moment I saw his face and felt him pulling me through the portal, a whole new life opened up to me.

He took me into his arms. I leaned against him, my legs weak. I hadn't eaten in days and my wrists and ankles were raw from the Order's iron shackles. Still, my heart swelled with love and gratitude.

Behind us, Lea shouted for help.

I turned to get my first real look at the scene. The blue light of the portal radiated out from a wide circle of black roses. Through the blinding light, I could just make out the

Peachville ritual room on the other side. A black, inky darkness began to spread along the right side of the light, like an eclipse.

That's when I noticed Lea standing beside the portal, a silver sword grasped in her hand. She swung the blade toward the black roses, severing them from their stems with furious precision.

"Come on," she yelled. "I need help. If we don't move fast enough, they'll regrow."

Mary Anne fell to her knees before the portal, wincing as her injured leg hit the rocky ground. She pulled a tiny dagger from her belt and began cutting the roses one-by-one.

Jackson sprang into action, grabbing another sword from a large duffel bag on the ground at our feet.

Disoriented, I watched as they worked to close the portal. With each severed rose, more of the blue light darkened to black. A strange fog began to ooze from the opening in the portal, moving across the area with startling speed. A vicious wind roared around us as the fog grew thicker. The swirling vortex blew me backward like a tornado. I struggled against it, throwing myself onto the ground and crawling toward the circle of black roses.

Frantic, I began pulling the roses from their stems, not even caring as thorns sliced into my palm. Black petals flew all around us as we worked, but just as Lea reached the last handful of black roses, something broke through from the Peachville side.

The figures moved so fast, I could only make out two streaks of orange, moving like flames across the fog. I screamed as one streak collided with Jackson, sending him straight to the ground.

I scrambled toward him, then froze as my eyes adjusted and the figure on his back came into clear view.

A tiger. And not just any tiger. One of the shape-shifting twins who had come after me in the field when the Order of Shadows first captured me. One of the tigers who had stood outside my cell at Shadowford for the last week, making sure I would never go free.

SOME KIND OF NIGHTMARE

The orange and black tiger bared its sharp teeth, lowering them toward Jackson's throat.

Forgetting my exhaustion, I lunged toward them. I wrapped my arms around the tiger's middle and tumbled over the top of it, wrenching it away from Jackson's body. The entire left side of my body hit the rocks at full speed, and I cried out. The tiger, unhurt, straightened itself and hissed at me.

I felt like I had entered some kind of nightmare. Time moved slowly, and the tiger leapt toward me, vicious claws extended. Instinctively, I threw my arms up to shield my face, but before the tiger could reach me, a stream of black energy raced toward it, slamming into her with such force that by the time she hit the ground, she was in human form again.

I looked over my shoulder at Jackson. He stood tall, his chest heaving with each breath. Black smoke flowed from his hand to the auburn-haired girl, holding her to the ground.

I stood, every muscle in my body protesting. "She has a

twin," I said, looking all around us. All I could see was the dark fog that surrounded the entire area around the portal. From where we stood, I couldn't even make out where Lea was. All I could see was the faintest blue of the portal's light somewhere to our left.

"I know," he said. "I'm sure they came through together, those two are inseparable."

Panic coursed through me. "What about Mary Anne? We have to find her." I took two steps toward the portal, bracing myself against the fierce wind. "Mary Anne," I screamed.

No one answered.

I knew Lea was capable of taking care of herself, but against one of the twins, Mary Anne would be in serious danger. We had to find her.

When I turned back to Jackson, he had wrapped his black energy tightly around the first twin. She was bound in smoke-like chains, struggling hard against them but getting nowhere.

"Will those things hold her?"

Jackson nodded. "For a little while," he said.

"Then come on," I said, gripping his arm. "We have to find the others."

We ran toward the portal's light.

Lea sliced at the black roses with her sword, but before she could clear them all, the ones at the beginning had begun to grow back. Frustration twisted her features. "I can't get the portal to seal," she said. "These damn roses are growing back too fast."

"Keep working," Jackson said, searching for his lost sword. "We can't let anyone else come through."

I swayed on my feet, my head spinning. I thought of the days of no food, lying on the hard wooden floor of Shadowford's attic, waiting for death. Please, tell me I hadn't escaped that only to end up right back where I started.

Through the bright light of the portal, I could see another one of Priestess Winter's servants preparing to enter the shadow world. Even in my exhaustion, I understood what it would mean if more of the Order broke through this barrier and dragged me back through. In Peachville, I was a dead girl.

I couldn't let them win. I wanted to live.

I had to find a way to keep the witch from coming through. My aching muscles protested as I lifted my arms to cast. I wasn't sure it would work, but I thought of the shield Zara had taught me to use. What if that shield could work like a barrier? It might give us the extra time we needed to put a more permanent seal on the portal.

I summoned every drop of energy I could find and concentrated on creating the shield. I knew I wouldn't be able to hold it long, but I hoped it would give them enough time to destroy the circle of roses.

Just as my shield went up, I heard a loud roar behind us.

I couldn't hold my concentration and the shield dropped. I cursed and bit back tears.

From the corner of my eye, I saw the second tiger twin pounce toward Jackson. This twin's coat was similar to her sister's but was colored with orange and white instead of black.

"I've got this one," Jackson said, fury and hatred in his eyes. "You help Lea."

I turned back to the portal just as the tiger dove forward. It took a lot of willpower not to look back to see what was happening. I had to just trust that Jackson knew what he was doing. For now, it seemed to just be these twins who had broken through to the demon world. If Lea couldn't seal this portal, we would all die. We couldn't fight off an entire coven of witches, especially if Priestess Winter was one of them.

I had to find a way to connect to my true power. I lowered my weary body to the ground and sat crisscross against the cold obsidian rock. I steadied my breathing and let all of the noise around me fade away. In my mind, I pictured one of my mother's cherished white roses. Finally connecting to the energy inside of me, I tried again to create a barrier against the witch's attacks.

And this time, it worked.

A DARK POWER

Spells blasted into my shield, leaving the taste of dark magic on my tongue.

On the Peachville side, the witches worked to bring down the barrier I had created. My strength wavered, but I forced myself to hold on. Just a few more seconds. My body screamed as my energy slipped away. I wanted to sob. I wanted to give up.

I wanted to lie down and sleep for a hundred years.

But more than any of that, I wanted to survive.

I exhaled, feeling the last of my power slide through my fingertips. When I thought I couldn't give more, the portal shifted, sealing with a sucking noise. A deafening silence settled on us as the wind stopped.

Beside me, Lea leaned over, trying to catch her breath. Black petals and stems were strewn across the ground in every direction. She had finally managed to close the portal, and for the first time since I'd met her, I actually wanted to hug her.

But we weren't out of danger yet. The twins were still on

the shadow world side. I turned to find Jackson and Mary Anne as the fog cleared.

Jackson had the white tiger pinned to the ground and she quickly shifted back to her human form.

Her dark green eyes practically glowed as she snarled up at me. "You'll never be able to hide from us," she said. "The Order won't stop until you're dead. All you're going to do is get your friends killed right along with you."

"That's a chance we're willing to take," Jackson said, wrapping a smoky black ribbon around the girl's mouth.

"Let her go," someone shouted. A flash of movement off to our right caught my eye as the other twin shifted into her orange tiger form, lunging toward Jackson with such speed I didn't have time to do anything but watch.

Her claws scraped Jackson's arm, streaks of blood staining his t-shirt. He cried out and let go of his hold on the first twin as she shifted into her white-tiger form. Both tigers now moved with incredible speed, circling me in an instant.

I tried to run, but they kept me trapped between them.

Lea laughed, and I jerked my head toward her. Seriously? With Jackson injured, me trapped, and Mary Anne nowhere to be found? How could she be laughing at a time like this?

Apparently, the twins were wondering the same thing. The orange tiger stopped circling and turned to stare at Lea. "You think it's funny that your precious Prima is going to die?"

"No, actually, I was just wondering what you think you plan to do with her now that you've got her surrounded," Lea said, smiling and raising an eyebrow. "In case you didn't notice, I sealed the portal. Trust me, there's no way anyone's going in or out of that thing for a while. How exactly are you planning to get Harper back to Peachville?"

The white twin growled low and bared her pointed teeth at me.

"We'll kill her here and now," the orange twin said.

"You won't kill her," Lea said. "If the Order simply wanted her dead, they would have killed her a long time ago. No, the Order has gone to a lot of trouble to keep her alive, so they could transfer her essence to a new Prima. Don't ask me why. For some reason, her essence is special to them. You need her alive, so they can complete their ritual."

The white twin shifted into human form and grabbed my arm so hard I knew it would leave a bruise. I tried to pull away, but the events of the past few weeks had finally caught up with me. I had no strength left. Only anger.

"You underestimate the power of the witches on the other side of that portal," the twin said. "They will break through soon, and when they do, all of you will die. Including Harper. Only her death will happen in the ritual room while yours will happen instantly."

"The Order doesn't have the upper hand in this world," Jackson said. I'd never seen such rage in his eyes before. Blood dripped from his shoulder, but he barely seemed to notice. "Nothing they can do will open that portal for at least another few hours. Do you really think you'll still be alive by then?"

As they argued, I scanned the area, searching for Mary Anne. She had to be here somewhere. Maybe she had gotten scared and run off to hide? But where? Around us, the black rock seemed to stretch on for miles. Far in the distance, I could see some type of forest, but there was no way she would have been able to see that in the fog.

No, she had to be close.

Then, I caught sight of a small form collapsed against the

rocks about fifty feet away. My stomach twisted. Oh, God. It was her. And she wasn't moving.

Tears burned my eyes. They spilled down my face and soaked into the fabric of my dirty white ritual dress.

"See?" the orange twin said, amused by my tears. "Even Harper knows there is no hope now. Open the portal and maybe we can convince the Order to let you live."

"What did you do to her?" I asked, my voice a whisper. I had meant to put more sound behind it, but I was breathless and scared. I tried again. "What did you do to Mary Anne?"

At first, the twins both stared at me, as if they had no idea what I was talking about. Then, the white twin followed my gaze over to where Mary Anne lay motionless against the rocks. She stifled a laugh.

"Oh, her?" she said. "The little bird tried to peck my eyes out. I had to put her in her place."

Rage boiled up within me, searing my skin. Mary Anne had risked everything to save me. More than once. She didn't deserve this, and it was all my fault. She'd come here to keep me safe. How could I have let this happen?

Deep inside, a dark power burned through me like liquid fire. I acted on instinct, knowing only anger. They needed to pay for what they had done.

I burned like a fever, my flesh becoming like hot coals. The white twin let go of me and stepped back, staring at her blistering hand in horror and confusion. Slowly, I lifted both of my hands upward. The ground beneath us rumbled and all around, pieces of black rock rose into the air. The force of my hatred consumed me. It seemed to rip me apart, splintering me into a million little pieces. I wasn't myself. I was something dark and furious. Anger rolled through me, consuming me. In my mind, all I could see was Mary Anne's unmoving body. All I wanted was revenge.

I focused all of my anger on the white twin. Without even thinking, I summoned the crushing weight of all those rocks on her.

The rocks flew through the air at lightning speed. Before anyone could react, the white twin was crushed and buried between a mound of rocks six feet high.

The sister threw herself onto the pile, screaming and clawing at the rocks. When I realized what I had done, I lowered my hands and fell to my knees. I had killed someone.

The strength drained from my body, leaving only an empty shell.

I struggled to stay upright, but suddenly, I was falling down, down into a sea of never-ending blackness.

The last thing I heard before I slipped out of consciousness was the sound of Jackson calling my name.

FOR FOREVER

A fire roared nearby, sending shadows dancing across my eyelids.

My eyes fluttered open, protested against the light, then closed again. I moaned, my body aching against the hard rock.

A warm hand touched my cheek.

Jackson.

I didn't even have to open my eyes to know it was him. His hands were slightly rough and smelled of evergreens and firewood. I smiled, my dry lips cracking painfully.

"How long have I been asleep?" I asked. My throat was sore.

"Almost two days," he said.

That woke me up. My eyes flew open in surprise, and I struggled to sit up.

"Whoa, take it easy," Jackson said, his arm slipping around my back. "You've been through so much in the past couple weeks."

Every muscle in my body protested as I came to a sitting position. Ouch. I guess lying on a cold stone floor for two days straight hadn't helped the situation. To be honest, it wasn't much better than the torture room they'd held me in at Shadowford. At least here my hands weren't shackled. I rubbed my wrists absently. They were still sore and bruised from the chains the Order had kept me in.

Then, I remembered.

The twins. Mary Anne.

I teetered backward, my stomach turning. Jackson's strong arm held me up.

"Thanks," I said, tears stinging the corners of my eyes. I looked around the dimly lit cave. "Is Mary Anne..."

Jackson motioned toward the back corner of the cave, and relief filled me as Mary Anne came into view. She was lying down, but there was no mistaking the rise and fall of her chest with each breath.

"She's going to be okay," Jackson said. "She has a pretty mean scratch across her face and a bite on her side, but she's going to be okay. A few scrapes and bruises, but she'll heal. Like you."

Would I heal? I stared down at my tattered and bloodied dress. Yes, the wounds on the outside would heal, but I had killed someone out of hatred and anger. That was going to take some time to deal with.

"The twins?" I asked, my voice cracking.

Jackson reached into a black backpack and pulled out a large bottle of water. "Here," he said. "Drink this."

I stared down at the backpack. Had he brought that with him through the portal? I hadn't noticed it before.

The water was lukewarm, but beautiful. It slid down my

sore throat like rain on a barren field, healing all the cracked parts. By the time I finally came up for air, there was only a small sip of water left in the bottle.

"Thanks," I said.

"Do you want some food?" he asked, avoiding my eyes. He rummaged through the backpack instead.

My stomach growled at the thought. I was empty. A shell.

But I wanted to know the truth about what happened. About all of it.

"Just tell me," I said. "Did I kill her?"

Jackson paused, his head hung low. The fire crackled. "You can't blame yourself for what happened," he said. "She was going to take you back to the Order. You had no choice."

I shook my head, the tears coming now. "That isn't true. You guys weren't going to let her take me back," I said. "I don't know what got into me. When I saw Mary Anne there on the ground, I just snapped. I never meant to kill her, I swear I didn't."

Jackson wiped away a tear as it slid down my cheek. "I know you didn't," he said. "She wasn't a good person, Harper. She was evil, just like the rest of them. And if she'd had the chance, she would have killed us all."

I knew what he was saying was true, but it didn't make me feel any better. The power I'd used to move those rocks had come from a deep dark place, and I never wanted to go there again. I'd completely lost control.

"What about the other one?"

Jackson sighed. "When you collapsed, all I cared about was getting you to safety," he said. "The other twin was out of her mind, screaming and pulling on the heavy rocks. I knew once she saw her sister's dead body, she would come after you. And I had a feeling she wouldn't care about the Order's rules."

"So, you just left her there?" I asked.

He nodded. "I don't even think she noticed we'd gone," he said. "I scooped you up and Lea grabbed Mary Anne, then we came here."

I studied our surroundings again. We were in some kind of cave. Behind Jackson, there was a small opening, and I could see Lea sitting at the entrance keeping guard. A warm fire blazed in the center of the room. The walls were made of the same black rock we'd seen on the ground near the portal, so I guessed we were still somewhat close to where we started.

"Where are we?"

"We're on the coast, a couple of miles from where the portal to Peachville opens," he said. "We couldn't risk taking you too far, with both of you injured. Lea and I know this place from when we were kids. We'll be safe here for a little while."

I put my hand on his knee and his eyes flickered toward the entrance. Toward Lea. Awkwardly, he shifted away. "I'm really glad to see you awake."

"Awake and very hungry," I said with a nervous laugh. I had a feeling I still didn't understand everything that was happening here. Why had he moved away from me?

Jackson reached into his backpack and handed me some crackers. "Take it slow," he said. "You haven't eaten in a while and if you eat too fast, it's just going to make you sick."

I looked at the bag of crackers in my hand. Then, I lifted my head and studied the rest of the cave. Several blankets were laid out like sleeping bags. Lea's duffel bag full of swords lay toward the back of the space. The food, the water, the supplies.

How long had they been preparing for this trip to the shadow world?

I took a bite and chewed slowly, questions swirling in my brain.

"What exactly happened back there? In Peachville?" I asked.

"What do you mean?"

I shook my head, trying to find the right words. "I mean, one second I thought I was going to die and the next you were there, pulling me through the portal. Was that planned? Or just some rash decision?"

"After the Order took you away, we searched for you," he said. "We thought they might take you to the headquarters for the Order, but we couldn't find you anywhere. No one had heard or seen anything. Then one day at school, Mrs. King pulled Mary Anne to the side and warned her that the Order had locked you away on the third floor of Shadowford. They had the room heavily guarded at all times. We tried to find a way inside, but they placed a strong seal against the door inside Shadowford and there was no way in. Luckily, Mary Anne overheard Mrs. Shadowford talking to the priestess about their plan to take you to the ritual room and transfer the line."

I nodded, listening. I tried not to let him see that my hands were shaking.

"That's when we knew the ritual was our best chance," he said. "We knew that if we rescued you and tried to run, the Order would find us eventually. You weren't safe in the human world. Here, though, we would have the upper hand. We knew we could find a way to keep you safe here."

"So, what's our plan?" I asked. "Now that we're here? Do you think they'll send anyone else through after us?"

Jackson took out a bag of chocolate and popped a few pieces into his mouth. "We're pretty well hidden where we are right now. I don't know if they've broken through the portal just yet, but you can bet they'll have someone looking for us. If not one of the witches from their side, someone on this side for sure."

I frowned. "This side?"

"Yeah, they have lots of servants on this side, both demon and witch," he said. "If I had to guess, I would think they'll be sending hunters after us."

"What are hunters?"

"Witches who have been here for over a hundred years," he said. "They're the ones who decide which demons are taken to be slaves in your world."

"So, they're humans?" I asked, confused. "How do they live so long?"

"They were human at some point," Jackson said. "But I wouldn't really call them that anymore. They've performed dark magic for so long, they've been corrupted by it. Plus, time is different here in the shadow world. Humans who are bound to demon energies will live a lot longer here. And the hunters, sometimes they're bonded to more than one demon."

I shuddered. More than one demon? That had to make them both extremely powerful and extremely evil. I didn't like the sound of someone like that hunting me in a strange world.

"How long do you think we'll stay here?" I asked.

Jackson looked toward the mouth of the cave, his gaze lingering on Lea. "Another day or two, max," he said.

I leaned back against the wall of the cave and ate a few more crackers. We would probably have to stay out of Peachville for a long time. At least until we could figure out a way to either defeat the Order or free Aerden. But at least we'd be back in the human world soon.

"Then what?" I asked, hoping he'd already come up with some kind of brilliant plan for getting back without the Order finding us.

"Then we're heading to a place called the Underground," he said. "We'll be safe there as long as we can convince them to let us in."

"Why wouldn't they?"

Jackson shifted uncomfortably. "The demons in the Underground aren't exactly fans of most humans considering most of the humans they've ever known were members of the Order," he said. He looked at Lea again. "I'm sure we'll be able to get in, though. Lea has some pretty serious connections in this world."

I paused. "Wait, so this place isn't back home?" I asked. "It's here in the shadow world?"

Jackson's shoulders slumped, and he bit his lip. "Harper," he said, pausing as if to find the right words. "You can't go back home. I thought you understood that."

I stopped mid-chew. What was he talking about? I studied his face, trying to make sense of it. Then, my hands began to tremble. "For how long?"

It took him a long time to answer, and when he did, it cut me straight to the core.

"For forever."

HOW CAN YOU BE SO SURE?

Had I heard him right? There was no way he expected me to live in the shadow world for the rest of my life. That was ridiculous. I must have misunderstood.

"What do you mean forever?"

"I mean, you can never go back there, Harper," he said. "The Order of Shadows is too powerful. They'll find you no matter how far we run."

"So, we find a way to fight." I pulled my knees up close to my chest. Despite the fire, I was shivering. "And what about Aerden? Do you just plan to leave him over there all alone? Eventually I will die, you know. Even here. Then what?"

Jackson closed his eyes, his jaw clenched as if trying to keep himself from saying something.

"I won't just sit back and let them win, Jackson."

His left hand balled into a tight fist. "You're not listening to me," he said. "They'll kill you. Or did you forget everything that happened a few days ago? If we hadn't shown up and brought you here, they would have killed you."

"But you did show up," I said. "Alone, I might not have a chance, but if we all stick together—"

"We barely made it out of there alive," Jackson said. "We didn't even have the power to fight them all. They're too strong. All I did was freeze them just long enough for us to pull you through the portal. If we had stayed to fight, we'd all be dead right now."

"Maybe so," I said, practically shouting at him. "But it was four of us against a few dozen of them."

Toward the back of the cave, Mary Anne shifted and moaned. I took a deep breath and lowered my voice.

"What if we built an army?" I asked. "If we find enough witches and demons to fight with us, we could win with sheer numbers."

"And how are we supposed to do that?" he asked. "Every time we get a coven of witches on our side in the human world, the Order kills them all without hesitation. And here in the demon world? There're a handful of rebels, but most demons are under the rule of the King of the North who would rather ignore the Order's entire existence while our citizens are stolen out from under us."

"Maybe we could talk to the king. Reason with him. Tell him what we've seen the Order doing to the demons. Maybe he just doesn't understand."

"The king isn't going to listen to a human," Lea said, taking me by surprise.

I hadn't heard her move from her spot at the mouth of the cave. She stood next to the fire and nudged a log with the tip of her boot, sending sparks up into the air.

"Then maybe he'll listen to you and Jackson," I said.

"We are the last demons he would listen to," she said. "Besides, he isn't going to change his mind about the Order. He's a coward when it comes to fighting them."

"How can you be so sure?" I said, lifting my chin defiantly.

Lea laughed and shook her head.

"Because he's my father."

RIVALS

"You're a princess?"

"You say that like it's so hard to believe," Lea said with a sly smile.

In her leather pants and tight corset top, she didn't look like any princess I had ever imagined. Plus, she didn't exactly seem refined and regal. She was definitely more biker chick than royalty. Of course, I had no idea what royalty even meant in the shadow world. Maybe their princesses were supposed to be tough and snarky and difficult in every way.

"Close your mouth," she said. "You look like an idiot."

I hadn't even realized I had my mouth open. I shut it quickly, embarrassed. "I'm sorry. I'm just surprised I guess."

"Don't be," she said. "My father didn't think I was good princess material either. I was a constant disappointment to him and my mother both."

"Is that why you left?" I glanced from her to Jackson. I had a feeling I knew why she left, but I wanted to hear her say it.

She shrugged and sat down. "Partly, I guess." She looked

down at her boots. "And partly because Jackson had gone. Aerden was my friend too, you know. We all grew up together. And my father? Well, he refused to help after Aerden went missing. He was too scared of what the Order might do to his kingdom if he invaded their territory."

I bit my lip. She'd gone because of Jackson, not his brother. I felt pretty certain of that. "So, your father is the king of the entire shadow world?"

"No," she said. "The world is divided into two kingdoms. The north and the south. My father is the King of the North."

"And what about the King of the South?" I asked. "Would he be willing to help us?"

Jackson and Lea exchanged silent looks.

"What?" I hated it when they did that. It always made me feel like they were keeping things from me. Or maybe what really bothered me is that they were obviously sharing in something I couldn't be a part of.

"Forget about the entire Southern Kingdom," Jackson said. "They won't help us."

His answer wasn't good enough for me. I knew he wasn't telling me the whole truth. "Why not?" I pushed.

"Because the two kingdoms are rivals," Lea said. "Enemies of the worst kind. If anyone so much as crosses the border between lands, the king has them thrown into his dungeons to rot. Wars have been fought in the lands between the kingdoms, leaving nothing but ghosts and monsters. Even if we wanted to, we'd never make it there alive."

I swallowed nervously. The way Lea's voice cracked a bit when she said ghosts terrified me. If it was something she was this obviously afraid of, it was something I wanted no part of.

"Does the Order take demons from their side of the shadow world too, then? Or is it just the north?"

Another look passed between Jackson and Lea. I wanted to confront them about it, but I was so tired of being angry.

"We don't know," Jackson said. "I would assume so, yes. But there's been no communication between the two sides for a very long time. The Southern Kingdom is completely separate from us, as if they were a part of a totally different world."

"I never came across any demons in the human world who were from the south," Lea said. "But that's not saying much, especially since I couldn't find a way to communicate directly with any of the demons who were already slaves. It was rare to find a free demon like Jackson or myself."

"So it's possible that the Kingdom of the South would want to fight against the Order," I said. "Even if it meant pairing up with some of the demons in the north for a little while."

Lea rolled her eyes. "You don't know what you're saying," she said. "This rivalry is ancient. There is hatred so strong between my father and the King of the South that nothing, not even a common enemy, could bring them together."

Frustrated, I leaned back against the wall of the cave. How would she know if no one had ever tried? If no one had talked to the demons in the south for more than a hundred years, how could they possibly know what was going on over there?

"It's complicated," Jackson said. "Don't forget that demons are immortal in this world. Here, we don't pass into the Afterworld unless we choose to, or unless our lives are wrongfully taken from us."

"Immortal means forever," Lea said. "And trust me when I say that forever is an awfully long time when it comes to holding a grudge."

I had so many more questions, but I was having a hard time keeping my eyes open. Besides, it seemed like each answer just led me to another question. And since we weren't leaving this world any time soon, I figured I had time to ask more questions later.

"I'm going to lie back down," I said. I curled up close to the warm fire and willed my mind to stop spinning.

Lea got up and walked back toward her post at the cave's entrance.

Jackson leaned over me and placed a warm kiss against my forehead. "When Mary Anne wakes up, we'll try to get on the road," he said. He placed a blanket over me, and I pulled it close. "Get some sleep. I'll be up front guarding the entrance to the cave if you wake up and need anything, okay?"

I nodded, then closed my eyes and fell fast asleep.

SHATTERED

A gentle nudge woke me the next morning. The fire had long since gone out, but a shimmer of light gleamed in from the mouth of the cave. I yawned and looked up, surprised to see worry on Jackson's face.

"What is it?" I whispered. "What's wrong?"

His eyes darkened, but he forced a smile. "I want to show you something."

I pushed the blanket from my body and sat up, wincing as my bones cracked and my muscles protested. I wondered how long it would take before I started to feel normal again.

I still wore the white ritual dress the Order had put me in on the day they intended to sacrifice my life. It was stained with blood and dirt and a long tear ran up the side. I could only hope Jackson wanted to show me a fresh pair of clothes and a place to take a shower.

Mary Anne and Lea both slept toward the back of the cave, and we were careful not to disturb them.

My feet ached against the rocks at the cave's entrance. No

shoes. I frowned down at my dirty feet, pale against the craggy black rock. This was going to be a problem.

Jackson wrapped his arms around me and pressed his lips to my ear. "Look," he whispered.

I had been so busy looking at the ground I hadn't even noticed the shadow world beyond the cave. When I lifted my eyes, the beauty of the place took my breath away.

The sky shone in silvers, blues and pinks that shimmered against the water of an endless ocean. I knew we had been hiding out in a cave, but for some reason, I hadn't noticed the sound of the water crashing against the rocks below. All that stood between us and the ocean was a small ledge about ten feet wide that ran in a winding path up and down on either side.

"It's beautiful," I said, wishing I had stronger words.

In some ways, it was like earth, but it was also different. The colors were brighter and more alive. More shimmery and full of motion. And somehow everything just felt... bigger.

Daring to look down, I stepped carefully onto the rocky path and leaned out over the edge. The side of the cliff was steep and cut an almost straight line down to the water. If I had to guess, I would say it was at least two hundred feet down. Still holding on to Jackson, I turned and looked up, shocked to see the top of the cliff was almost just as far away.

"How did you even find this place?"

He smiled. "Aerden and I found this cave when we were really young. We used to explore all over the place back then. Besides, it's not quite as scary when you can fly."

I laughed. He had a point.

"So, this is close to where you grew up?" I turned back

toward the water and sat down on a smooth black rock at the edge of the cave.

Jackson sat down next to me, but when I moved to take his hand, he pulled away.

"Relatively close," he said, acting like nothing had happened. "We're close enough that we could get there before nightfall if we walked it. But Lea and I wanted to make sure we were far enough away that we could avoid being detected by the Sentinels."

"Sentinels?" I asked. I tried to keep the conversation going, but I couldn't help but feel something was off with him.

"The king's guards, I guess you could call them," he said. "They're supposed to patrol the countryside and protect all of the towns, but they really only protect the king and his council. When we first came through the portal, we were trying to avoid casting any magic, hoping they would never know we'd come through. After the tigers came after you, though, we had no choice."

"What's wrong with magic?" I asked, not understanding.

"Our magic leaves a signature here," he said. "Something others can trace, even from great distances."

I stared out over the water, speechless as a second sun rose, sending a blast of lavender-colored light across the silvery clouds. There was so much to learn about the shadow world and how things ran here. I had so many questions; I knew there was no way to get them all answered this morning. I chose my questions carefully.

"How come Lea doesn't want to see her father?" I asked. "Wouldn't we be safer in the city if we had the Sentinels to protect us?"

"It's complicated," he said. "When Lea left to come to the

human world, she was in direct disobedience to her father's orders. The king doesn't take well to being disobeyed."

"You're saying he would hurt her if he knew she was home?"

"No." He bit his lip and ran a hand through his hair. "I don't know. Maybe? He would definitely punish her, probably lock her away for a while and never let her leave again. For her, that would be the same as torture."

"So why even risk coming back here?" I asked softly. I knew she hadn't come back because she cared about me. It was obvious Lea didn't give a crap about me. In fact, I was pretty sure she hated me. So why risk everything?

"Because I asked her to," Jackson said.

His words were simple, but to me, they cut like a knife. All he had to do was ask and she was willing to risk her entire life's work? Leave her best friends behind in the human world? Ever since Jackson had first introduced me to Lea, I knew there was more to their story than just an old friendship. Now, with him acting weird and pulling away from me, I wondered just how much there was between them.

I wanted to ask, but I was too afraid to find out the answer.

"Thank you," I said finally. "For coming to get me. You saved my life back there."

Hesitating, he took my hand in his and brought it to his lips, kissing my skin softly. "I was so scared when they took you away from us. I couldn't bear it if something happened to you."

The feel of his lips against my skin felt amazing, but I was confused. What was really going on between us? I turned to meet his eyes.

The sadness that crossed his eyes twisted my gut. "They held you captive for eight days," he said. "Those were the worst eight days of my life. I wasn't sure I'd ever see you again. I'm so sorry, Harper. I told you I would keep you safe, and I just let them take you."

I scooted closer to him on the rock and put my arms around him. He stiffened, then slowly returned my embrace, hugging me tight.

"It wasn't your fault," I said. "I never should have gone wandering around in that field. I never should have left the camp. I got too confident that we were okay after all that traveling. I completely underestimated the Order." I looked down at my tattered dress. "I won't let that happen again."

Footsteps sounded behind us, and Jackson pulled away as if I'd burned him.

"Can I talk to you for a second?" Lea asked, tension in her voice.

Jackson sighed, then excused himself.

Together, they walked back into the cave, whispering too low for me to hear. Lea seemed to be lecturing him about something, and whatever it was, Jackson wasn't happy about it. A dark feeling came over me when Jackson returned, his expression tight.

His jaw tensed, and he began to fidget. "Harper, there's something else I brought you out here to talk about."

The seriousness in his voice made my insides twist. I shifted on the rock, suddenly feeling very uncomfortable.

"We're leaving today to go to this place I was telling you about earlier," he said. "The Underground."

"Okay," I said, waiting for the bomb to drop.

"I just thought it would be good for you to understand how things work down there," he said. "As far as rules and magic and politics."

I cleared my throat, finding it difficult to swallow.

He rubbed his palms against his jeans. "There are some rules I'm going to need you to follow."

He pulled a small vial from the pocket of his jeans. The liquid inside glowed deep purple.

"What's that?"

"Joost made potions for you and Mary Anne before we left the human world. They will make you see all the demons down here as if they were human. It will also make you hear everything in English rather than the demon language. He thought it would help make your transition here smoother."

"That was nice of him," I said, taking the vial from Jackson and uncorking it. "How long will it last?"

"For as long as you're here in the shadow world," he said.

I stared down at the liquid. Part of me was curious to see the demon world exactly as it was. I'd seen Aerden's true form a couple of times before and even though it was different, he hadn't really scared me. Still, an entire city of demons speaking in a foreign language might get to be a bit overwhelming. Especially if they all were staring at me like they hated me.

I took a deep breath, then emptied the vial into my mouth and swallowed. Surprisingly, it tasted sweet.

"What else?" I asked. The first part hadn't really been a rule, I noticed, but I let him continue.

"We can't cast any magic until we get down there," he said. "It's too easy to track."

I nodded. No magic. Easy enough as long as we weren't being attacked.

"You said it was just until we got to the Underground though, right?" I asked. "Can we do magic once we get down there?"

"Yes, they are so deep under the surface and buried under a special stone that blocks the trace from being seen or felt by anyone up on the top," he said. "Once we get down there, magic use will be fine. Still, you'll want to play it very low key, okay? It will be very important that you listen to me and do what I tell you."

I chewed on my inner lip. I had never been one to respond well to the phrase 'do what I tell you'. But I would try to behave.

"What else?" I asked, suddenly feeling that the worst was yet to come.

He looked up, staring out across the ocean. His knee jerked up and down. There was still something he was nervous about having to tell me.

"Just say it," I said, my stomach full of butterflies. "How bad can it be?"

Jackson ran his fingers along his forehead, then finally met my eyes. "You know how I feel about you, right?"

Ouch. That was never a good start to a conversation. "Yes," I said, a tremble in my voice.

"Once we leave this cave, we can't let anyone know we have any sort of relationship beyond the fact that you're connected with my brother."

I swallowed but felt a lump of worry stick in my throat. Was he breaking up with me?

"It's forbidden for shadow demons to have romantic relationships with humans," he said. "The way my people see it, that's how we got into this mess with the Order in the first place. Friendships are tolerated, when the human is sympathetic to our cause, but never more than that."

I tried to breathe, but despite the open air, I suddenly felt very claustrophobic. I couldn't find my voice.

Jackson stood up and stared out at the water, his body tense. "It's not like I wanted things to be this way," he said, finally turning toward me. "But we don't have any choice. The Underground is the only place where I can guarantee that you'll be safe."

Safe. And completely alone. It was obvious he and Lea had already discussed this, which only hurt me more. The idea of staying down there forever was bad enough when I thought we were going to be together. But the thought of never kissing him again or feeling his arms around me? Or worse—watching him fall in love with Lea? What kind of life was that going to be?

"I won't go," I said. He couldn't make me go somewhere I didn't want to go.

Jackson's face grew red. "Yes, you will," he said. "I won't sit back and let the Order take you away from me again."

I stood, scowling. "No, but you'll willingly take yourself away from me in the name of safety. How is that any different?"

"At least this way I can watch over you," he said. "You'll be alive and safe."

"And completely miserable?" I shook my head. "That's not the life I want."

"You'd rather have no life then?" he shouted. "Don't be stupid, Harper."

Tears welled up in my eyes, and I swiped at them. "I don't understand why we can't just keep running," I said. "If you really love me, why wouldn't you do everything you could to be with me? There has to be someplace else where we could hide. The mountains. Somewhere out there on the ocean. This can't be the only choice."

Jackson put both hands on my shoulders and held me tight. "Harper, don't you know that I would give anything to be with you?" he said. There were tears in his green eyes for the first time. "Believe me, if I thought there was any chance we could run from the Order, I would run until the end of time. But they would find us. They would kill us both. The Underground is our only chance. It's the only place you'll be safe."

I pulled away and leaned against the side of the cliff. This couldn't be happening.

"Harper, please." Jackson stood behind me, the warmth of his body against my back. He leaned his forehead against the back of my head, but despite his closeness, I could already feel a deep well growing between us. "Please."

Tears streamed down my face. There was no winning this argument. He had already made up his mind.

"Okay," I said. My heart shattered deep inside my chest. "I'll go."

I didn't want to look at him. I just wanted to stare out at the ocean and let the sorrow crash over me like a wave.

But Jackson pulled me closer. "Harper, look at me."

I met his clear green eyes as he leaned in to kiss me one last time.

Our lips were wet with salty tears, and for a moment, I thought I might drown in them. I wrapped my arms around his neck and pulled him close as if he were my life-raft. The kiss deepened, and he pulled me tighter, both of us desperate for it to never end.

But eventually, all things must come to an end.

THE CLOSEST THING I HAVE LEFT TO A FAMILY

B ack inside the cave, I sat beside Mary Anne and waited for her to wake up.

Jackson and Lea moved toward the entrance to discuss plans for the journey to the Underground, but I wanted to be as far away from them as possible right now. Inside, my heart was breaking. How could Jackson do this to me? How could he sweep me away to this place, give me hope of a better future, then take it all away? It wasn't fair.

I couldn't imagine a life where I would be standing next to him, yet forbidden to touch him.

I would go to his Underground. Get my strength back. Learn to take control of my own magic so that someday I would be able to leave and fight the Order on my own. There was no way I could stay there for the rest of my life.

Beside me, Mary Anne shifted and moaned. I leaned over her and felt her forehead. Her fever seemed to have passed, but her skin was still deathly pale except for the red scratch across her cheek.

Jackson was hoping to leave this afternoon, but I wasn't so sure she'd be ready to travel.

Her eyes opened slowly, and she squinted up at me. "Harper?"

"Hey," I said with a smile. "How are you feeling?"

"Like I got bit by a tiger," she said. She laughed, then winced and grabbed her side. "There's something I never thought I'd say."

I shook my head and felt the guilt tear through me. "I'm so sorry," I said. "I got you into this mess."

Mary Anne placed her hand on mine. "It's not your fault," she said. "I came here of my own free will."

I paused. "Why did you come?" I said it softly, not wanting her to think she wasn't wanted. I just didn't understand why she risked her life to come save me.

She held both hands out to me so I could help her move into a sitting position. It took her a few seconds to get herself upright, but when she did, the color started to return to her cheeks. "You're the closest thing I have left to a family," she said simply. "I wasn't about to let them hurt you. Besides, eventually the Order would have figured out that I was the one who told Jackson where to find you. I don't think they would have liked me too much, at that point."

I raised an eyebrow. "You have a point there."

"So, what are those two up to over there, all secret-like?" She nodded toward Jackson and Lea at the cave's entrance.

I turned to look at them, an instant pang biting into my heart. Lea was a demon and therefore, completely fair game for him. He said his feelings for me wouldn't change, but who knew what might happen after years of being in the Underground? And the two of them already had a past I didn't understand.

I did my best to shake it off. "They're planning our trip to the Underground."

Mary Anne grabbed a bottle of water and just nodded. Apparently, the Underground was not news to her. They must have talked about their plan before they left our world.

"What do you know about it?" I asked. "The Underground?"

She shrugged and swallowed. "Not much, I guess. Just that it's deep under the surface and that magic can't be tracked down there. Some kind of shield blocks it from the upper world," she said. "Jackson said we'd be safe there for as long as we needed to stay. I just hope they let us in."

"Did he tell you that they don't like humans?"

"Yeah," she said. "But only because they've never really known any humans that weren't a part of the Order. I think they'll warm up to us pretty quickly. Especially after they hear about what we've done to fight back against the Order."

I nodded, but I was worried. What if we'd just traded one miserable life for another?

IT REALLY IS YOU

Miserable or not, there was no turning back now. Jackson and Lea decided on a route that would take us to one of the Underground's portals. They were used to traveling fast by demon form but using their magic would set off warning signals to both the Order and Lea's father. It was too risky. Especially if Lea's father had already realized she was here. He might already have his Sentinels out searching for her. We would have to walk it.

By the time Mary Anne felt well enough to walk on her own, the first sun was already setting. Walking in the dark made me nervous, but Lea said we would do better under the cover of darkness, anyway. Since one of Jackson's many talents was that he could see in the dark, he led the group up the side of the steep cliff.

My feet argued with each step I took on the black rock. I tried to maneuver to the smooth places, but every once in a while, I would hit a jagged part and the pain would shoot through my entire leg. In a way, I almost didn't mind the pain.

I felt numb after hearing Jackson's news, so the pain in my feet was a reminder to keep moving forward.

I kept one hand on the cliff wall at all times. Somehow, we all made it to the top. When I stepped out onto the blue-green grass of the nearby field, I realized just how tense I'd been holding my body. My shoulders were practically attached to my ears.

I took a deep breath in and out, letting the panic melt away. No amount of breathing could get rid me of my fear and sadness, though.

"We're heading toward the Obsidian Forest," Jackson said. He pointed off to the east. "See there?"

In the far distance, I could see a wall of trees, black as night and thick as any forest I'd ever seen.

"Ominous," Mary Anne said.

"We should keep moving," Jackson said. He was all business. "Stay close, and be as quiet as you can."

"Yes, sir," Mary Anne said. She followed closely behind Jackson, but the way she limped made me wonder if she really was up for this trip. Lea had offered to carry her part of the way, but she'd refused and said she was fine.

I hung back from the group a little bit. Being too close to Jackson right now just made me ache.

The grass slid under the bottom of my feet like oily snakes. Had it rained here? The ground squished with each footstep, and I had small seeds snuggling between my toes. Definitely an improvement over the solid rock, but I kept glancing down to make sure there were no bugs crawling on me.

Soon, though, the second sun began to slip below the horizon, leaving nothing but darkness and the light of a single amber moon that rose slowly above the trees of the Obsidian Forest.

No one spoke as we walked, and unlike home, there were no crickets or frogs to sing into the night air. The only sound in my ears was the sound of the light wind as it hissed across the tips of the grass. I let the steady rhythm of each footfall lull me into a kind of hypnosis. I wanted to forget the horror of the attic at Shadowford. The nightmare of facing death. The heartache of forbidden love.

Walking here, in the grass under a foreign moon, might be my last real taste of freedom for a long time.

I opened my heart to it, letting myself be vulnerable to the night for just a moment. I tried to remember a simpler life, but when had my life ever been simple? Maybe in the very earliest of days before the first fire. Before my powers had ever manifested. But my memories of those days were few and far between. It was easier to remember the tough times. The bad foster homes and the fear of knowing I was different.

My whole life, I'd longed to fit in and belong somewhere. I'd wanted to find other girls like me, who could move things with their mind and see the world the way I saw it.

Be careful what you wish for.

I sighed. Who would ever have thought that finding those girls would lead to all this?

As we walked in silence, I wondered what Lark and the others were up to back home. Had things gone back to normal? Did they ask about me? Or had the Order wiped their memories? I thought about the fact that somewhere in that town, I had a half-sister. A real flesh-and-blood family member. Everything had happened so fast after the night I'd first read my mother's journal, I hadn't had time to think about my sister very much.

She might only be a half-sister, but I wanted to find her more than anything. She was my father's daughter, and maybe if they both were still alive, we could have a normal family someday.

Well, normal except for the witch thing. Was my sister a witch? I guess I'd never given it much thought. Just because she'd been born in Peachville didn't mean she was part of the Order.

Still, as I looked up at the rising amber moon, I wondered when I would ever get back there to look for her.

Up ahead, Jackson froze, then crouched down toward the ground. He put a finger to his lips and motioned for us to get down. I broke away from my thoughts and dropped to my knees in the tall grass. I looked all around, trying to figure out what had him spooked.

I held my breath, not wanting to make a sound in the near silence. Somewhere in the distance, the grass rustled with movement. My legs tensed, ready to run. I didn't know who I was more scared of. The sentinels, the hunters, or the crazed twin whose sister I had killed. My heart raced.

I turned my eyes to Jackson, waiting for some cue to run or fight.

After a few minutes, he stood and gestured for us to follow again. This time, I kept my attention in the present, not wanting to make a mistake that could cost us our lives. We only made it another half-hour before seven flames appeared in the distance.

Jackson must have seen them the split second after I did. Quickly, he ducked behind a large boulder, furiously signally for the rest of us to hide.

I watched as the flames drew closer. I could see now why

Jackson looked so frightened. Walking in a straight line across the field were seven men in matching black and red uniforms. The Sentinels? It had to be. Magical orange flames hovered in the air beside each of them, illuminating the area like large torches.

I held my breath and crouched even lower to the ground. Everyone else in our group was dressed in dark colors, but my white dress stood out against the night. If the light caught it at all, the Sentinels would see us for sure. Then what would become of us? Jackson made it sound as if we'd all be thrown into the dungeons.

The Sentinels drew closer, their light reaching almost to the rock where we hid. Five or six steps to the right and the flames would have given us away.

The four of us huddled close, a mass of tension and beating hearts. Even Lea seemed frightened of her father's men. I don't think any of us took a single breath or moved a muscle until the men had safely passed us by.

"That was close," Lea said.

"Too close," Jackson said. "We're going to have to try to move faster. I think we'll be safer once we get into the darkness of the forest."

I stood and stretched out my aching legs. I reached my hand out to Mary Anne, helping her up from the ground. She winced and held her side for a moment.

"Are you okay to keep going?" I asked her.

She nodded, but I could tell she wasn't feeling well. "Let's just get somewhere safe," she said. "I'll be fine."

Not wanting to waste another moment, Jackson once again led us toward the outline of trees in the distance. Even though we'd already been walking for a while, the forest still looked far away. It was going to be a very long night.

I wasn't sure how much time had passed when I could have sworn I heard a twig break nearby. I turned around, frightened and half-expecting to see a Sentinel standing behind me. But the area was dark and silent.

Jackson came back around to me, following my gaze toward a couple of outlying trees. "What is it?" he asked.

"I heard something," I whispered. "Like a branch breaking under foot."

He listened for a moment, then shook his head. "I don't see or hear anything," he said. "Maybe it was just an animal or something."

"Yeah, maybe," I said. A feeling in my gut told me otherwise, but maybe it was just my fear talking.

Then, about twenty minutes later, I thought I heard footsteps behind me in the grass. Just in front of me, Mary Anne flipped her head around. Judging from her wide eyes, I'd say she heard it too.

"Jackson," I said. "There's someone following us. I heard footsteps."

"Me too," Mary Anne said. "But I don't see anyone."

Worry darkened Jackson's features. He looked toward Lea. "What do you think? Do you sense anyone? See anything?"

Lea turned in a circle very slowly, taking her time to study the areas around us. "If someone is following us, they're very good at concealing themselves."

She motioned toward a cluster of small bushes and rocks just ahead, then whispered something in Jackson's ear. He nodded, then told us to follow him as if nothing were wrong.

When we reached the bushes, Lea stealthily dropped from

the group and hid behind them while the rest of us kept moving forward. I wasn't sure exactly what was going on until a few seconds later when she leapt out from behind the bushes and placed her hands around the biceps of an unusually small man with spiked hair and a very large nose.

As soon as we saw what was happening, the rest of us ran back toward her.

"Why are you following us?" she asked, her eyes locked on the man's face with a deadly focus.

"Princess," the man said in a breathy voice. "It really is you. Your father has placed a reward for anyone who finds you, you know."

He struggled against her grip, suddenly breaking free. His body started to turn to black smoke as he shifted to his demon form, but before he could complete his transformation, Lea reached into her pocket and threw a glittering powder on him. The man froze like a statue in mid-shift, half-man, half-smoke.

"Damn," Jackson said. "What do we do now?"

"We keep moving," Lea said. "Only faster this time. The powder will only hold him for an hour. Maybe two if we're lucky."

"There's no way we'll make it to the portal in an hour," Jackson said.

"Not if we keep wasting time," Lea said.

Without even discussing it, she lifted Mary Anne onto her back and began to run toward the tree-line. Jackson turned to me, our eyes meeting in the near-darkness as he reached out and lifted me into his arms. I threw my hands around Jackson's neck and buried my face in his shoulder as he ran.

I tried not to think about our past or how this would probably be the last time I felt my body pressed against his. I focused only on the rhythm of his feet against the ground.

When we reached the edge of the Obsidian Forest, we stopped and looked back, the silhouette of the frozen man black against the night sky.

OUT OF THE SHADOWS

Under the canopy of the Obsidian Forest, all light ceased to exist. I kept waiting for my eyes to adjust and for something to come into view. A tree. A shadow. Something. I could put my own hand two inches away from my face and never see it.

"I can't see anything," Lea said. "We'll have to set them down and walk together."

Jackson helped me back to my feet. "Harper, hold Mary Anne's hand. Lea take Harper's free hand and use your other one to grab onto my arm," he directed.

We formed a chain and began to move through the darkness. Jackson moved fast, and I struggled to keep up, my heart pounding as I tried to catch my breath. The journey through the forest was terrifying. Around us, the wind howled, and animals moved in the trees. It took some serious willpower not to jump every time a vine slipped across the skin of my leg.

An eternity seemed to pass before finally, up ahead, the faintest strip of moonlight appeared in the distance. Around me, the shadowy figures of the trees, low bushes and under-brush began to form.

"How much farther?" I asked.

"We're getting close," Jackson said. He pulled a tattered piece of paper from his pocket and unfolded it. "The map says it should be just past the edge of the forest on this side."

Minutes later, we finally emerged from the forest. Even the moonlight seemed brighter after the pitch darkness we'd been in. I broke off from the others and stood on my own, staring up toward the amber colored moon, noticing that now, there were two moons in the sky. One amber and one lavender. It was breathtaking.

"We have to keep moving," he said, taking off down a path that led along the edge of the forest.

Soon, we came across a small bridge that floated over a stream running with icy blue water.

"This way," Jackson said. He motioned for Mary Anne and me to cross first.

I stepped up onto the bridge, half expecting it to wobble since it was just floating in the air, but it was surprisingly sturdy. I was over to the other side in five steps. The grass beyond was strange and stiff, almost white, as if it were frost-bitten.

I studied the new terrain as the others crossed the stream.

A field of white grass was cut into an almost-perfect circle. All around it were large red stones, like markers of some sort. In the center of the circle was a cluster of something black, but from this distance I couldn't quite make out what it was. I stepped out onto the stiff white grass, my legs instantly breaking out in goosebumps.

"Wait," Jackson called, then jogged over to me. He pulled

me back off the grass. "It's enchanted with frost. If you tried to walk all the way to the middle, you'd be a frozen block of ice before you got there."

My eyes widened. "You can't be serious."

"I'm deadly serious," he said. "See the ring in the middle? That's where we're heading."

"And how do we get over the enchanted grass without using magic?" I asked.

"You don't," a voice said, coming out of the shadows just beyond the stream.

I turned, my muscles tense and on high-alert. The man who spoke was tall and lean with dark tanned skin and hair as black as night. His eyes gleamed almost white. He squinted at us in the darkness, weapon drawn.

"Jericho," Jackson said. "Old friend. Don't you remember us? Denaer and Lazalea."

It took me a moment to realize Jackson was giving this demon their true names. I realized, with a pain in my heart, that I had never heard his true name until this moment.

Denaer. So much like his twin brother's name. It sent chills through me, making me feel as if even after I'd felt so close to him, there was so much I still didn't know about him.

The demon he'd called Jericho straightened, then stepped closer, shaking his head. "It can't be," he said. "But you disappeared years ago. We haven't heard a word from you in ages."

Lea moved to him, extending her hand. "Jericho, don't tell me you've forgotten me already?" There was a sweet coaxing to her tone that I'd never heard before.

Jericho bowed his head to her. "Princess Lazalea," he said, his voice cracking a bit on the words. "It's an honor to see you again."

"Thank you," she said. "But please, you don't need to bow. We're the ones who have come here to ask a favor of you. And I'm afraid we're in a hurry."

Jericho's eyes searched the small group. His attention flicked from Mary Anne to me, not even trying to conceal his distaste. "Human witches?" he asked. "Are they your prisoners?"

"No," Lea said. "They are our friends, and they're in serious danger. The Order of Shadows is searching for them as we speak. It's extremely important that we gain entry to the Underground."

Jericho lifted his head, surprise on his face. "Princess, you can't ask such a thing of me," he said. "Humans are not allowed below."

Lea's patience was growing thin. I could see the frustration and determination in the set of her jaw and the way her feet were planted firmly into the ground just outside the white grass. "Listen to me, in a few minutes this forest will be crawling with Sentinels. My father knows I'm here, and he's going to come looking for me," she said. "Now, if that happens and he finds me here with two human girls, we both know he'll throw me into his dungeon. Then, he'll probably leave these two witches to fend for themselves here in the shadow world, and believe me, it won't take the Order long to find them."

"I'm sorry Princess, but I—"

"This witch in particular," she said, cutting him off and pulling me forward, "is extremely important to the Order of Shadows. Believe me when I say they will do anything to capture her. We can't let that happen, Jericho. She is bound to Aerden and we have promised to protect her life. If you feel any loyalty to me at all, I ask you to please let us in."

Jericho's eyes shifted back and forth between Lea and me. He looked frightened and unsure. "She's important to the Order?" he asked.

"She's critical to their plans," Jackson said, stepping forward. "As enemies of the Order, we have a duty to protect her. Now, please. We're running out of time."

The demon seemed to be at war within his own mind, wringing his hands together nervously. Finally, he nodded. "Okay, then, let's get underground as soon as we can," he said. He moved to the white grass, then turned to look at me over his shoulder. "Stay on the black path at all times."

I opened my mouth to tell him that I didn't see a black path, but before I could say a word, he lifted his hand and a black oozing smoke drifted from his fingertips down to the grass, slinking along the white toward the middle, turning everything in its path a shimmering black.

He moved quickly along the new path, so we all followed. As we approached the center, though, I hesitated, my heart skipping a beat. There, in the center of the frosted grass was a perfect ring of black roses.

"What's wrong?" Lea asked.

I shook my head and pointed to the center. "I'm sorry," I said. "I just have some bad memories of black roses."

Lea narrowed her eyes and looked from me to the circle of black roses. "Don't you remember the roses at the portal when we first came in?" she said. "It's perfectly safe."

Mary Anne shifted beside me, obviously uncomfortable with the roses too. It was her family who had been using the black roses. They'd gotten the dark magic from old spell books of the Order of Shadows. Mary Anne had probably seen them used several times in her childhood.

Jackson spoke up. "Harper, the roses work a bit differently here than back in the human world," he said. "The black roses act as a conduit, pulling the essence of a witch or a demon into the black rock below. It's the same kind of rock you saw in the human world. A soul stone."

I was listening, but so far, he hadn't convinced me.

"The difference here is that instead of a small soul stone that traps the power inside, the entire ground below this area is made of this special magical rock," he said. "When a demon's being passes through the stone, the black roses on the other side, underground, help pull them through and out the other side. I promise, it's safe. Just a little scary at first."

"We don't have time for fear," Lea said. She moved forward without hesitating even for a second. She stepped over the roses and into the circle. "I'll go first."

Lea disappeared in the blink of an eye.

"She's fine," Jackson said. "She's in the Underground below us now."

I peered over the edge of the roses and noticed that in the center was an iridescent black rock that looked exactly like the soul stone the crow witches had used to steal Caroline's power back in Peachville. Jackson's explanation didn't make complete sense to me, but I knew we didn't have another minute to waste.

"Okay," I said. "I'll go next."

I knew Jackson would want to go last, and I wasn't about to let Mary Anne go through until I knew for sure it was safe.

I took a deep breath and with shaky legs, stepped into the circle.

THIS WILL BE DIFFICULT

A subtle energy hummed through my body, starting with the bones in my feet and traveling up my legs, hips, torso, down each arm and up through my skull. It was nothing like the painful torture of the black roses in the woods near Shadowford.

I turned to meet Mary Anne's eyes and was about to tell her that everything was okay when an overwhelming feeling of lightness and separation came over me. For a split second, I ceased to be. Everything went dark. I knew the sensation of falling, but I couldn't feel my body anymore. It felt as if I were a ghost passing through a wall. A mist of a person. I separated, then came together again, landing on my feet at the bottom of a cool dark cave.

I stumbled. Tried to catch my breath.

"Are you okay?" A woman's voice.

I was too disoriented to answer. All I could do was hold on to the wall and close my eyes, praying for the world to stop spinning.

"She's fine." Lea this time. I could tell by the level of sarcasm.

My stomach twirled and twisted, but I refused to throw up down here in front of Lea and this stranger. Most demons I'd met already thought of me as a weakling. I didn't want to give them the satisfaction of thinking they were right.

I took a long breath in, counted to three, then let it out; slow and steady. I pushed away from the wall and stood strong on my own two feet. "I just need a second," I said. "I'm fine."

I let my eyes focus on the girl standing next to Lea in the small corridor. She was petite and beautiful. Her black hair was braided into at least two dozen thin braids that hung all the way down to her waist. Her lips were painted a dark red and her eyes were as black as coal.

"I'm Harper," I said, ignoring the fact that she was staring at me like I was diseased.

"Marlana," she said, not meeting my eyes. She looked up toward the ceiling, then placed her hand on a dark stone embedded in the wall beside her.

Mary Anne popped down beside me. She wobbled. I reached out to her and held her steady.

"Just give it a second," I said in her ear. "You're safe, it just takes a minute to get over the dizziness."

Her breaths were shallow and quick. Her eyes were closed shut as if she were scared to open them and see where she'd landed. I held tight to her to give her some reassurance that everything was going to be okay. Her hands trembled slightly, and she brought her elbow in close to her right side, wincing.

I looked down toward her wound and saw a fresh red blot of blood spreading across her shirt. I looked at Lea, alarmed. I didn't say a word because I didn't want Mary Anne to freak out, but this didn't look good. Lea stared at me in confusion until I nodded toward the wound.

I pulled Mary Anne closer, careful not to bump her wounded side. I looked up at the ceiling like the demon girl had done, wondering when it would be Jackson's turn to come down here. He'd said magic couldn't be traced this far below the special stone. It worked like a barrier of some sort. I prayed that meant he could use his healing powers to heal Mary Anne's side.

The ceiling of the corridor was covered in black roses. They hung upside down, seeming to grow out of the soul stone. I had no idea what Marlana had seen when she looked up there before, but apparently, she could see something my human eyes couldn't. After a few seconds, she glanced up there again, then placed her hand on the dark stone on the wall. It had to be some kind of lever that opened the passageway.

Jackson came through in a rush of cool air, completely unfazed by the process. He took one look at my face and knew what was going on. "Mary Anne?" he asked, touching her shoulder. "How are you feeling?"

She didn't say a word, but her lip trembled. She laid her head against my chest, and I could feel her small frame shaking.

"Can you help her?" I asked.

"What's the problem?" Marlana asked, stepping forward.

"She was injured by a witch when we first came through the portal to the shadow world," Jackson said. "I thought she was healed enough to come through the soul stone, but it might have been too hard on her. I can do a little bit to stop the bleeding, but I'm not a full-scale healer. Would it be possible to get her to your shaman?"

Marlana frowned. "The shaman isn't going to want to help a human," she said.

The disdain in her voice made me want to punch her. I opened my mouth to give her a piece of my mind, but Lea spoke before I could.

"Perhaps I can convince her to help," Lea said. She nodded to Jackson and he lifted Mary Anne's shirt over her wound.

Not caring about the blood that trickled through his finger-tips, he placed his hand directly on the gash in her side. The black energy of his magic manifested and surrounded her middle section. Mary Anne moaned, gripping the sleeves of my dress tight.

"You're hurting her," I said.

Jackson ignored me, his eyes locked on the wound. When the tension in his arms relaxed, so did Mary Anne's body. She slumped against me, and I struggled to hold up her weight. I glanced down at the bloodied place in her side and sighed with relief when I saw that the bleeding had stopped.

"That will hold for a little while," Jackson said. "But we really should get her to the shaman."

"Andros will want to speak with you first," Jericho said.

I turned in surprise. I hadn't heard or seen him come through the soul stone. Marlana had been standing beside us, and I was certain she hadn't pressed the dark stone to let him in. I wondered how, exactly, the portals here worked and how they kept unwanted demons or humans from coming through. But now wasn't the time to ask a lot of questions.

"Then please, go and get him and let him know we are here," Lea said, her voice commanding.

Marlana stayed with us as Jericho shifted into smoke and flew down the passageway.

I helped Mary Anne into Jackson's arms and he cradled her close as we waited.

"What is this place?" I asked Marlana. "Did you guys build it?"

She turned her face away from me, refusing to acknowledge me. I took a deep breath and tried to remind myself that the only humans she'd probably ever seen were witches from the Order who had come to this world to do terrible things.

"The Underground was discovered rather than built," Lea said, filling the awkward silence. "The demons who live here now call themselves the Resistance, and they began moving into this place about seventy years ago, when they first discovered it. No one really knows how long the Underground has existed, though. It's believed to have been built by an ancient race of trolls that went extinct in the shadow world over six thousand years ago."

Trolls? Not exactly what I'd been expecting to hear.

"Does the king know about it?" I asked.

"He didn't fifty years ago," Jackson said, looking to Marlana. "Does he now?"

She shook her head. "No, we've managed to keep our whereabouts a secret, but he knows the Resistance exists, of course," she said. "There are many portals throughout the Northern Kingdom and we are very careful to make sure no one knows where they lead."

Silence descended on us again as we stood, waiting for Andros to arrive. I wasn't sure, but I guessed he must be the leader of the Resistance. At the very least, he seemed to be the one making the final decision about whether we could stay here or not.

When he finally did arrive, it was in a rush of black smoke. He took form as a tall, very handsome man with long black hair and olive colored skin. His eyes were shockingly blue and seemed to have a glowing light that came from within.

"Princess Lazalea," he said, bowing to her and taking her hand. "You have no idea how happy I am to see you."

Next, he turned to Jackson and clapped him on the shoulder.

"Andros, thank you for seeing us," Jackson said. "I know we're putting you in an awkward position by bringing two human witches to the Underground, but once you hear the whole story, you'll understand that we had no choice."

Andros glanced at me, then at Mary Anne, still cradled in Jackson's arms. "This will be difficult to explain to the council, but considering our long friendship and your status among our people, I am going to place my trust in you."

I let out a long breath, relieved to hear that we could stay. At least for now.

"I'm sorry to ask more from you," Jackson said. "But this girl is injured badly and needs to see a shaman."

Andros held up his hand. "Of course, my friend," he said. "I will have rooms prepared for all of you and once you are settled, I'll have the shaman sent to your quarters immediately."

"Thank you," Lea said.

"All I ask is that you stay in your rooms until you are called for," he said. "You'll be perfectly safe and comfortable there."

"Whatever you need," Jackson said. "We really appreciate this."

Andros nodded, then disappeared down the hallway.

The four of us waited there with Marlana for a little while until Jericho finally reappeared.

"I'll show you to your rooms," he said. "Follow me."

I walked behind the others as we made our way down the long corridor.

In the distance, I could make out a brighter light where the hallway seemed to open up into a larger area. As we got closer, I could make out the sound of voices. Clanging metal. Footsteps. The hiss and sizzle of food being cooked. It was the sound of everyday life. Of movement and laughter and work.

It was the sound of the Underground.

THE SECRET OF THE STONES

We stood at the top of a large marble staircase overlooking a marketplace so large you could fit six football fields inside of it. The ceilings were more than fifty feet high. I stared out, open-mouthed. Who could have ever guessed something this grand and beautiful existed so far under the ground?

The room was shaped like a giant rectangle with long sides extending from where we stood at the front of the space. The sides of the room were lined with staircases leading to dozens of tunnels carved into the sides of the rock.

The floor looked like it had once been some kind of grand ballroom, but now the area was filled with hundreds of colorful tents. Demons moved about, traveling up and down staircases, moving below us from one tented shop to another. The sounds of everyday life and movement echoed through the hall. The smell of food wafted up from a few makeshift restaurants scattered throughout the room. Clanging sounded from a blacksmith's shop below, where a big burly man pounded on a large silver sword.

"What is this place?" I asked.

"This is the Grand Hall," Jericho said. "It's our central marketplace. All our shops are here. Food, clothes, supplies, everything. You should be able to find anything you need here, but for now, I'd like to get you all to your rooms."

"Of course," Jackson said.

Jericho turned quickly on his heel and motioned for us to follow. He led us down the long stairway to the left, along the edge of the tents below, past three tunnels, then finally up the fourth staircase and into a new tunnel. All along the way, demons stopped to stare at us. Some of them probably recognized their Princess, but most of them kept their eyes trained on me and Mary Anne. Human witches invading their space.

I felt very exposed in my thin white dress with its rip up the side and streaks of dirt and blood.

So much for a great first impression.

I did my best to walk with my head up and not show my fear or embarrassment. It seemed a little bit ironic that the one safe place Jackson could think of to bring me to was full of demons who despised humans. He'd said they would come around once they learned more about me, but I wasn't so sure. The way they looked at me now made it very obvious they didn't want me here. Some even looked openly afraid of me.

Stepping into a quieter corridor, I relaxed a little. The hallway was deserted except for our small group of travelers. Jericho led us down toward the very end of the hall, and all along the way we passed dozens of stone doors. I shivered as this place reminded me of the Hall of Doorways in Shadowford's attic. I wondered where all of these doors led.

We finally came to a stop in front of a set of double doors at the very end of the hallway.

"We have plenty of extra housing down here," Jericho said. "Andros decided to put you on one of the empty halls. The ladies will all share this one suite of rooms if that's okay. I understand if you'd rather be in a room separate from the humans."

"I'm sure this will be fine," Lea said.

Jericho wasn't very good at hiding his disappointment. He frowned, then let his eyes flicker over me, no doubt wondering why in the world a Princess would want to live with two human witches. I honestly just wanted to stick my tongue out at him.

"Can we get inside?" Jackson asked, his voice tense. "I have a girl here who needs medical attention, and I don't think we have any time to waste."

"Of course," Jericho said. He took a small green stone from his pocket, then placed it up against a carved symbol in the stone beside the doors.

Both of the large double doors opened inward to reveal a gorgeous suite of rooms beyond. I tried not to act impressed, but it was hard. Jericho led us inside, and I had to press my lips together to keep my mouth from hanging open.

The floors were pure white marble, smooth and cool and polished to a high shine. The walls were a bluish-gray slate and were decorated with golden sculptures and paintings made of colors so real and bright, they looked like windows to some outdoor landscape. A crystal chandelier hung from the ceiling in the center of the room, but it wasn't like any chandelier I'd ever seen before. It was a mess of geometric shapes and crystals in about seven different colors ranging from aqua to dark purple.

Jackson laid Mary Anne down on a soft fur-covered couch in the living room. "I take it the shaman is on her way?"

He said it more as a demand than a question. He seemed to be losing his patience with Jericho. It definitely didn't seem like he was in any hurry to help Mary Anne.

"I'll take care of it right away," Jericho said. "And I left one of my stones on the table there for you just in case."

Lea glanced toward the table in the main area and nodded.

I walked over to the table as she moved to see him to the door. I hadn't noticed him lay it down, but now there was a very small, round gemstone lying in the center of the white table. A ruby from the looks of it. I picked it up and rubbed my index finger over the smooth surface of it.

It seemed gemstones were used everywhere here in the Underground. First, there was the dark stone that Marlana kept touching to bring us down through the soul stone. There was the soul stone itself, covering the area above this entire hidden fortress. There was the key to this suite—a green stone pressed against the strange symbol outside. And now Jericho had left a small red stone here so that we could contact him if we needed anything.

My mind raced. What was the true power of all these stones? And how did it relate to the portal stone in each of the demon gate towns? How did it relate to the power of my own lost pendant?

I set the ruby-red stone back on the table. Maybe hiding down here wouldn't turn out to be a complete loss. I couldn't help but think that the answer to some of my many questions about the Order lay in the secret of the stones.

PAST AND FUTURE PAIN

The three of us sat in the living area just staring at Mary Anne as she slept. We all jumped up when the knock sounded. Lea was the first to reach the door, and she looked relieved to see the woman standing there with her beaded hair and long, flowing dress.

"Thank you for coming, Priestess." Lea took the woman's hand and brought it to her lips.

The shaman bowed her head. "It's my pleasure, Princess," she said. Her gaze took in the room around her. "I don't have much experience healing humans, but if this girl is truly a friend of yours, I will do everything within my power to make her better."

I stood as still as a statue, not knowing whether I should bow to this woman or leave the room. Would my presence here make her uncomfortable? I looked to Jackson for some kind of clue, but he wasn't paying any attention to me. His eyes were glued to Mary Anne.

Feeling that I would be better off out of the way, I moved

to the very far corner of the room and sat in a large blue chair, watching.

The shaman priestess moved quickly to Mary Anne's side. She pulled a vial of bright orange liquid from her bag. "Where is she wounded?"

Jackson lifted Mary Anne's shirt on her right side. I winced at the ugly wound, the tiger's teeth marks still prominent against her bruised skin. There was so much blood everywhere.

"The only other wound is the one you see on her face," he said. "But that one doesn't seem to give her much trouble other than her appearance."

The long scratch across Mary Anne's face had healed really well. It was scabbed over and the color of rust, but it wasn't infected like the gash in her side.

The shaman woman uncorked the bottle in her hand and closed her eyes. She began to chant, and the bottle rose up into the air over Mary Anne's side, moving in slow circles. I couldn't make out what the woman was saying. She spoke low and close, as if she were speaking only to Mary Anne. The orange liquid bubbled and steamed, sending a sweet-smelling smoke into the air. The shaman priestess rocked forward, wafting the steam into her own face.

Her eyes opened suddenly and instead of the blue eyes I'd noticed when she first walked into the room, her eyes were now a bright, fiery orange. She stared ahead as if seeing into some other dimension. She began to hum something so sad, it brought tears to my eyes. Mary Anne shifted on the couch.

With trembling hands, the shaman woman wrapped her long fingers around the mouth of the floating bottle. I flinched at the sound of burning flesh, but the woman hardly seemed to notice that the bottle was steaming hot. Her grip was firm as she tipped the bottle over and poured it onto Mary Anne's wound.

The scream that tore from Mary Anne's lips ripped through me like a chainsaw. I bolted from my quiet spot in the corner and threw myself at the shaman. Before I could reach her and stop her from hurting my friend, Jackson's arms closed around my middle, one hand slapping across my mouth to keep me from interrupting the ritual. I struggled against him, anger bubbling within me.

Couldn't he see that this woman was making it worse? She was going to kill her!

But my tired body lost energy quickly. I slumped against him, my chest heaving with each breath.

"Shhh," he whispered, his warm breath against my skin breaking my heart further. "She's going to be better, just wait."

I watched as Mary Anne settled back onto the couch. Her eyes were still closed, but her body writhed against the fur of the couch. The shaman placed both of her hands on Mary Anne's injury, rubbing the orange liquid into the wound.

The pain on Mary Anne's face tortured me. I could only hope she was too far gone to know what was really happening.

When it was over, the shaman priestess lifted her hands from Mary Anne's side. I couldn't tell if the wound was better or worse. It was covered in a thick orange paste. The woman stood, wiped her hands on a towel, then placed the empty vial back in her bag.

She stood and nodded to Lea. "I have sealed the wound," she said. "I am sorry to say that this young one would have died if you had not brought her here when you did."

I pulled away from Jackson's hold. "She's going to

be okay?"

The shaman woman looked at me, and instead of frowning or looking at me like I was a cockroach, she actually smiled at me. "Yes, my dear, your friend is going to be just fine," she said. "And so will you, in time. Wounds of the heart take much longer to heal."

I stared at her, surprise rooting me to the spot. My gaze flicked to Jackson, then down to the ground. How did she know? Was it really that obvious?

Lea walked the woman to the door. "Is there anything special we need to do for her?"

"Just make sure she leaves the paste on the wound for at least a week," she said. "And under no circumstances can she come in contact with the fur of another tiger for the next several months."

Lea smiled and raised an eyebrow. "Well, that shouldn't be a problem," she said. "Unless you guys have a lot of tigers down here."

The shaman smiled. "None that I'm aware of," she said.

Before she left, the shaman looked at me one more time and smiled. I nodded to her and she nodded back. The look in her blue-again eyes said this woman could see deeper inside of me than even I could see. But what was it that brought on this sad, knowing smile?

It was a smile that said she knew my fate, my past and future pain. She knew my destiny.

As she disappeared behind the closing double doors, I felt a powerful urge to run after her and ask her what she saw. What she knew.

But fear held me to this spot, not wanting to know the truth.

NOT IN FRONT OF HIM

Once the shaman left and Mary Anne was sleeping soundly on the comfort of the couch, I decided to explore the rest of the suite. Lea claimed a room in the very back of the apartment. There were two additional bedrooms, each on an opposite side of the living room.

I peered into the first one. Decorated in pure white linens and furniture, the walls in this room were the same slate blue-gray color as the walls in the rest of the suite. The floors were pure white marble like most of the floors in the Underground seemed to be so far. I sighed in relief as the coolness of the tile soothed my weary feet.

"How are you feeling?"

Jackson stood behind me in the doorway, but I didn't turn around.

"Fine," I said, stiffening. "Did you need something?"

Okay, so I was giving him a bit of cold-shoulder treatment, but how else was I supposed to get over him and move on? If he kept touching me and whispering in my ear, there would be no end to the torture.

"I just wanted to make sure you were okay," he said, sadness in his tone.

I walked around the room, running my hand over the pure white wood of the desk and opening one of the drawers. Pretending his presence had no effect on me.

"I'm fine, just checking out the rooms," I said. "I wanted to see which one looked more comfortable for Mary Anne."

"I think they're both exactly the same," he said. "You should each have your own bathroom."

He stepped into the room and opened a door just beside the bed. Beyond the frame, I could make out a small shower.

"I guess if they're the same, I'll just take this one, then," I said, staying on the opposite side of the room instead of walking over to inspect the bathroom. "If you don't mind, I'd like to get showered and see if I can find something else to wear."

"Oh yeah," he said, taking a few quick steps to the bed. He crouched down and pulled a drawer out from under the bed. "Jericho said Andros had someone from the marketplace tailor some clothes for you and Mary Anne. They should be down here."

He reached in and pulled out a stack of clothing, laying it out on the bed.

"How do I know if these are mine or Mary Anne's?" I held one of the shirts up and it looked too big for either of us.

"Magic," he said, pretending to examine the shirt. His hand brushed mine, and I stepped away, letting the shirt fall to the bed. "They should be made so that once you put them on, they form themselves to your body in a perfect fit."

I sat down on the heavenly soft comforter to get a closer look at the clothes and sank in deeper than I imagined I would. It was like sitting on top of a cloud. I couldn't help but smile, despite the tension in the room. I wanted to lay back in it and disappear inside of it for the next twelve hours.

But when I caught Jackson's eye and saw him smiling back at me, I tensed. Wasn't this exactly the kind of thing we weren't allowed to do? If the demons here didn't approve of me, they surely wouldn't find it appropriate for him to be standing here with me in my private bedroom. Our eyes locked, but I looked away, not wanting to start a conversation that would only lead to tears. I wanted to be strong, not some weepy little girl who couldn't face reality.

"Thanks," I said. I made a point to look at the open door behind him. "I think I'm all set here then."

Jackson stood and nodded. "Sure," he said, sadness darkening his eyes. "If you need anything I'll be down the hall in the apartment marked with a clear stone. It's on the left side of the hallway."

I nodded and reluctantly stood up from the comfort of the bed. I walked him to the door and put my hand on it, so he knew I intended to close him out as soon as he cleared the doorway.

"I might be in some meetings for the next few days, so I'm not sure how much I'll be able to come around," he said, lingering just inside the room. "I'll come by to check on Mary Anne when I can, and I'll make sure Jericho keeps the kitchen stocked for you."

I lifted my chin. "I can take care of myself," I said. "And Mary Anne. You don't have to worry about babysitting us."

Jackson cleared his throat. "I know you can," he said. "I

just want to make sure you're comfortable, since you aren't allowed to leave the suite."

I nodded, understanding the gravity of his words. We were stuck here in this suite indefinitely while he and Lea talked to the council. I suddenly felt very alone and very trapped. I felt the sting of tears but refused to let them show. Not in front of him.

"Okay, well, have fun with your meetings," I said, my tone short and cutting. I closed the door, slowly pushing him out of my space.

"Harper," he said, pleading.

I didn't let him finish whatever it was he wanted to say. I simply closed the door and leaned against it, waiting for the sound of his boots against the tile before I let the tears begin to fall.

NEVER FORGET

I stepped into the small shower in my private bathroom. The warm water felt like heaven as I washed about a pound of dirt off of my body. I chose a fruity-smelling shampoo and lathered up my greasy, dirty hair, laughing as the water at my feet ran brown. I was suddenly grateful I hadn't come across any mirrors in the week since we'd first gotten to the shadow world.

With every speck of dirt that slid off my body, I thought of the days I'd lived since that fateful day at Shadowford. Had it really only been a few days? Why did I feel so different?

Maybe it was because I'd been reborn. Given a second chance at life. Or was it third or fourth at this point? Either way, I wasn't going to let this one go to waste. I had never been as sure of my own death as I had been in the ritual room that day. I had never felt so helpless.

Hopeless.

And I never wanted to feel that way again.

As I scrubbed, my laughter turned to anger. No one had

any right to have that much power over me, much less thousands of other witches. The Order of Shadows recruited us with smiles and promises of unlimited power, fun spells, and timeless beauty. Then, when it was too late, they revealed their true methods, the slavery of demons. When it was time to make our choice, the choice itself was taken away.

I thought of Brooke's initiation ceremony. The way they dragged her into the room, her screams of protest echoing through the woods, was torture. She didn't want to be one of them. She didn't want to change her goals and dreams for the Order.

And yet, as soon as it was done, she was different. She'd been brainwashed somehow to believe that the Order's wishes were now her own. It wouldn't be long before they did the same thing to Lark and to Allison and to every other girl in every other demon gate town.

What gave them the right to steal our lives and our power? What gave them the right to steal our choices?

I had escaped, but not every girl had that chance.

If it were up to Jackson, I would stay here, hiding out from the Order of Shadows for the rest of my life. I knew he only wanted me to be safe. But I couldn't stay. Not forever. I would live here just long enough to get my strength back, and then I would return to Peachville. Somehow, I would have my revenge and put a stop to their ways.

Of course, it would be easier with Jackson and the others fighting by my side, but even if I had to fight alone, I would do it.

I turned off the hot water and wrapped myself in a soft towel that smelled of fresh flowers. I walked into my new room with its fancy furniture and unbelievably comfortable bed. I was lucky to be here, I knew. But that didn't mean I belonged here.

Not by a long shot.

Proof of this lay on the floor at my feet. I leaned down and scooped the dirty ritual dress off the tile. As I held it in my hands, I made a promise to myself. I would never be that helpless again. I gripped the tattered garment tighter in my fist.

I was going to learn to be powerful. Somehow, I was going to find a way to free Aerden and myself. And if I survived long enough, I would close the Peachville gate and make sure that the Order never enslaved another demon or witch in the name of my ancestors.

With passion and determination burning in my chest, I ripped a strip of bloodied cloth from the hem of the white dress and wrapped it around my wrist like a ribbon. Then and there, I vowed to wear it until I either died or won. It would serve as a constant reminder of my new purpose. My new destiny.

I will never forget.

TWINGE OF PAIN

Despite my renewed passion, there wasn't much I could do to fight back while I was trapped here in this apartment. Jackson had made it pretty clear that Mary Anne and I needed to stay in the suite. He had someone come by each day to stock our kitchen with exotic fruits and vegetables. There was also some kind beef jerky stuff for us to chew on, but we were definitely not eating anything gourmet. Personally, I wondered how they were able to get fresh fruits and such way down here. Did they have a garden somewhere?

These were the kinds of things I spent my days thinking about since there was absolutely nothing to do down here. We didn't have any magazines or TV or books. Mary Anne spent a lot of time in her room sleeping, but she was slowly getting her color back and starting to act more like herself. Still, I spent a lot of time alone.

And alone time is not exactly something I needed. I'd gotten enough of that during my prison time at Shadowford.

Of course, being caged in an opulent suite of rooms with my own shower and bed was much more comfortable, so I knew I shouldn't complain.

Over the course of the first week we spent in the Underground I barely saw Jackson at all. He came by a couple of times to briefly check on Mary Anne, but he never stopped to really talk to me. Our eyes would meet, and I knew there was a lot left unsaid between us, but neither of us said what we were really feeling. I missed him like crazy. I just didn't want him to know that.

"I'm getting cabin fever," I said to Mary Anne on our eighth day of quarantine. "I don't think I can take this much longer."

We'd been sitting together on the fur couch playing a game of twenty questions. After six games, I'd had enough.

"I know what you mean," she said. "This place is nice and all, but it's starting to feel a bit like prison."

I nodded, picking at a hangnail on my index finger. "So, I guess the question is what are we going to do about it?"

Mary Anne shrugged. "I guess we should talk to Lea or Jackson next time they come by," she said. "See if they have any ideas."

I sighed and sat up. "And how long before they come back?" I asked. "We haven't seen Jackson in days, and Lea only comes home crazy late at night. We're lucky to see her at all most days."

"I know," she said. "But what choice do we have?"

I looked toward the counter where Jericho's red stone sat against the white tile. "What if we contacted Jericho?" I asked, standing to retrieve the stone. "How do you think this thing works anyway?"

She shook her head. "I don't think that's such a good idea," she said. "He left that stone for Lea, not for us."

I sighed again and put the stone back down on the counter. "I'm going to go insane."

Then, as if he'd been listening to us, Jackson walked through the door of the suite.

My stomach fluttered at the sight of him, followed by an immediate twinge of pain in my heart. I returned to the couch and tried to act like his presence didn't affect me.

"Hey," he said, coming to lean against the back of the couch. "How are you two holding up in here?"

"We're bored out of our minds," I said.

"We were just talking about wishing we could get out of these rooms for a while," Mary Anne said.

"Well, that's sort of what I came to talk about," he said. "Andros has asked you to join us for dinner."

My I-don't-care act went flying out the window at his announcement. I sat up, crossing my legs under me and practically bouncing up and down. "When?" I asked.

"A real dinner out?" Mary Anne asked. Her face lit up and her eyes sparkled at the thought.

"Yes, a real dinner out." Jackson smiled, making my stomach flip again. But when he turned to meet my gaze, I stopped smiling and looked away. "Tonight," he said, disappointment in his tone. "If you're up for it."

"Oh, we're definitely up for it," Mary Anne said with a giggle. She hopped up from the couch and ran toward her room, all traces of her injury gone from her step. "I just have to figure out what to wear."

She disappeared into her bedroom, leaving me alone with Jackson for the first time in a week. His hand lingered on the back of the couch, just inches from my own. Even though we weren't touching, I could feel the heat of him near me. My entire body was still tuned to him like some kind of hyper-sensitive magnet.

No one was watching, yet we couldn't touch.

Could he feel it too? The tension between us? The desire? Or had his feelings changed now that he was home and with his own people again?

His hand inched closer to mine, but I quickly stood and moved away.

"I'll go get ready, too," I said.

As casually as I could, I walked by him toward my room. I wanted him to reach out to me, grab me and pull me into his arms and tell me he was wrong to think he could be apart from me. But he didn't move, except to turn and watch me go.

THE BITTER TASTE OF UNSAID WORDS

We entered the Grand Hall and Jackson led us down the staircase, through a couple rows of shops, and finally to a small restaurant at the far end of the hall. Rather than a tent like I had expected, this place was carved into the solid rock. A few tables were occupied outside, but Jackson led us through the rounded entrance and straight up to the hostess.

I was amazed at how many things here were similar to my world. Sure, we were deep underground and the restaurant was carved into thick black rock; but there was still a hostess and tables and chairs just like any normal restaurant.

"We're here to see Andros," Jackson said.

The hostess raised an eyebrow, then looked at Mary Anne and me with curiosity. "Follow me," she said. "We have a private room set up for you in the back."

She stepped out from the podium and passed by me, her judgmental gaze lingering just a bit too long on my face.

We obediently followed to the back of the restaurant. As we walked by, I took in the rich smells of the food. I couldn't catch any specific smells that I recognized, but everything smelled so delicious it made my mouth water. I don't think I'd ever been so hungry in my life.

The hostess disappeared through an archway at the very back of the restaurant. Inside was a small room with one large round table. She motioned for us to take our seats, then disappeared back the way she'd come.

Sitting down at the table were three demons. Andros, was one. Beside him sat a woman with short, pixie-cut blonde hair. She was small and had pale skin, almost as if she were designed to be her partner's exact opposite. Instead of black eyes like Andros, hers were almost snow white.

The final guest at the table was a young girl who looked no older than four or five years old. Of course, I had no idea how old that was in demon years. After all, Jackson only looked eighteen, but in truth he was over two hundred years old.

I smiled at the young girl and she smiled back. Her face was sweet and beautiful, and her smile was happy and genuine. My heart warmed. This little girl was the first demon who had truly welcomed me since I first got here.

Andros stood and held his hand out to me. Tentatively, I took it, amazed at how much his view of us had seemed to change in the past week.

Jackson greeted the blonde woman, then took a seat next to her. Even though there was an empty chair by his, I stepped to the side and took the seat next to the child instead, leaving two empty chairs between him and me. The little girl immediately took my hand in hers as if we'd always been best friends. I couldn't help but smile, thankful to be treated so nicely among strangers.

Mary Anne sat next to me, leaving one seat still open.

Lea came in just moments behind us, looking as beautiful as ever in her leather ensemble with her long black hair free-flowing down her back.

"Hope I'm not late," she said, smiling. She embraced both Andros and the blonde woman, then took the seat next to Mary Anne and Jackson in the circle.

"I am sorry you've been locked away in your room for so long," Andros said. "Many were concerned you were spies who might report back to the Order. It took some time to convince the council to allow you all to stay here long term under our protection."

"Does that mean a decision has been made?" I asked.

Andros laughed, taken aback by my honesty. "Right to the point," he said. "Yes, as a matter of fact, just this afternoon the council voted to accept you into our community. Jackson and Lea have been telling us a lot about your struggles against the Order."

I noticed Andros had called him Jackson instead of his demon name.

"It's definitely our pleasure to have you here with us," the blonde woman at his side said in a very sweet voice. "It isn't every day that we hear of a witch who wants to fight back against the Order. And from what I hear, you are quite a powerful witch for someone so young."

I bowed my head and stared at the scarred wood of the circular table. I didn't know how to respond. Was I powerful? I certainly hadn't felt that way lately.

"And you must be Mary Anne?" Andros asked, turning his

attention to her. "I don't sense any kind of connection to the Order within you, is that right?"

Mary Anne cleared her throat. "Yes," she said nervously.

"Jackson and Lea have told us a lot about you," the blonde demon said. "I felt awful knowing you were in those rooms all alone with nothing to do. As soon as the council's vote came in, I made sure to arrange this dinner right away."

"Thank you," I said. "The rooms are very beautiful, but still, it's been a little bit boring, if you'll forgive me for saying so. We are very thankful for a place to stay, though."

"Yes," Mary Anne said. "Thank you."

"You are most welcome," the blonde said. "My name is Ourelia, I am Andros' mate. And of course, you have met our daughter, Sasha. I hope we'll be seeing much more of each other now that we've sort of broken the ice."

"It's nice to meet you," I said.

The conversation around the table continued on in this very polite way, no one really saying anything important or deep. Mostly, Andros wanted to know about Peachville and how life was different in the human world. We avoided topics like demon slavery and the fact that almost every demon down here hated humans.

More than once, I caught Jackson's eyes on me, but I quickly looked away.

A waitress in a silky blue dress entered the room and poured glasses of wine for everyone. I hesitated as Andros raised his glass in a toast. The only wine I'd ever had was with Jackson that day in the pecan orchard and it had made my head swim. I didn't think now was the right time for me to be clouding my own judgment. Still, it would be rude to refuse when these demons were obviously going out of their way to serve us.

I raised my glass.

"To old friends," Andros said. "And new ones."

Everyone leaned in to the center of the round table to knock our silver cups together. At first, I drank only a sip, not intending to have much of the wine. But it was surprisingly sweet and bubbly, and I was so thirsty.

The wine seemed to loosen everyone up. By the time the food arrived, Jackson and Andros were sharing funny stories of their childhood.

"Remember the time you and Aerden slipped past the castle's guards and set off those homemade fireworks from the east tower?" Andros said, laughing so hard there were tears in his eyes. "I will never forget the look on your father's face when he caught up with you two."

"Oh, man, that was such a long time ago," Jackson said.

I watched as they talked, an outsider gazing in. Their childhood didn't seem all that different from a normal human experience except for their stories of magic and castles and kings. And the fact that their childhoods lasted for about a hundred years.

I think I would have laughed with them and enjoyed their stories except for the way that Lea kept smiling and talking about how much time she used to spend with Jackson and his brother. I knew they had a past together, but I never realized that it was a hang-out-everyday-best-friends kind of past. I willed myself not to care, but it didn't work.

Thankfully, once the dessert came—a beautiful pie with some kind of sweet blue fruit inside—Andros turned the conversation back to the present.

"You wouldn't believe the changes in the Kingdom since you left, my friends," he said, shaking his head. "The laughter has been replaced by fear."

Ourelia sighed, a dark sadness in her eyes. "Especially after what happened in Genestra. Nothing was every the same after that."

"Genestra?" Jackson asked, sitting up straighter. "The king's northernmost city?"

"A few years after you left, a group of citizens in Genestra decided to set up watch against the hunters," Andros said. "They patrolled the city streets, waiting. One night, a demon on watch set off the alarms. One of the hunters had come for an innocent girl, the new mate of the city's head guard. Many rose up against the hunter, and even though they weren't strong enough to kill her, they did manage to wound her and banish her from the city. At first, they considered it a great victory, sure they had scared the Order away from their city."

"What happened?" Lea said. The earlier smiles had been wiped from her face and replaced with worry.

"It was horrible," Ourelia said, her voice shaking. "The Order of Shadows brought an army into Genestra about a week later. Human witches and hunters both. In a matter of hours, every single demon in the town was either dead or captured and sent to the human world to be a slave."

Jackson's eyes grew wide. "How could that happen to such a large city?" he asked. "I mean, Genestra had what? Three thousand demons living there? There's no way the Order was strong enough to take them all."

"Never underestimate their power," Andros said. "Their darkest magic is enough to kill us all, especially when their attack is a surprise. The city was helpless against the power of the Order of Shadows."

"Who did this horrible thing?" Lea asked. "What was the name of the head witch? Do you know?"

Andros shook his head. "No one survived to give any specific details of what happened there that night."

I shivered and glanced at Lea. Her eyes met mine, and I know we were both thinking of the memory she'd shown me of Aldeen, Kansas. The Order had killed everyone in the blink of an eye. We knew what they were capable of, but how were we supposed to fight back?

"This happens in the human world too," I said. For most of the night I had sat back and been a spectator, but this was a conversation I was passionate about. "The Order gets rid of anyone who opposes them, even if it's their own people."

Andros looked confused. "You mean, they kill their own witches?"

"Yes," I said. "Entire cities of them. I've seen it with my own eyes."

"Why don't your people fight back?" Ourelia asked. "Are they also afraid?"

"Well, fear is part of it, but it's also misinformation," I said. "The Order doesn't exactly go around advertising the fact that they killed one of their own covens. Instead, they find an enemy to blame it on, making sure the other towns hate whoever it is they think really did the killing."

"Very smart," Andros said, rubbing his forehead. "They build loyalty through their lies, using it to take out any groups who oppose them."

"Yes, and they get the rest of the covens to rally against any enemy they choose, whether those enemies did anything wrong or not," I said. "The Order is the Order, no matter which side of the portal you're on. They hold all of the power because none of their true enemies ever communicates or works together."

Maybe I'd had too much wine. My tongue was loose, and I could feel my cheeks getting warm. Across the table, Jackson tensed and tried to change the subject.

"It's been a long night," he said. "And this isn't really the time or place to be discussing politics and other unpleasant things."

"Perhaps you're right," Ourelia said, pushing her half-eaten pie toward the center of the table. "Our evening so far has been so nice, let's not ruin it with talk of the Order of Shadows."

With that, I knew my chance to speak my mind had come and gone. There was so much I wanted to say. I wanted to ask him why we couldn't find a way to work together. I wanted to explain that there were other witches like me who would be willing to risk their lives to expose the Order for who and what they really are.

But the conversation was already back to pleasantries and smiles.

I sat back in my chair, the bitter taste of unsaid words on my tongue.

ALMOST FREEDOM

B ack in our suite, a set of wrapped presents was waiting for Mary Anne and me. We found them on each of our beds. Two identical small boxes wrapped in shiny red foil wrapping. Excited to see what was inside, we both met up in the living room and tore them open at the same time.

Inside, we found a black armband with a red dragon embroidered on it. Confused, I looked to Lea and Jackson for some kind of explanation.

"I told Andros you were having a hard time being stuck in these rooms," Jackson said. "The dragon is his family's insignia. If you wear that in the marketplace, people will know you are there as friends of Andros."

"Basically, no one will mess with you," Lea said. "They probably would not have, anyway."

"It's more for my peace of mind," Jackson said. I noticed that with Lea in the room, he rarely met my eyes. "I'm sorry you had to stay in here for so long, but now that we have the council's approval to stay, things should be much easier."

"Thanks," Mary Anne said. She hugged Jackson, but I kept my distance.

Jackson reached into his pocket and pulled out a pair of matching black cards that were also decorated with a red dragon. "Here," he said, handing one to each of us. "These cards work like money down here. Or more like a credit card, I guess. I mean, it's not free rein to go buy anything you want, but if you go to the marketplace, you can at least shop around a little bit and try out some of the restaurants."

"Great," I said. "Thank you."

The prospect of being able to go to the marketplace anytime we wanted was a huge relief. With these new armbands, we might still get some strange looks, but no one was going to be too mean to us. At least not to our faces. It was like we'd been handed keys to our freedom.

"Just keep it to the marketplace, okay?"

I sighed. Almost freedom. Yes, the marketplace was better than nothing, but his statement immediately made me wonder what other places he was trying to keep me away from.

THE CYCLE CONTINUES

The next morning, Mary Anne knocked on my door early.

"Want to go exploring?" she asked. Sleep and food seemed to agree with her, because she was back to her normal self this morning.

"As long as exploring means getting some breakfast, I'm in," I said. "Just let me get ready."

I was showered and dressed in no time, making sure I had the red and black armband securely over my clothes. The two of us made our way to the Grand Hall marketplace. I wasn't sure what time it was exactly, but the place was booming. There were more people bustling around the shops than any other time we'd been in here, so far.

"Where to first?" Mary Anne asked.

"Somewhere they serve food," I said.

"How can you still be hungry after all that food we had last night? I'm still stuffed."

I laughed. "I guess my stomach is making up for two weeks of being starved."

I looked to the left and right, searching for a place that looked promising. Finally, I just picked left. Mary Anne followed by my side.

We passed all kinds of shops selling everything from handcrafted weapons to what looked like prayer beads of some kind. In a way, it reminded me of going to the Farmer's Market in Atlanta with all these independent vendors set up in tents selling their wares. I hadn't expected there to be such a big economy down here. I wondered where they got all their supplies. Did they constantly have people going up to the surface to get things?

When we got to the end of the first row, Mary Anne turned right and led us down another row of shops. A store selling bags of all sizes caught my eye, and I stopped. I really needed a bag of my own. I wasn't sure how long I was going to stay here, but if I decided to leave, I'd need a way to carry my new clothes and some supplies.

"Excuse me," I said to the old female demon sitting in the corner. Behind her, a row of bags were sewing themselves at her direction. Each of the sewing needles moved together in unison.

When she looked up at me, they all stopped in unison too. "Yes?"

She pressed her cracked lips together tight and held her body rigid. Her eyes flickered over our armbands.

"I was just wondering how much one of your backpacks costs," I said. It was a silly question, really. Especially since I didn't have the first idea about their money system down here. She could have said it costs a million thingamajigs and I wouldn't have had a clue what that meant. Still, it seemed like the polite thing to ask.

"My bags are not for sale today," she said. She turned back to her sewing, obviously wanting us to move on.

"Please," I said. "I know you don't really know us, but I promise you, I'm not your enemy."

The woman's back straightened and she pulled her elbows in tight to her sides. I was trying to reason with her and let her know that I was a good person, but I could tell from her body language that all I'd done was make her angry. Was it going to be this way with every shop we came across?

Mary Anne tugged on my arm and backed away from the tent's entrance.

"I'm sorry," I said, stepping back. "I didn't mean to offend you."

Behind me, Mary Anne screeched, then tumbled backward, straight into the arms of another demon.

He laughed and helped her get her footing.

"I'm so sorry," she said, her cheeks bright red. "I must have slipped on the edge of the fabric. I didn't mean to—"

"It is no problem," the guy said. He was of medium height with dark hair that was longer in front than in the back. His eyes were every bit as blue as Mary Anne's and instead of looking at her with disgust, he was actually smiling at her. "I have heard very much about you. It's very lucky running into you today."

His speech was strange. Different from the other demons we'd met so far. But he was friendly, which was also a nice change.

Mary Anne seemed to realize she was still clinging to this

stranger. Nervously, she backed away, straightening her hair and staring down at her feet.

"We never get to see humans down here," he said. "I never thought I would see you in my own shop. Did you find something to your liking?"

I looked from him to the small tent. "This is your shop?"

"Yes," he said, puffing out his chest with pride. "Well, my family's shop. We are tailors. In fact, I helped make the clothes you are wearing now. Do you approve of them?"

Mary Anne ran her hands along the sleeves of her silky black shirt. "I love them," she said, blushing again.

I couldn't help but smile, watching the two of them stare at each other, then look away as if they were embarrassed.

"There was a bag inside," I said. "A backpack that I really wanted to buy, but the woman inside, she wouldn't sell it to me. Is that your mother?"

I wouldn't have mentioned it except for the fact that I really needed that bag. I was hoping this guy could maybe convince her to sell it to me.

His eyebrows came together in a point and he shook his head. "I am so sorry for my mother's behavior," he said. "But she has had much sadness in her life. My father was taken by the human hunters, and we have never seen him again. She doesn't trust any humans."

I nodded. I completely understood why she wouldn't trust us, and I didn't blame her for it one bit. It had to be hard to live in a world where anyone you loved could be taken away from you at any moment. "I'm sorry," I said.

"I'm sorry too," Mary Anne said.

"It was many years ago," he said. "Besides, you are not like those hunters. I know that our princess and our leader would never let any of those types of humans into the Underground. I will get you a bag. Please, wait here just one moment."

He disappeared into the tent, and we heard some whispering, then some arguing. Finally, he emerged carrying a pair of backpacks made from a heavy cloth.

I smiled. "Thank you so much," I said. "You have no idea how much this means to me. Here, please, let us pay."

I tried to hand him my black card, but he waved it away.

"It is my pleasure," he said. He looked at Mary Anne, his eyes sparkling. "You may repay me by spending the day with me, telling me all about your world and what you have been up to since you arrived in the Underground."

I had to hide a smile. We seemed to have run into the one demon here who didn't hate us. In fact, I think he had quite the crush on Mary Anne. I waited for her to respond, but she just stared up at him.

"That sounds like a fair trade," I said. I held my hand out to him to shake. "My name is Harper, and this is Mary Anne."

He took my hand and bowed slightly to me. "My name is Essex. It is such a treat to meet you both. Where would you like to see first?"

"Can you show us a good place to get some breakfast?" My stomach growled.

He nodded. "Come with me, I will show you my favorite place in the entire Underground."

We spent the next hour at a small tent cafe on the far corner of the marketplace. There were only six tables in the entire place and most of them were empty, so we didn't have to worry about anyone bothering us, which was nice. We had a great breakfast. Their version of eggs down here was delicious.

I watched the cook preparing them and was amazed at the bright pink color of the shells.

"What kind of eggs are these exactly?" Mary Anne asked, taking a big bite of her egg sandwich.

"Angelbird eggs," he said.

I wondered what an angelbird must look like. I couldn't remember seeing any birds on our trip so far. "Where do you guys get all of your supplies down here?" I asked since it had been on my mind so much lately. "Do you grow your own food below ground?"

Essex shook his head. "Not all of it," he said. "We do have a garden district one level below this one, but we do not raise our own animals."

"So, someone goes out to hunt?" Mary Anne asked.

"Yes," he said. "Most of us have a job to do down here just like on the surface. Some are gatherers of food; others trade for supplies like cloth or leather. Many are members of the Resistance and spend their days training."

"The Resistance?" I asked. I perked up a bit at the mention of training. "They're the fighters, right?"

Essex tilted his drink to his mouth and finished it in one gulp. "Yes," he said. "They are an army of fighters who train all day so that they can fight back against the Order."

"Do they ever actually go up and fight?" Mary Anne asked.

I was glad we were alone in the cafe. I had a feeling this was exactly the kind of conversation most of the demons here thought we shouldn't be having. Especially since there were those who still thought we might be reporting back to the Order.

"From time to time the alarm will sound and our Resistance members will head out, but they rarely report to us about what is happening on the other side," he said. "Sometimes when they come back, they are cheering, and their numbers are still high, but other times they return with wounds and many missing, never to be seen again."

We ate in silence for a minute. I let Essex's words sink in a bit. Why didn't they keep everyone up to date on what was happening with the Resistance? It seemed strange to keep it all a secret and make everyone wonder what had really happened.

"Do you hear anything at all about their missions?" I asked. "Like where they were going or who exactly they were fighting?"

Essex shook his head. "No, but this is normal," he said. "The council believes there is no need to worry the rest of the community with this kind of information about the surface. It only will lead to suffering and worry."

"But what's the point of being down here if not to try to build up a community of demons who can fight back against the Order?" I asked. "What's the purpose of being left in the dark?"

"Most of us are not choosing to be down here because we want to fight," Essex said. "We are here to be safe from the hunters. As long as we can provide some service to the community, we are welcome here even if we do not want to fight."

"Like bag making or tailoring?" Mary Anne asked.

"Yes," he said with a smile full of pride. "Exactly like bag making. It is an important service we do for the Resistance. We provide them with bags and armor and boots. This is our contribution to the fight. My mother and I are very lucky to be here. We come from a small village in the far north."

The purpose of the Underground was becoming clearer to

me as we spoke. From where I sat, I could see a good portion of the marketplace. As Mary Anne and Essex changed the subject to his work and how he learned to be a tailor, I studied the demons of the Underground as they traveled from shop to shop or did their work.

Some had come here to fight back, but most of them had only come to seek safety from the Order of Shadows. This was more of a refugee camp of sorts than a staging ground for an army.

No wonder the Order of Shadows had such free rein to take the demons in this world. Very few demons were willing to stand against them. They wanted their safety, but they weren't willing to risk their lives to insure safety for all of their people.

Was this really any different from the human world? Many of the members in the Order didn't agree with the way they did things, but no one would speak out. They either didn't want to lose their power, or they didn't want to risk losing their lives.

And so the cycle continues, forever.

Without an organized army of demons and witches willing to die for the freedom of future generations, the Order would continue to rule us all.

CHANGE THE WORLD

Later that night, back in my room, I couldn't get the idea of an army out of my mind. Was it impossible to think demons and human witches could work together to defeat the Order? Isn't that how this all began? Not with slavery and death, but with a demon and a human woman falling in love and working together?

Somewhere along the way, it had all become corrupted, but what if we could go back to our roots? What if we could work together by choice instead of force?

Of course, my mind wandered to thoughts of Jackson. There was a part of me that still hoped someday we could be together again.

We could change the world. Both worlds.

SURVIVAL TACTIC

Another week passed, and even though I had the freedom to explore the marketplace, I still felt trapped down here. No sunshine. No fresh air. No one to talk to.

Mary Anne and Essex had hit it off immediately and when he wasn't working, he was in our suite or they were walking around and talking. I tagged along a few times, but mostly felt like I was getting in their way.

I scoured the marketplace for something I could read or an equivalent of an mp3 player, so I could listen to music, but entertainment items weren't exactly a priority down here. Most of the shops were for more practical items like weapons, clothing, food or other necessities.

The demons in the Grand Hall slowly became used to seeing me walking around, and I got a few smiles here and there instead of threatening looks. I had become friendly with some of the food vendors, but I hadn't met anyone I would really consider a friend. Not the way Mary Anne had, anyway. Sometimes, seeing her with Essex made me even angrier with Jackson. If this stranger was willing to risk ridicule from his fellow demons to spend time with a human, why wouldn't Jackson spend any time with me?

Of course, wasn't I the one who'd been pushing him away ever since we got down here?

It was a survival tactic. I believed that being close to him and pretending to only be casual friends would be harder than simply cutting him out of my life. Now, however, I was missing him like crazy.

Every time I saw him these days he was deep in conversation with Andros or some demon I didn't recognize. I had no idea what they talked about, but I guessed it had to be about the Order and Jackson's hope to free his brother. At first, when we'd see each other in the marketplace, our eyes would meet, and he would hold my gaze for a split second longer than he should. I was always the first to look away and now, he'd practically stopped looking all together.

To try to push the worry and sadness from my mind, I started writing in a leather-bound journal I'd bought from one of the vendors. I spent my afternoons at the small cafe brainstorming possible ways to fight back against the Order.

HUMAN WORLD:

1. Find a way to expose the Order's lies to all of the Primas around the world.

2. Find proof that the Order killed its own people and then lied about it.

3. Educate future candidates about what initiation really means.

4. Search for a way to break the spell between a Prima and her demon without killing either of them.

DEMON WORLD:

1. Talk to Andros about forming a joint army between demons and humans.

2. Try to convince the King of the North to fight back.

BY THE END OF A WEEK, I had a notebook full of ideas but wasn't really any closer to coming up with a true solution. As I looked over my notes, I realized just how crazy I was to think I could do this all on my own. These were huge dreams that would take years of planning and training. I needed help to really accomplish anything important.

I was tired of sitting back and doing nothing proactive or productive. Without something to occupy my mind all I thought about was Jackson. And that only made me sad. I needed a project or a plan. Something I could do that would make a difference.

The items on my list were big, but maybe the difference needed to start somewhere smaller. Closer to home. Maybe the change needed to start within me. No one cared to listen to a young human witch without any real battle experience or knowledge of how to fight with magic. Yes, I had managed to end a few lives, but only in the most desperate of situations and only with help from Aerden or Jackson.

If I truly wanted to make a difference, I needed to learn how to fight.

What little training I'd had with Zara back home in Peachville was so minimal, it hardly counted. Besides, I knew I couldn't trust anything the Order's witches had taught me. After what Lea showed me in Aldeen, I knew the High Council of the Order was capable of a lot more than they ever taught their fellow witches. They preferred to hold on to the secrets of their most powerful magic so that, if need be, they could use it against anyone who dared to voice opposition.

They were afraid that if everyone knew just how powerful they could be, they would rise up and overturn the leaders of the Order. So instead, they taught their Primas just enough to scratch the surface of their power, but never enough to make them a real threat. Never enough to allow them the strength to fight back.

Well, this was one Prima who had her eyes wide open. I knew exactly what witches like me were capable of, and I desperately needed to learn how to access that magic and power within myself. I might not have the same kind of strength and demon power as a Prima who had already passed through initiation, but I knew there was a reservoir of untapped power inside me.

I had seen it that day we came through the portal. I still didn't know what had come over me when I killed the sister tiger. I wasn't thinking. I was only acting on instinct, but the power that had raged inside of me was foreign and terrifying and incredibly strong. If I could find a way to access that kind of power but still have control over it, I would be capable of so much more.

I touched the strip of white cloth around my wrist, feeling a rush of certainty fill me.

No matter how helpless I felt down here, there was one thing I always had access to. My own power.

It was time I learned how to use it.

THE INFORMATION YOU ARE SEEKING

Alone in my room, I started working on my magic. Nothing fancy, just learning how to reconnect to my power. I practiced glamours, lighting candles, going invisible, moving things from one side of the room to another. My skill had definitely gotten rusty, but slowly, it all came back to me.

When I'd nailed down the basics of what I'd learned in Peachville, I started experimenting with slightly more daring magic. For example, I spent a few hours learning how to make my leather jacket hover high in the air, then quickly dive-bomb to the floor at breakneck speeds. Of course, a soft jacket was harmless at those speeds, but what about a brick? Or a knife? If I could learn to control both the speed and direction of any item, then I could almost always find a weapon no matter what situation I found myself in. Hell, what would stop me from learning to lift an entire person high into the air and then send them into a wall or a rock?

Despite hours of practice, I'd still been unable to match the speed and power of the rocks I'd thrown at the tiger. I was making progress, though, and that was all that mattered.

With my limited materials and space, I was only able to get so creative with my own magic. What I needed was a good teacher and a good place to practice. Essex said they had training grounds here in the Underground where they took their best students of the Resistance and taught them techniques to fight against the Order. I wondered if there was any way I could find those classes and watch what they did. I doubted the demons would want me learning their fighting techniques, but what if I could make myself disappear and observe them from some hiding place?

Then again, all demons seemed to have their own unique powers and abilities. All it would take is one demon who could see through my invisibility glamour and my fate down here would be in serious danger. Hiding out to watch their secret training sessions would definitely make me look like a spy. It was too risky.

I pushed the doubts from my mind and instead, channeled my frustration into my magic. I stood with my back against the door and slowly chose several items one after the other and lifted them into the air. My jacket. The backpack. A hairbrush. My pillow. One of my black boots. It took every ounce of my concentration to keep all five items lifted and controlled.

Slowly, the jacket began to fall toward the ground and I switched my concentration over to it, lifting it back into the air. As soon as I did, the other four items collapsed in a heap on the floor. Damn. I sighed and leaned against the door. I'd been trying to perfect this one skill for at least an hour. I did okay when it was just four items, but the second I added a fifth, everything fell apart.

I knew that if I ever wanted to have a chance to defeat the Order, I was going to have to bring my focus to a whole new level. I needed to develop a concentration so sharp that no one and nothing could break it during battle. Right now, my mind was still too scattered.

In the other room, I heard the front double doors open. I froze, listening for who had come through. Mary Anne giggled, and I relaxed, glad it wasn't Jackson. If he discovered me in here practicing magic on my own, I knew he'd be pissed.

I poked my head out my bedroom door and saw Mary Anne and Essex sitting on the couch, heads huddled together looking at something.

"Hey guys," I said.

They turned toward me, then separated like kids caught making out in their parents' living room.

"Hey," Mary Anne said. "I didn't realize you were home. Essex just got off work, so we came here to hang out for a while. Hope that's okay?"

I shrugged and came deeper into the living room, curious about what they'd been looking at so secretively. "Sure," I said. "I don't mind."

Essex turned shyly toward me and put up his hand in a half wave. On his lap, I could just make out a blue book with a tattered binding. "Hello, Harper, I trust you are having a pleasant day."

"It's been fine so far," I said. "I just wish there was more for us to do down here. I mean, even just a place to exercise or a small library or something, you know?"

He fidgeted and moved the book under his thigh, looking nervous. "Yes," he said. "It can be quite dull down here if you don't have a trade."

I moved around to the front of the couch and sat down on the large white marble coffee table. "What's that you've got there?"

It was obvious he hadn't wanted me to see the book, and maybe it was rude to call him out on it, but I wanted to know where he'd gotten it and what, exactly, was in it that he didn't want me to know about.

Mary Anne shifted her feet underneath her. She looked around, double checking that the doors to the suite were closed. "Is Lea here?" she whispered.

I shook my head. "I haven't seen her since yesterday afternoon."

She bit her lower lip and seemed to make a decision about the book. "Show her," she said finally. "She won't tell anyone, I promise."

Essex kept his eyes trained on the ground. In his lap, his left hand trembled slightly. I realized I'd misjudged how important this book was to him. He wasn't just nervous. He was terrified.

"Hey," I said, leaning my head down to try to catch his eye. "I didn't mean to upset you. I just saw the book and was curious. Is it something important?"

He nodded slowly and looked up at Mary Anne, as if asking her if she really did trust me.

"It's fine," she said. "We're like sisters. I swear you can trust her."

Essex took a deep breath in, his chest puffing out. He finally released it, allowing his shoulders to relax a little. With a nervous twitch of his hand, he lifted the book and set it out on the couch between the two of them.

"What is it?" I asked.

He glanced toward the door again, then finally turned and met my gaze. "What I am telling you is restricted information," he said. "I heard some members of the Resistance talking a few days ago about a mission from which they had just returned. They spoke in quiet voices, telling the story to a soldier who had not been at the battle. They spoke of a hunter they had fought in one of the many battles on the surface. Sometimes in battle, the hunters are killed, but most of the time, if the Resistance is able to defeat them, the hunters still manage to get away with only a few wounds. They are very much difficult to kill."

I listened with patience, waiting for him to talk about this book.

"At this battle, the Resistance managed to capture one of the hunters," he said. "The soldiers spoke of this event as if it were very rare."

"What did they do with her once they captured her?" I asked. At this point, I was sitting on the very edge of the coffee table, my hands sweaty with anticipation.

"They forced her to take them to the place where she lives," he said. "A cave of some sort high in the snowy mountains above Gollier."

He paused, putting one hand on top of the book.

"This book is one of the things they found as they searched her home," he said. "According to the soldiers, an entire box of books had been found there in the cave."

"What kind of books?"

"Spell books," he said. "And more importantly, records."

A chill slipped down my spine. "Records?"

"Notes about each demon the hunter had ever taken from our world to yours."

I leaned back, my mouth dry. I wondered why they would even be keeping records. "How did you get hold of one of them?"

Essex shifted in his seat. He didn't answer. He simply looked down at the book and picked at the tattered edges of the binding.

"He stole it," Mary Anne blurted out.

"I am planning to return it," he said quickly. "I only needed to see if my own father's name was included in one of the books."

"And was it?" I asked, trembling.

When he looked up, the pain in his eyes was heartbreaking. "No," he said. "My father's name was not there, but many others from my village and the villages near mine. It must have been a different hunter who took my father."

"I'm sorry," I said, not sure what else to say. "What happened to the hunter? The one they captured?"

"I do not know," he said. "They did not say more about her. Only that they found these books in her cave. I was too afraid to question the soldiers about what happened. I did not want them to know I had been listening."

"Where did you get the book?" I asked, wondering what other books might also be stored there. "Is there some kind of storage room where they keep them all?"

Essex nodded. "Yes," he said. "In the council's meeting hall. It is a large room here where all of our books are stored."

"Sounds like a library," I said. "Can we not just walk in and ask to see some of these books?"

His eyes grew wide and he shook his head fast. "No. Going inside the council's chamber is strictly forbidden unless you are a scholar or a translator or a member of the Underground's council," he said.

"I don't understand," I said. "How did you get the book in the first place if it's so hard to get inside?"

"It was an accident," he said. "Or perhaps it was fate. One of the soldiers telling the story that day dropped it in the marketplace very near to my tent. I picked it up quickly, before he knew it was gone. When I discovered what was inside, I knew I must study it before I could let them know that I had it."

I thought for a minute, letting Essex's story sink in. "You said they also had spell books?" I asked.

He nodded.

"Did they say anything about what was in those books? Anything at all?"

Mary Anne sat up straighter. "I think I just got what you're thinking," she said to me. "If the hunters here live for hundreds of years, who's to say some of those spell books wouldn't be extremely old?"

"Or extremely rare?" I added, excitement pulsing through my veins. "What if one of the books they found had some kind of clue about how to break the spell that ties me to Aerden?"

"Aerden?" Essex said, confused. "You are tied to the twin of Denaer?"

"Yes," Mary Anne said. "Only we call him Jackson, not Denaer. Harper is the future Prima of the demon gate town where his brother Aerden is being held captive. Her family has been tied to Aerden's power for a hundred years."

"All I want is to be able to break the spell that holds us together," I said. "I spent some time in our world looking for any kind of clue as to how to do it, but the only things we found would mean that either Aerden or I had to die."

"I wish I could be of more service," Essex said. "I have not known about the way things work in your world, so I have not known of any way to break this spell you are talking about. However, I do know that the Underground's council holds hundreds of tomes that once belonged to the Order of Shadows. Some of them date back to when the Order first crossed into our world over two hundred years ago. Maybe one of these books could contain the information you are seeking?"

My breath caught in my chest. Could this really be happening? Had I really just stumbled onto the one secret here that might save all of us?

One thing was certain.

I had to get into that library no matter what it took.

IT'S COMPLICATED

I sat in the hallway until the sounds of the marketplace died down and the Underground went to sleep. It was hard to keep my eyes open, but I needed to see Jackson. Since I had no way of contacting him directly, my only option was to sit outside his room and wait.

I was glad we were the only ones living in this hall or else people would have started getting suspicious. So far, I'd been out here for at least four or five hours. What was he up to all the time that he almost never came back to his room?

With a twinge of jealousy, I realized Lea was never in her room either. Did that mean they were together a lot? Had his feelings for me changed so much that he would honestly prefer being around her more than me?

Luckily, I didn't have to wait much longer before he came walking down the corridor. If I'd had to be out there much longer, alone with my thoughts, who knew what I might have come up with to worry about? Of course, it didn't help that when he finally did appear, he wasn't alone.

"Hi," I said as he and Lea approached.

"What are you doing out here?" Lea asked. "It's practically the middle of the night. Did you get locked out?"

"No," I said, not letting her snarky attitude frazzle me. I turned to meet Jackson's eyes, ignoring Lea all together. "I need to talk to you, and since I never see you, I figured this was the best chance I had of getting you alone."

Jackson looked to Lea as if asking for permission. My cheeks grew hot, and I fidgeted while I waited for him to respond.

Lea rolled her eyes. "It's fine with me," she said. "Just don't do it out here where someone might see you. Bring it inside, okay?"

I looked around, wondering who exactly she thought was going to see us in an empty corridor in the middle of the night. I didn't protest, though. I just wanted to talk to him. I didn't care where.

I turned toward his room, expecting him to invite me inside, but he moved in front of the door and shook his head.

"Let's go to your suite," he said.

The three of us walked into the bright light of the suite. Lea said goodnight and slipped into her bedroom. Mary Anne had gone to bed hours ago.

After weeks of being apart, Jackson and I were finally alone again.

My mouth grew dry and butterflies fluttered in my stomach. Every inch of space between us burned with tension.

"What is it?" he asked. "Did you need something?"

His business-like tone hurt me. "Why are you acting like this?" I asked, apparently missing the filter that should have been working between my brain and my mouth.

"Like what?" he asked, shifting his weight and avoiding my eyes.

"Cold," I said. "Like there's nothing between us."

He looked up, a split second of regret in his eyes that was immediately replaced by annoyance. "You do realize that you're the one who was acting cold to me first, right?"

My face grew tense. "What did you expect? You broke my heart," I said.

He closed his eyes and ran a hand through his hair. "Is this what you waited up to tell me?"

I drew in a long breath and tried to calm my rocketing pulse. "No," I said. "I wanted to talk to you about the possibility of joining in with you guys on whatever it is you're working on down here."

He snapped his head up, surprised. "Joining in?"

"Yeah," I said, pacing. "You're obviously meeting with Andros and the council a lot, and I have to assume you're talking about plans to fight against the Order, right?"

"Something like that," he mumbled.

"Okay, so I want in."

He shook his head and walked over to the couch, leaning against the back side of it. "It's not that easy, Harper. The council accepted you as a resident. That doesn't mean they want you in on all their secret plans."

"Am I not a part of this?" I asked. "Have I not proven my commitment to destroying the Order? Or is it just that you don't think anything I do is going to make a difference?"

Jackson sighed. "It's not about what I think."

"Yes, it is," I said. "I've seen the way Andros hangs on every word of yours. He trusts you. He listens to you."

He shook his head and paced the area in front of me. "It's

complicated, Harper," he said. "I wish I could help, but things take time down here. I need more than a couple of weeks to convince them to change the entire way they think about human witches."

Bullshit.

I didn't believe him. There was some other reason he was shutting me out. I could feel it. And I could tell he was struggling with it to. But why? Did it have something to do with Lea? He was always looking to her for permission these days, as if he answered to her.

"Fine," I said. "But what about training? Can you get me into any of the Resistance training classes?"

Jackson's eyes grew wide as if I'd just asked him to fly me to Mt. Fuji. "Why would you want to do that? And how do you even know about the training classes?"

"Do you think I want to be weak and powerless for the rest of my life?" I asked. "If I'm stuck down here, I want to at least make the most of it. I'm bored to death down here. I feel like a prisoner."

He lifted a hand in the air as if he were going to say one thing, then he put it down and turned his back on me, changing his mind. After a few moments, he finally turned back to me and said no. "I can't even ask for permission for such a thing right now," he said. "The training is for their soldiers, Harper. They don't even let all the demons down here into the training. They're certainly not going to let a human in."

I walked to the door and opened it for him, so frustrated I wanted to scream. "I don't know what's gotten into you," I said. "But you're not yourself. The Jackson I knew back home would have fought for me. I don't know what it is that's changing you here or why you can't just tell me what's really going on, but I miss you. I miss the real you."

Jackson stood there, just staring at me. I could tell I'd struck a chord with something I'd said, but he still didn't tell me what was going on in his mind.

"Everything I've done," he said, walking toward the door. He paused right in front of me, his face so close to mine it made my heart ache. His green eyes were filled with secrets and sorrows. "I've done to protect you."

I watched as he made his way back to his room, not once looking back.

RIGHT PLACE AT THE RIGHT TIME

The marketplace hummed with life. The late afternoon crowds filled the makeshift streets. Barely anyone noticed me anymore. I had become a permanent fixture in the Grand Hall over the past couple of weeks. I don't know if that meant they had begun to trust me, exactly, but at least they no longer seemed to fear me.

Today and every day since Essex first told me about the library, I'd spent at least a few hours here watching the soldiers and the council members come and go. I wanted to know how often the soldiers seemed to go on missions. And I wanted to see where it was the council members kept disappearing to. Since the council's library was such a restricted place, I knew I couldn't just walk up and ask where it was.

In some ways, I had become exactly what they'd all feared I was all along. A spy.

The difference was that the last thing I wanted to do was spy for the Order. No, I gathered information for myself only.

If Jackson and Lea had insisted I be included in all the

meetings and treated as an equal, I never would have gotten myself into this situation of spying and sneaking around to get my own information. But since they had decided to shut me out and treat me more as a visitor than an actual participant in this war against the Order, what choice did I have?

So, I watched.

I made notes in my journal.

Since I didn't have a clock or a sun to keep time for me, I kept time based on the rhythms of the people. In the mornings when I heard the door of our suite slam closed, I knew Lea had left for her daily meetings or whatever it was she and Jackson did all day out of sight from the rest of us. In my mind, I labeled this as the beginning of the morning. I spent this time working on my magic. When the smells of food on the grill stretched all the way down to the suite from the marketplace, I figured it was about noon. Lunchtime.

Then, when the voices grew louder, and the market buzzed with conversation and excitement of another finished workday, I knew it was quitting time. Somewhere around five or so in the afternoon. This was when the soldiers and the council quit their work and emerged from their secret caves like tiny ants from their hill.

It took me a few days to pinpoint the exact location of the training area. At first, it seemed the soldiers just magically appeared out of nowhere. I recognized them by their matching black uniforms and serious looks. I had expected the army to be made up of mostly men, much like the army back home. I was pleasantly surprised to see an equal number of men and women had joined in the training and fighting against the Order.

Around this time in the afternoon, I tried to position

myself in different parts of the market, hoping to get a glimpse of the soldiers pouring out of some secret corridor or area. It wasn't until the fourth day that I found myself in exactly the right place at the right time.

I got to the marketplace a little early and walked around toward the very back, as far away from the entry staircase as I could get. I walked along the back wall, which, as far as I could tell, was just a solid wall with no caves or entrances of any kind. I was actually trying to get to the other side of the market when part of the wall next to me rose up like a trap door. Startled, I jumped back and wedged myself between the fabric of two nearby tents.

Immediately, my fear was replaced with secret joy. A group of soldiers emerged from the hidden door, talk of the latest training session on their lips. I stayed hidden for the next half hour as hundreds of soldiers gradually poured from the corridor.

When they were all through and the door was closed for the night, I stepped out of the dark alley between the tents and took a mental picture of my location. Just across from a purple and orange tent that sold jewelry with red stones inside. I memorized every detail of the area, then ran my hand along the wall, trying to feel the outline of the door, but there were no grooves or cracks to show it had ever existed. A magic door.

Later, I sat down in my favorite little cafe and drew a map of the marketplace, marking a special X for the secret training ground of the Resistance army.

FOLLOW YOUR FRIENDS

F inding the library was not as easy.

Unlike the soldiers, the scholars and council members didn't wear matching outfits, which made them much harder to spot. I tried to remember the faces of the demons I'd seen walking with Jackson from time to time, but I soon lost my patience and decided to stop in to see Essex at his work.

"Hey," Mary Anne said with a smile as I walked into the tent. She was sitting on top of the sales counter watching Essex direct a bunch of needles to make matching shirts in a variety of colors. "What have you been up to so far today? I feel like I've hardly seen you at all lately."

"Oh, just walking around," I said casually. I had kept my activities from Mary Anne because I didn't want her mixed up in it if I got caught. I leaned in and whispered so that Essex's mother couldn't hear me, just in case she was close by. "What about Essex's mom? Does she still give you the evil eye?"

Mary Anne giggled. "Not really," she said. "I think she's

getting used to me. Look, yesterday she even gave me this leather cuff. I think it was a sort of peace offering in a way."

She held out her wrist and showed me a black leather cuff that clasped tight around her entire wrist. On the top, it was embroidered with the initials M. A. in silver thread that sparkled when she moved her wrist from side to side.

"That's beautiful," I said.

A jolt of regret ran through my heart. If an old woman with obvious prejudices toward humans could accept the fact that her son had made a very close friendship with a human girl, why was Jackson so certain no one here would understand our relationship? It didn't make any sense. Something wasn't adding up between us. There had to be more to his reasons for breaking up than what he told me.

For the most part, I'd done really well at not falling apart about the whole Jackson scenario. I'd thrown myself into other projects and found goals for myself like finding the library or working on my own magic. But with as much time as I spent alone these days, there were definitely a lot of late nights when I lay in bed just thinking about him.

What was he doing down here every day? Were they planning something important? Was he going to go back for Aerden? Why was he keeping so much from me? Did he miss me the same way I missed him?

"Are you all right?" Mary Anne asked.

I came out of my thoughts and smiled. "Sorry, I think I spaced."

"You did more than space," she said. "You went into some kind of sadness coma. What's going on with you lately? I thought you'd be glad to be out of Peachville and away from all that crap the Order put you through."

I sighed. "I am glad," I said. "I just think about Lark and my other friends a lot. I wonder what they're up to. I hate not knowing what's going on in Peachville."

This wasn't exactly a lie. I did think about Peachville a lot, wondering if anyone had spoken up about their plans to sacrifice my life and transfer the line. I knew Mrs. King didn't approve, and I was sure Lark and her mother were dead set against the idea. But did they speak out? Had they been punished? Or did their fear keep them quiet?

Between worrying about them and thinking about Jackson, it was amazing I was still holding on to my sanity at all these days.

Honestly, it was the idea of having a plan of my own that kept me waking up and going through the motions each day.

Mary Anne put her hand on mine. "I know what you mean about Peachville," she said. "I thought I'd be so glad to get out of there that I would never look back, but I can't help thinking about Courtney. I didn't get a chance to explain anything to her about our plan. She probably has no idea what happened to either one of us."

I nodded, ashamed to admit I hadn't been thinking about Courtney in all of this. "To tell you the truth, I bet they just wiped her memories of us, like they did with me when I first got there."

"Well, I kind of hope they did," she said. "That should at least keep her safe from them."

She had a point. My hope was that all of my friends and allies in Peachville would be safe and sound when I finally returned. I couldn't bear it if they'd gotten hurt because of me and the choices I'd made.

But I hadn't come here today to talk about Peachville. As

much as I cared about the people back there, I also knew there was nothing I could do for them until I was strong enough to fight against the Order. For me to find that strength, I needed two things. Training and information. If I could find the right spell book, I could end this whole thing forever. I could free all of the Primas from their demons and change the entire game in one instant. In my heart, I knew that spell existed. I just had to find it.

"Listen, I need to ask Essex something about the library," I whispered, looking around to make sure there were no customers in the tent or people lingering outside.

Mary Anne's eyes grew dark. Worried. "Here?" she asked. "Can't we talk about this back in the room later or something? I don't want to get him into any trouble."

"It'll just take a second, I swear."

She chewed on her lower lip and finally nodded, motioning for Essex to stop his work for a second. He walked over to us, a sweet smile on his face. He placed his hand down on the counter beside Mary Anne and I noticed her pinky slide over to touch the side of his palm ever so slightly.

"Ask him quickly," she said.

"What do you know about the council's meeting place?" I asked. "I've been trying to find the entrance to the library by following some of the council members around, but other than Andros, I'm not completely sure who is on the council. And what about the scholars you talked about? What do they wear?"

Essex looked around nervously. Then, he leaned in close to me. "You'll never see the scholars," he said. "They never leave the council's wing as far as I know. They are like monks. Hermits."

I blew out a hard breath of frustration. Crap. "So how else am I supposed to find the library?"

The question was more for my own benefit. I hadn't been expecting Essex to actually have an answer for me.

"Follow your friends," he said. "The princess and the twin. They are going there every day."

My eyes widened. "How do you know this?"

"My shop is in a very good location here on the end of the row," he said with a sly smile. "Many believe they are talking in secret, not understanding that those of us inside the shop can still hear them. I hear many things, and one thing I hear is that the council and your friends are meeting in the library almost every single day to discuss a new plan for our people. There are many whispers on the streets of these events. Follow them and you will find the library."

A customer walked into the shop, not hiding her surprise at finding two humans talking so casually to the shop owner's son. She almost turned around to go, but then changed her mind and turned back toward us, an attempt to smile coming out as more of a grimace.

"Hello, Essex, I was hoping you could help me with a new dress for a party I'm attending this month?" she said. She kept glancing my way, obviously uncomfortable in the presence of a human.

"I was just leaving," I said. "Thank you for your help with the new backpack. I sincerely appreciate it."

Essex bowed to me. "Anything for a friend of Andros," he said. As I walked away, he turned his attention to the lady customer. "Now, what kind of design did you have in mind?"

I slipped outside and made my way back toward the suite.

Following Jackson and Lea wouldn't be easy. Especially

since Jackson could usually sense my presence from a mile away. But that gave me an idea. He might be able to sense my presence, but I was usually able to sense him too. The feeling had been somewhat diminished here while I was so far away from Aerden, but still, I might be able to use that connection to find Jackson.

It was too late in the day to try anything now, but after my magic practice tomorrow, that's exactly what I was going to do.

CLOSE ENOUGH TO FEEL

My new goal was to re-establish my connection with Jackson's energy. There had been a time when I could feel him like he was a part of me. An extension of my own energy. I knew part of that connection had to do with his twin brother, Aerden. Since Aerden was a part of me, bound to my family's line for a hundred years, it was only natural for that to extend to Jackson as well.

But I knew our connection was more than that.

No matter what was going on between us now that we had come to the Underground, it didn't change the fact that I loved him. We had saved each other's lives. Surely that counted for something. Wouldn't that kind of thing leave a mystical connection?

I was counting on a combination of all those things.

I sat alone in the comfort of my bedroom, my legs crossed under my body and my palms facing upward. I became centered, focusing on the feel of my own power coursing through my bones. When I was sure and solid in my own power, I switched my focus from myself to Jackson. I sought him out with my mind, extending my magic like hidden fingers that stretched out to the entire Underground. I searched for any sign of him, wanting to feel that connection and hoping to be able to recognize him even in a crowded space of a thousand other demons.

That first day, despite hours of meditation, I failed. I couldn't feel him at all. Was he too far away? Meeting somewhere deep in the bowels of this place? Far from my reach? Was the soul stone above our heads messing with my focus somehow? Or was I simply too far away from Aerden to feel any connection to his brother as well?

The next morning, I spent my typical magic practice time in meditation instead, with the same bitter results.

It wasn't until the fifth day of trying that I finally found him. In my quiet state of meditation, a whisper of him crossed into my mind. My body lit up like a firefly, the tiny hairs on my arms standing up. Somewhere, he had stepped into my range and my body had reacted.

At first, I couldn't tell where he was, only that he was close enough to feel. I pushed my excitement down to the bottom of my mind and instead focused on what I knew of the Underground. I started by imagining the suite, then the hall where we all lived together. I rebuilt the place in my mind, like a ghostly map, uninhabited and shadowy, but clear. The process was a bit disorienting at first. My body was here in this room, but my mind was floating, free from the restrictions of flesh.

I didn't sense him in any of these places, so I stretched my thoughts even further, struggling to stay focused despite the slight dizziness I felt. Finally, near the small cafe where I liked to write in the afternoons, I saw him.

In my vision, I could see impressions of other energies bustling past, but Jackson's form glowed bright and steady.

He stood in the marketplace talking to someone, but I wasn't good enough yet to identify anyone else by feel. For all purposes, I might as well have been standing there beside him. I could feel him that strongly. And the longer I focused on him, the stronger my focus became.

I swam in it, letting the closeness of his essence surround me like water.

When he moved, I moved with him, sensing his path step-by-step with amazing clarity. Then, he stepped into a cave on the far north side of the marketplace. A cave I had never been in before.

Like a light switch being turned off, he was gone.

No matter how hard I tried for the rest of the day, I couldn't find him again. Was it simply that he'd gone somewhere my mind's eye couldn't envision? Or was there some kind of block set up in that particular cave?

That afternoon, I strolled through the marketplace, looking for the cave he'd disappeared into. The problem was it didn't exist.

DO YOU KNOW THIS WORD?

I ran my hand along the stone wall.

Just like the hidden door where the soldiers went for training, the cave where Jackson spent most of his days was equally as hidden. There was no trace of it from the outside. Similar to the other one, this hidden door was also in a far corner of the marketplace, tucked behind a few tents where no one would notice people coming in and out.

I couldn't help but wonder why there were so many secrets in a place like this. Hadn't everyone come down here with the same idea and purpose? Why would it be important to keep the activities of the soldiers and the council hidden from the rest of the community?

For that matter, why would they have a library that no one could see? Why didn't everyone have a right to learn what they could about the Order of Shadows? Was the council really that paranoid about spies?

I kicked my boot against the stone wall. Nothing in my plan was coming together like I'd hoped.

The only thing I'd accomplished so far was learning a few extra magic tricks and establishing a new connection to Jackson. A pretty much useless connection now that I knew I couldn't follow him through this door.

Still, I wasn't going to give up. I may be in hiding from the Order, but that didn't mean I couldn't be working on ways to fight them.

My two main objectives hadn't changed. I wanted to watch the demons here train and see if I could pick up on some real offensive magic I could use to fight. And I wanted to find the books the Underground's Resistance army had taken from the Order's hunters.

All of this would have been a lot easier if Jackson had stuck by my side and worked harder to include me in his plans. As I made my way back to my room, this thought made me more and more angry. Why hadn't he at least introduced me to the members of the council? I was confident that if I'd had my chance to speak to the council members individually, I could have convinced them of my dedication to destroy the Order.

Anger fueled my steps as I tore through the marketplace with increasing speed.

If I had to resort to more drastic measures, it was his fault really. He could have made this all a lot easier for me, but instead he deliberately made it impossible for me to do anything down here except sit in my room like a prisoner.

Well, I had been a prisoner most of my life in one way or another. First, a prisoner to all the horrible foster homes, never really given any freedom to be myself. Then, a prisoner in Peachville, forced into a life I never wanted as future Prima. And finally, when the Order realized I wasn't going to bow to their will, a prisoner on death row at Shadowford.

I'd had enough of being locked up.

I wanted to be free, and the only way I was ever going to do that was to get more knowledge. I needed to know how to fight, and I needed to know how to break the spell that bound me to Aerden. And down here in the Underground, with or without Jackson's help, I had a chance to learn both.

I reached the suite and threw open the door.

Mary Anne and Essex sat on the couch together playing some kind of game I didn't recognize.

"Hey, Harper," Mary Anne said, raising a hand in hello.

I ignored her, anger and hurt sending me straight toward my room. Then, I decided, what the hell? It was time for drastic measures, right?

I turned back toward them, my gaze landing on Essex. "What do you know about invisibility?"

He drew his eyebrows together and stared blankly toward me. "What are you meaning by this?"

"You know, being invisible," I said. "Going from being able to see something to not being able to see it at all."

"Okay," he said, tilting his head to the side. "What is it you are asking?"

I sat on the arm of the couch beside Mary Anne. "Say I was to go invisible right now and start walking around the marketplace," I said. "How many of your kind would be able to see me?"

"If you are disappearing?" he asked. "No one. Isn't that the point of disappearing?"

I couldn't help but laugh at his logic. "Yes," I said. "But the point of the dark is that you can't see anything, but some shadow demons see perfectly fine in the dark."

He nodded, as if finally understanding my question. "You

are wanting to know if anyone here has the special powers of seeing through invisibility."

I thought about the wording of his statement. "Sort of," I said. "The only way I know to make myself invisible is to use a glamour. Do you know this word?"

He brought a hand up to his lips and narrowed his eyes. "I am not certain, what does it mean?"

"A glamour is when you change your outer appearance to something different," Mary Anne explained. "Not really changing it deep down, only on the surface."

He opened his mouth and nodded again. "Yes," he said. "You are meaning an artificial self, in a way. Like the way you see me because of your potion. Human."

"Right," I said. "Can everyone see through those things? Like if I made myself look like Mary Anne and walked around the marketplace, would people know it was really me and not her?"

Essex shook his head. "I do not believe this is a magic most of my people would be able to see unless they were specifically looking for it," he said. "Up on the surface, they might be more careful with such things, but down here, I think you would be unnoticed."

I decided to practice without letting him know I was practicing. "Thank you," I said, standing up from the couch.

"Wait," Mary Anne said. "Why are you asking about all this?"

I shrugged. "I was just curious."

Mary Anne cut her eyes toward me suspiciously, but I just turned and walked back to my room, careful to leave the door wide open.

In the living room, they resumed their game. I moved

quietly into my bathroom and sat down on the floor, concentrating until my power was strong enough to let my body become enveloped in a glamour of nothingness. My body disappeared from the room, and once I was sure it was going to stick, I stood and walked quietly into the living room.

I took each step extremely slow so that I didn't make a single sound.

I moved around the couch and stood inches from them, watching them play their game for about ten minutes before I finally cleared my throat.

Both of them jumped sky-high, pieces of their game scattering around the couch. Essex was so frightened, he was halfway to the door by the time I released my glamour and let him see that there was nothing to be afraid of.

"I didn't mean to scare you," I said, trying not to laugh. "I just wanted to see if you'd see me."

"Well we didn't," Mary Anne said, laughing. She held a hand up to her heart. "Jesus, you scared the crap out of me."

Essex still stood halfway between the couch and the door, a blank expression on his face.

Crap. I'd probably pissed him off.

"Are you okay?" Mary Anne asked, hopping off the back of the couch to go to his side. She took his hand, and it was the first time I'd seen them touch so openly.

Her hand in his seemed to wake him up from his shock. "Yes," he said, shaking it off. "I have never had this experience before now. I honestly did not see you or even sense your presence in any way. You startled me."

I apologized again, but in my heart, I was satisfied. It had worked.

Now, all I had to do was make it work in front of about five hundred demon soldiers.

THE HIDDEN DOOR

Early the next morning, I slipped out of the suite long before even Lea was awake.

I didn't want to miss it when the soldiers went into the training room for the day. Since I'd mostly just watched them come out in the afternoons, I had no idea what time the doors opened. I guessed it had to be pretty early.

I hid myself between the folds of the tent, just as I had last time, and waited. About an hour later, as my eyes drooped with sleep, the first soldiers arrived at the hidden door.

I pulled myself together and was able to make myself invisible just as the door slid open. My heart racing, I stepped from the safety of my hiding place and waited. To my surprise and great happiness, no one noticed me. I hung back and waited for the last of the group to file inside, then I followed close behind.

And just like that, I was inside.

MAGIC I COULD USE

TRAINING DAY 1, DISTRACTION

Today the soldiers learned about the art of distracting their enemies. I watched as they each practiced distracting their enemy with one type of magic while they prepared a death blow from behind. The soldiers practice with floating dummies that look eerily human. They are not alive but are animated with some kind of magic to make them act like living targets. One girl in particular caught my eye, and I watched her very skillfully throw a fireball directly at her target while simultaneously lifting a dagger from the floor behind the dummy. The dummy easily defended itself against the fireball but was defeated by the well-placed dagger stabbed through its heart from behind. Watching this gave me chills.

TRAINING DAY 2, Momentum

It seems that many of the demons here have some connection with one or more of the elements. Some used fire in their *training today while others chose wind or water. Except not all demon power seems to use a pure version of the elements. I noticed that some use lightning instead of fire, much like Agnes. Others use ice instead of water. It reminded me of the way Jackson had so quickly frozen the archers in the woods the night we were attacked by the fake witch. I wondered if every demon had its own talent where the elements were concerned or if they each just picked one they liked and went with it? What were the rules of how the different elements could be manipulated? Maybe energy is a better word than elements.*

I watched today as they learned different ways to create momentum with their chosen energy. Fires that began small were infused with power to become raging infernos of rolling fire that reached from floor to ceiling, which is saying a lot considering how high the ceilings here are. One boy with particular skill in wind control created a tornado so large it swept several other students up into the air before the instructor calmed him down.

Training Day 3, Black Smoke

Out of all the magic I've seen so far, this was probably the one that I'll never be able to attempt. Today, the recruits learned to use their raw demon power as a weapon in and of itself. I remember seeing Jackson and Lea's power manifest itself in ribbons of black smoke once they passed through the portal. Jackson had said it left a trace or signature behind, but he hadn't really explained how it worked.

Today, I got to see a lot more of this black smoke in action. Every time one of the demons casts a spell, the smoke seems to come from their hands. If the spell is small or weak, the smoke is thin and barely noticeable. If the spell is strong or powerful, the smoke becomes like billowing ropes that can be used to strangle an opponent or lift them into the air. Many students used their power today as a type of extension of their own hands, letting the black smoke reach out and touch something far away.

I was fascinated, wishing this was a magic I could use.

TRAINING DAY 4, *Danger*

I almost got caught today. I fell asleep during the afternoon session and fell against the rock behind me. I didn't lose my glamour, but I must have made a noise, because several students toward the back turned to look in my direction. For a moment, I was sure they could see me. I am going to have to be more careful.

A TINY GLOW

By the end of the week, my little notebook was almost completely full of journal entries from the training sessions I'd sat in on. Watching the shadow demons at work was fascinating. It was nothing like what we'd been taught on the Demons cheerleading squad. This training camp made ours look like child's play.

When I first followed the soldiers into the cave, I'd had to spend some time figuring out which class was the beginner's class. The training area was made up of about twenty smaller rooms and one giant room that was about a quarter the size of the Grand Hall marketplace. In each of the smaller rooms, individual classes met, each seeming to work at different skill levels.

Some of the classes were dealing with magic that scared me. I knew those classes were way too advanced for me, so I kept looking until I found one class that used types of magic I felt I could replicate. I found a dark place in the corner where I could sit and observe them throughout the day. I remembered as much as I could from the day's lessons, and in the evenings, I would spend a couple of hours in my room writing down in my notebook what I'd learned.

Holding the invisibility for so many hours each day was draining, but I was surprised to find that it didn't make me sick; the way it had back in the human world. Back home, I never would have been able to stay invisible for so long, but here it was much easier. I was still exhausted, but after a short break, my power came back to me. I wasn't sure where all this new power was coming from, but I liked it.

In the evenings after dinner, I practiced some of what I'd seen, trying to perfect the art of distraction or learn how to manipulate fire. Of course, since I was only in my small room in the suite, I had to be very careful not to catch the whole place on fire. The space limited what I could do, but at least I was working on new skills.

After that first week, though, I knew I needed a bigger place to practice. The best place would be the training room itself, but what if I got locked inside? Or if someone caught me in there? What if they had guards that walked through the rooms at night?

I worried about it for about five seconds before I decided to just do it. Hadn't I already come this far? The bottom line was that I needed the space to practice if I was ever going to learn to do these things myself.

That's when I decided to stay in the training room until every last soldier and teacher had left. It took about an hour of waiting after the last class before I felt confident that I was alone. The lights had been turned out and everything around me was silent as a tomb. I finally stepped out of my hiding place and let my invisibility glamour drop.

Drained, I had to sit down and meditate in the darkness for almost an hour before I felt my power return to me. Plus, I was starving. It was stupid of me to forget to bring any food along. I'd seen the demons eating some kind of power bars during their lunch break, so they didn't have to go back to the market-place for food. I lit a small orb and made my way to the front of the room where I'd seen the instructor with the bars. Unfortu-nately, there was nothing left in the box. I searched around a little more but figured out pretty quick that I was out of luck as far as food was concerned. Luckily, there was a large container of water in the hallway.

With my stomach growling from not eating since breakfast, I positioned myself in the middle of the large training space and got to work. For hours, I worked on the momentum magic I'd seen them learning last week. Not knowing which type of energy would be my strongest, I played around with all of them. I didn't want to limit myself, but I was also curious if I would naturally be better at one than another.

Fire was by far the easiest for me to manipulate. I'd been accused of playing with fire my entire life, ever since my adop-tive father died in a fire that I accidentally started. But I alone understood at the time that I hadn't created that fire. It was my ability to move objects around with my mind and my emotions that had set that fire.

The same thing happened with Agnes the night she died. She was the one who lit the candle in the lake house that night. All I did was use my powers to make it fall over. Still, the fire had spread much more rapidly than any normal fire should have. Was that because of me?

I remembered back to the old hospital the night the Others tried to kill Jackson. Hadn't I killed someone with fire that night as well? I'd sent the fire across the room like a wave to save Jackson's life.

A chill spread up my arms. I'd always thought my relationship with fire was purely accidental. An unfortunate result of my ability to move things with my mind. But there in the quiet darkness of the training room, I found something different to be true.

The easy way my hands manipulated the small fire I created told me in my deepest core that I had a real connection with this blazing light in front of me. The flames responded to my every thought, like an extension of myself. I moved my hands high into the air and the fire spread itself up like a giant wall in front of me. I spun around in a circle and the blaze followed, creating a perfect barrier around me. I held my hands out to my side and lifted them, amazed as the entire circle of flames rose from the ground to a spot just above my head. I was completely encircled in flame.

The control and power of it made me giddy and light. I brought the fire back down to its smallest self, a tiny glow in my palm. Then, with a happy smile, I leaned over and blew it out like a birthday candle.

A PIECE OF MYSELF

I slept in a dark cubby on the far side of the largest training room. After my practice the night before, I'd gone to the door and tried to find a way to open it, but it wouldn't budge. I was locked in for the night. So, I searched for a relatively safe place to curl up and sleep until morning.

I was a little bit worried that Lea or Mary Anne would notice that I had never come home, but there was nothing I could do about it from here. Tired from so much magic work, I went to sleep instantly, only waking in the morning when I heard the first voices enter the training corridor. I'd been sure to hide in a place where I'd never seen anyone practicing. Mostly, the various groups seemed to stay exclusively in the smaller rooms, rarely ever coming together in this larger hall.

Rested, I quickly worked up my invisibility glamour and made my way to my normal hiding place in the beginner's training room.

Things went on like this for a couple of weeks. Obviously, I couldn't stay in the training room every night. It was too hard on my body to go for so long without food. Instead, I would spend a couple of nights resting up my powers, then spend a night training, and so on.

One afternoon, Mary Anne knocked on my door and pushed her way inside. "What the heck is going on with you?" she whispered, shutting the door behind her.

Lea was home for once, so I hoped she couldn't hear. I motioned for Mary Anne to join me in the bathroom. I closed the door and turned on the shower and the faucet full blast.

"I can't tell you exactly," I said.

She opened her mouth to protest, but I interrupted her.

"If I get caught, it's better if you know nothing, trust me," I said.

Concern darkened the blue of her eyes. "What's going on, Harper? I came here to help keep you safe, not to watch you get into any kind of trouble."

"I know," I said. "But I can't just sit here in the suite and stay completely clueless like they want me to. The Order is still out there, here and back home, killing people and making demons into slaves and doing whatever they want to do. You guys didn't really think I'd just stay here forever and let that happen, right?"

Mary Anne lowered her eyes and shook her head. "I guess not," she said. "But Harper, how can we fight them? Even if we took an army with us back home, we still wouldn't be strong enough to stop them."

"How do you know that?" I asked. "Everyone keeps saying we'd never beat them, but when has anyone ever really tried? I mean, sure, small groups have fought back, but never a massive army. At least not that I've ever heard of. Instead the King of the North sits on his throne pretending nothing is wrong. The

King of the South, who knows what's up with him? The two are such vicious rivals they'd rather hate each other than work together to fight the Order. And back home? How is a demon gate town supposed to fight back when the entire coven's lives are bound to a single person? If the Prima dies, everyone dies. That's a serious weakness, and one that the Order uses to its full advantage."

"But—"

"But what if we could break the connection between a Prima and her demon? If we could find a way to do that, the Order would have to take us out one at a time. It makes the size of the army that much bigger in an instant, right?"

Mary Anne nodded, but there was still doubt in her eyes.

"I know what you're thinking," I said. "You and Jackson both think I'm crazy for insisting there's a way to break the connection, but I'm telling you, I know there is a way. And I won't stop until I find it."

"You think the answer might be in those books, don't you?" she asked. "The books the soldiers brought back from the hunters?"

I nodded. "I know it sounds like a long shot, but don't you think it's possible? I mean, these books could be hundreds of years old. These hunters aren't really human anymore. You heard what they said. They're bonded to several demons so they can live longer."

Mary Anne's face grew sad, and I knew she must be thinking of her own family. The old crow witch did something similar to stay alive for a hundred years by taking the power from other witches. These hunters were the same.

"I'm sorry," I said. "I wasn't thinking about..."

My words drifted off.

"It's okay," she said. "We all have our own family's past to deal with. I'm not proud of where I come from, but I'm not like them. I want to make something different of my life."

"You already have," I said.

Mary Anne wiped away a tear and smiled up at me. "I'll help you however I can," she said. "You know that, right?"

I hugged her small frame and nodded. "I know," I said.

"Please, tell me what you're doing," she said. "I hate being in the dark."

I suddenly realized, looking at the sadness in her eyes, that I was shutting her out the same way Jackson had shut me out. Yes, I'd been trying to protect her, but didn't she deserve to know?

We sat down together on the tile floor of my bathroom, and I told her about everything I'd been doing in the training room. She was surprised, but excited for me.

"I've barely used magic at all since we got here," she said. "I think my wounds are still healing, because I haven't been able shift. I tried to explain it to Essex, you know, my shape-shifting, but I couldn't make it happen. When I tried to cast my magic, my side hurt so bad I couldn't keep going."

"Just give it more time," I said. "You were hurt pretty bad."

"I know," she said. "I just worry that I won't ever be able to use magic again."

"You will," I said. "It's a part of you just like it's a part of me. Besides, it's the pain that's stopping you and that won't last forever."

She squeezed my hand. "Thanks."

"So, you'll cover for me if Lea ever realizes I'm gone overnight?" I asked.

Mary Anne giggled. "Maybe I'll tell her you found a nice demon to shack up with."

I playfully punched her arm. "Hey, speaking of shacking up, what's with you and Essex? Is there officially a romance there?"

She blushed and avoided my eyes. She shrugged like it wasn't a big deal, but I knew differently.

"Hey, it's not like you're the only one who ever loved a shadow demon," I said. "You don't have to worry about judgment from me."

"I really like him a lot," she said. "I never liked any of the boys back home. Not even a little bit. I always felt so different, you know? Like I didn't really belong there. But here, with Essex..."

"He feels the same way about you," I said.

"You think so?"

"Isn't it obvious?" I said. "Have you guys talked about it?"

She shook her head and started playing with the hem of her skirt. "I'm too scared to really bring it up after, you know, what Jackson said about the demons here being forbidden to love humans."

"It's a stupid rule, anyway."

"Yes, it is," she said. "Do you miss him?"

My breath caught my throat for a second. Did I miss him? Such a simple question for such a complex set of emotions. I nodded yes, but what I meant was that every day we spent apart, I felt like a piece of myself was missing.

"I try not to think about it," I said once I felt that I was in control of my voice again.

"Is that why you're doing all this?" she asked. "Risking so much to train and look for the books?"

I shrugged. "Maybe," I said, tugging on the white strip of fabric tied to my wrist. "But mostly it's because I am tired of being helpless."

Mary Anne gave me another hug and stood up, moving to turn off the water. "I've got your back," she said. "Whatever you need."

"Thanks," I said.

"And Harper?" She turned back just as she was almost out the door.

"Yes?"

"Promise me you won't leave here without saying goodbye."

I started to deny that I was planning to leave, but I knew she wasn't stupid. After a moment, I nodded.

"I promise."

I HAD TO KNOW

I'd learned so much about magic and fighting from my days in the training room, but there was still the matter of the library.

I knew I could spend the rest of my life training at the different magic levels and probably still not learn everything. After all, the shadow demons were immortal. They had no time limit to their learning, while I felt time slipping through my fingers with every day I remained stuck inside this underground fortress.

I had to find a way into the library.

My only guess was that it was somewhere down the same hallway I'd seen Jackson disappear the day I'd connected to his essence.

As reluctant as I was to stop my training, I knew my best chance at getting into the library was to follow a similar plan to the one I'd used to sneak into the training door. I needed to get there early. But I knew that there would be no throng of soldiers crowding in and out, making me much less noticeable.

Getting into the council's secret space was going to take a little bit more planning.

I followed the map I'd made in my notebook back to the place where I'd seen Jackson disappear into the wall. I studied the shops in the area, looking for someplace where I could sit and watch the entrance without looking too suspicious. Unfortunately, the only place I could find that had a clear view to the wall was a blacksmith's shop. I couldn't think of any reason why I'd be spending several days hanging out at their shop, so I needed a different plan.

I stood there for a minute, studying the area and trying to find a place where I could hide, but the tents here were more spaced out. Hiding between them might be a little riskier.

Then I looked up and saw that from here I could see the balcony of the stairs where we'd first come into the Underground. My heart skipped. If I had a clear view of it from here, then I should have a really good view of this wall from way up there.

I had to slow my steps to hide my excitement. As casually as possible, I made my way through the maze of tents, up the left side of the double staircase, and straight to the balcony area. Yes! I could easily sit here in the corner and peer down through the marble banisters. I had a perfect view of the wall and would be able to see exactly who was coming in and out. And more importantly, when they were coming and going.

The only trouble would be if there were other people on the stairs, but for the most part, no one came in and out of the Underground except to bring in food or supplies. As far as I had observed, that only happened every once in a while, certainly not every day or even every other day. Besides, if anyone saw me sitting here, I could easily explain that I was sitting up so high so that I could get a better view of the marketplace for my drawings.

Drawings I would work on while I sat up there for hours.

I used to love to draw. Before I came to Peachville, I would spend hours working on drawings of my mother or trying to draw things I'd seen in my dreams. Since I joined the cheerleading team, I'd barely taken the time to draw much of anything. It might be nice to sit up here on this balcony and get back into it.

The next morning, I woke up early and made my way to the hidden spot on the balcony. This early, there was never much activity in the marketplace. Mostly, it was just quiet and peaceful. A bakery somewhere on the south side smelled of heaven. My mouth watered, but I was anxious to get in place. I didn't want to miss anything.

I carried a blank notebook today. I didn't want anyone to question me and find that I had been taking notes and drawing maps this whole time. I needed my drawing excuse to look legit if someone saw me.

An hour passed before anyone made a move toward the wall. I didn't recognize the robed man who went inside. I'd never seen anyone dressed that way, and I wondered if he was one of the elusive scholars Essex told me about. No one else went through the wall for another hour or so, but I recognized the woman who went in next.

Ourelia. Andros' wife. She was alone, but in an obvious hurry. In her hands, she carried a couple of bags, but I couldn't see what might be inside of them.

Throughout the day, more demons came in and out, sometimes in groups and sometimes alone. There seemed to be no rhyme or reason to the times of day they chose. Everyone seemed to come and go as they pleased.

The first day, there was no sign of Jackson or Lea.

Day two was much more informative. Jackson, Andros, Lea, and Jericho all walked into the corridor together relatively early in the morning and didn't emerge until well after dinner time. What did they do in there all day?

On day four, I was tired of waiting and ready to make my move. Luckily, no one had noticed me on the balcony. I did, however, have several nice drawings of the marketplace that had kept me from being too bored while I was staking the place out.

I left my notebook behind the fourth morning. I waited until the area near the door was completely abandoned, then I made myself invisible and hid off to the side next to the blacksmith's tent. Within half an hour or so, an elderly demon came up to the door alone. Quiet as a whisper, I fell in behind him and stepped inside, undetected.

When I stepped into the corridor, the tiny hairs on the back of my neck perked up. Instantly, I knew something was different here. I could feel it in my bones. The hall was wider in general, and I think the ceilings were a little higher here as well. But more than just the way it looked, it was all about the way it felt. There was the feel of magic in the air.

I followed the old man until the hallway came to a cross with long corridors stretching out in front and behind and on both sides. The man turned left and disappeared behind a door about ten feet from where I stood watching. There was no other soul to be seen down any of the passageways.

Following some unknown instinct, I walked straight ahead. Instead of lamps, the hallway here was lit by glowing stones embedded into the rock walls. There was something almost holy about the quietness of the place.

I didn't pass a single doorway that I could see, but up ahead, at the very end of the hallway, a door appeared.

My heartbeat sped up as I approached. This door was different from any of the others. First of all, it was a very tall, very wide door made of pure green stone, like an emerald.

I paused when I reached the end, looking behind me to make sure no one had followed me down the corridor

I was completely alone.

I hesitated as I stared up at the huge door. Was this the council's meeting chamber? If I tried to open the door would an alarm go off?

I knew it was risky, but hadn't I risked everything already? What if the spell book I'd been searching for all this time was just on the other side of this door?

I had to know.

I placed my hand on the cool marble and pushed.

NOT ALL OF US HAVE TIME

Nothing happened.

The door wouldn't budge. I looked for some kind of handle, so I could try to pull it open instead, but the surface was flat. There was nothing to grab on to that I could see. Disappointed, I stepped back and studied the entire area around the door.

That's when I heard them.

Voices on the other side. Getting closer by the second. My breath caught in my throat and I looked around frantically for a place to hide.

The door began to swing open very slowly, and I ducked behind it, hiding in the shadowy space between the door and the wall.

"This is an interesting proposition," a man's voice said. "But it's also extremely dangerous."

"But you have thousands of followers here. Enough that you could build an army."

I gasped, then quickly covered my mouth with my hand.

Jackson. I'd know his voice anywhere. No wonder I'd been drawn to this hallway. I should have recognized that it was his closeness I was feeling. I pressed even closer to the wall, hoping I was well-hidden.

"We've been through this. Even with thousands of us fighting together, how could we hope to defeat an organization as powerful as the Order? They have more than twice our numbers," the other man said. I couldn't be sure, but it sounded like Andros.

The group leaving the room was far enough away now that I could see their backs as they walked down the hall. Jackson, Andros, Lea, and another man I didn't recognize.

"We're forgetting our power here," Lea said. "If we train and apply ourselves, I know we could come up with a plan that would succeed. Besides, we do have some human witches on the other side who would fight with us."

"If the Order doesn't kill them all first," Andros said, bitterness dripping from his lips. "I think it's better for us to wait. See what happens to the Order over the next fifty years. Watch them closely and see if we can find a weak spot. Remember, we have something they don't have."

"What's that?" Jackson asked.

"Time," Andros said.

"Not all of us have time," Jackson protested. "My brother, for example. What will happen to him when he's bound with a different family line? One who isn't as opposed to slavery as Harper?"

"Your human girl? This Prima?" the stranger said.

My mouth went dry at his mention of me.

"You're sure her loyalties are with you? It's not possible she's a spy for the Order? If bringing her here has compromised our secrecy, we could be in danger as we stand here talking."

At that, I nearly came out from the shadows to give this unknown man a piece of my mind. I had nearly died for this cause. How could anyone think I could be a spy for the Order? But I held back, figuring that jumping out of the shadows wouldn't exactly make me look more trustworthy.

Luckily, I had Jackson there to stand up for me. "There's no chance that Harper would ever betray us," he said. "I've told you this over and over. She wants to see the Order ended every bit as much as we all do. She may have a mind of her own when it comes to following the rules sometimes, but you can trust her, I give you my word on this."

I relaxed slightly. It felt good to hear him still defending me.

The voices faded as the group walked farther away. I nearly screeched as the marble door began to close. Any second, I would lose my chance at getting into that room. But how could I be sure I would ever be able to get out? What if I got stuck inside for days?

Panic shot through my stomach. I didn't want to lose this chance at getting inside. Without really thinking it through, I quickly slipped around the open door and into the darkness of the room beyond it.

Seconds later, the heavy doors closed, leaving me completely alone in the black.

TO TRANSLATE WORDS

I couldn't see anything, but I knew I had found the room. I could feel it in my bones.

Trembling, gratitude washed over me. After all this time, I was finally here in a room filled with priceless information about the Order.

First things first. I needed light. Blindly, I felt along the sides of the door, looking for a crystal or something that might give off light.

No luck.

It could take me all day to find a light in this place. I definitely didn't have the time or the patience for that. I created a small orb of dim light and held it up, stepping forward.

Rows and rows of intricately carved bookcases lined the room. Ancient tomes filled the shelves from end to end, top to bottom. I swallowed, feeling my heart rising. There were more books here than I ever dreamed there would be. I'd been expecting a row or two, but this? This was over a thousand books.

Were they all captured from hunters?

I made my way slowly through the stacks, looking for any kind of organizational system that might help me figure out which books held the spells. Instead, what I quickly came to realize was that many of these books were written in a language completely foreign to me. Apparently Joost's magic potion did nothing to translate words on a page the way they did the demon language.

In the center of the room there was a large black circular table that reminded me of stories I'd read of King Arthur and the round table. Was this where the Underground's council met? It was completely clean of papers or notes except for a single book sitting on one of the chairs. I picked it up and ran my hand along the binding.

I couldn't make out what it said, but the words were written symbols like hieroglyphics. I laid it on the table and flipped it open, letting my orb hover over the book. Inside was more of the same, only symbols, all handwritten very neatly in a dozen rows. I flipped it closed and sat down. How was I going to ever find the hunters' spell books in all of this mess?

Randomly, I walked around the room, pulling books from the shelf and peeking inside to see if it was written in a language I could understand. After more than a dozen tries, I finally gave up. It would take me forever to go through all of these books.

The library was floor to ceiling books in a room that was bigger than Shadowford's entire downstairs. I couldn't even begin to estimate how many were here in all.

I wanted to lay my head down on the table and just give up. After all the weeks of training and studying and planning, I was drained. Totally burned out.

I wasn't sure I had the energy to go through every row in this room, book by book. This room held answers, I could feel it. I just wasn't sure how in the world I was supposed to find them on my own.

Deep in thought, I almost didn't realize the door to the library had begun to open. Had they come back?

My pulse hammered in my veins. I had to hide.

I scrambled to my feet and ducked behind the next to last bookcase. The orb disappeared, but I had no idea if I'd gotten rid of it fast enough. Even the tiniest light would make an impact in this stark darkness.

My heart rose into my throat. I held my breath. If I was caught now, none of the demons here would ever trust me again. Why had I risked this?

Footsteps sounded against the marble floors. I jumped as the entire library lit up in a blaze of lights. I squinted up toward the ceiling, raising my arm to shield my eyes from the sudden brightness of it. Up in the air above the top of the book-cases, more than a hundred lit candles floated. Well, no wonder I hadn't been able to find the light.

I pressed my back deeper against the bookcase, wishing I could just disappear into the books.

I listened. From the sound of the footsteps, only one person had entered the room. Slowly, they seemed to be making their way through the center row of stacks. I estimated that I had about sixty seconds before they reached the end of my bookcase, where I would be very easy to see.

I summoned my power and quickly disappeared into noth-ingness, standing completely still.

That's when the person in the room spoke, freezing me to the spot.

I HAVE MY REASONS

"Harper? Are you really going to make me search this whole place?"

My shoulders slumped, and I let my head fall back, heavy with both regret and relief. Jackson. How had he known I was here?

He was probably going to kill me.

Reluctantly, I dropped my glamour and stepped into the middle aisle. Jackson stood about fifty feet away, a frown on his face.

"What were you thinking?" he asked. "I don't even know how you managed to get in here, but this is completely insane. How could you do something this risky?"

The anger in his voice made my stomach twist.

"I'm sorry," I said, unable to come up with something better to defend myself.

"You're sorry? You don't even know the first thing about being sorry," he said, his face red with rage. "Do you have any idea what would happen if someone else had found you in here?"

I hung my head. I didn't know what he wanted me to say. That I knew they would call me a traitor? A spy? Probably kick me out of this place.

Or worse.

"I felt your presence in the hallway earlier. Believe me, I rushed back here as soon as I could get away," he said. "The demons here don't know you like I know you. They wouldn't be so forgiving."

I crossed my arms over my chest. "And how do you think they are going to get to know me when all I do is sit in a room all by myself all day?"

Jackson shook his head in frustration and turned away. "That's not true," he said. "I've seen you in the marketplace plenty of times."

"Yeah, with all my new friends," I said, my tone biting. "Do you have any idea how lonely it is for me here? Or do you even care?"

"I didn't bring you here to make friends," he said. "I brought you here to save your life. Did you know that right now there's a hunter stalking the entrance where we came in? She's there, just waiting for you."

I felt like I'd had the breath knocked out of me. "One of the Order's hunters? How did she know where to find me?"

Jackson ran a hand through his hair. "I don't know," he said. "She had to have tracked you somehow, which doesn't make sense to me when you've barely even been casting any magic down here at all."

I froze, my body tense. "Magic?" I shook my head. "I

thought you said this place was shielded from the surface. That they couldn't track me all the way down here."

"Normally, that's true," he said. "But that's never really been tested with a witch's magic. I mean, we're usually thinking more about demon-only magic. It doesn't matter though; you haven't been casting that much, have you?"

I didn't know what to say. I hated to lie to him, but to tell him the truth would be admitting that I'd been watching the soldiers.

"Harper?" He took a step toward me. "Have you?"

I closed my eyes and drew in a deep breath. This was going to be painful.

"Oh, my god," he said. He walked around in a circle, his hands balling into fists. "You've been casting? A lot? Tell me now."

"First of all, let me say that I had no idea I could be tracked," I said in my defense. "You never told me that was even a possibility."

"Tell me," he demanded.

"Okay, yes, I've been casting," I said. "A lot."

I explained about the practicing in my room.

Jackson paced the room in front of me. "Still," he said. "I wouldn't think that would be enough. I mean, I would have thought it would take something more to get through the barrier. Something stronger, like all-out use of your power."

I fidgeted. "There's something else," I said. "And I know you're going to be angry, but you have to understand, I couldn't just sit down here and do nothing. I wanted to learn to be more powerful."

"What did you do?"

I knew I had to say it quickly, like ripping off a Band-Aid.

"I used my invisibility to follow the soldiers into the training rooms," I confessed. "I went every day for several weeks, sometimes staying overnight, after they left, to practice."

The shock on Jackson's face was complete and terrifying. He took a step backward, then collapsed into one of the chairs around the table. "How could I have missed this?" he asked himself. "I should have been paying more attention. I never thought... how did you even pull that off?"

When he looked up at me, I saw a mixture of anger and wonder.

He genuinely hadn't thought I was capable of something like this on my own. Didn't he know me at all?

"You don't think I'm strong enough to make any real difference, do you?" I asked, so angry with him for always believing I was weak. "Did you really expect me to just sit around down here like a little puppy dog? I don't want to be down here forever, no matter what you might think. I plan to go back and fight someday."

Jackson stood, taking several quick steps in my direction. "Why are you always so bullheaded and stubborn? Why can't you just be patient for once? You have no idea what the Order is capable of."

The anger in his tone felt like a slap across the face. I had no idea? How could he even say that after all I'd seen and been through? I pushed back the sting of tears. "You want to know why I can't be patient?" I asked. "What about the fact that I've got an entire army of witches looking for me? Witches who, by the way, want to kill me. Or what about the fact that every day we sit here on our asses, more and more demons are forced into an eternity of slavery?"

"You think I don't know all that?" he said. "But what do you want me to do about it, Harper? I have been trying to find a way to fight back for a hundred years. You think we can just change the world in two weeks? It doesn't work like that."

"No?" I said, lifting my chin. "Well, how does it work?"

Jackson didn't answer. He stared at me, his chest moving up and down with each heavy breath.

"You don't have a clue how it works," I said. I was in his face now, part of me wanting to punch him and part of me wanting to kiss him. "Just how far have you really gotten in one hundred years? Have you fought anyone? Defeated anyone? Changed one single thing?"

I saw the hurt in his face. His upper lip twitched slightly and the muscles in his cheeks pulsed as he ground his teeth together. I know I was throwing some low blows, but wasn't I right? How long were we all going to sit back doing nothing?

"What do you propose we do then, oh, mighty sixteen-year-old, Harper?"

"I'm seventeen now," I mumbled. I didn't have some brilliant plan to offer, either, I just wanted us to start looking for better answers.

"Oh, excuse me, seventeen," he said, clapping his hands together. "I'm sure that extra year has provided you with the wisdom of the ages, right? So, what's your big plan to save my brother and the entire shadow demon race? Do you think we should all go over there and just start fighting?"

"At least that would be something," I said.

"It would be mass carnage," he said. "For both sides probably. Is that really what you want?"

"No," I said, my voice softening. He couldn't really think that was what I wanted. "Of course not. But I want to do something. I'm so sick and tired of always being kept in the dark by you. Why can't you just talk to me? It's like you don't believe I'm strong enough to hear the truth. You don't think I'll have anything to contribute to the conversation. You don't think I can help. You just take it all on your own shoulders, thinking you can protect everyone, but you know what? That's bullshit."

"That's not the way I feel at all," he said, sadness darkening his eyes.

"How would I know?" I said. "It's not like you talk to me about how you're feeling. Since we got to the shadow world, it's been nothing but secrets between you and Lea."

"All I've ever done is try to protect you, Harper," he said. "That's all that matters to me."

"That's not true," I said.

"Yes, it is."

"So, you're saying there isn't some small part of you that thinks I'm incapable of doing anything important to help?"

He paused, and I felt the seconds tick away like a bomb in my gut. When he finally lifted his eyes to mine, I knew I had gotten it right. Even after everything we'd been through. Even after I'd saved him from the Others and fought back against the crows. He still didn't think I was powerful enough to make a difference. To him, I was just a weak young witch who needed to be sheltered and protected.

And wasn't I?

Hadn't I almost died at the hands of the Order? If Jackson and the others hadn't come for me, I would have died that day in the ritual room. No doubt about it.

I couldn't hold the tears back any longer. They streamed down my face like a waterfall.

Jackson reached for me, but I stepped away, holding my hands up.

"Harper—"

"Don't," I said. I wiped at the tears on my face. "I know you don't understand why I came here or why I keep breaking your rules, but you have to know that I am just not the kind of person who can sit back and wait while everything falls apart. I want to at least try to make a difference. If you wanted me to give up, you should have just let me die."

My words hung between us like a thick cloud.

"You don't understand anything," he said. "You're seeing it all wrong."

"Then how should I see it?" I asked softly.

Jackson stared at me, his eyes telling me he had something he wanted to say, but something seemed to hold him back. The moment passed, and he turned away.

"Why this room?" he asked. "What were you hoping to find here that was worth risking so much?"

I sniffed. "I heard that at least one of the hunters caught along the way had some spell books in her cave," I said. "I thought maybe, if they were old enough books, they might hold some of the Order's secrets."

He shook his head. "You're still determined to find a spell that will release Aerden?"

"Aren't you?" I asked.

"I've seen the books you're talking about," he said. "But there's nothing new in them. Nothing we haven't seen before."

My heart fell, and the tears threatened to come again. I suddenly felt so incredibly tired and defeated. "Why didn't you at least tell me about it?"

He met my eyes and I could see in his expression that he understood the pain in my heart.

"Just because you don't want anyone to know about what we had together, doesn't mean you had to completely cut me out of your life," I said. "That was your choice."

His face grew tight and I noticed his hand trembling slightly. "I have my reasons," he said.

I nodded. "Yeah, you always do."

Jackson held up his hand and turned back toward the doors. "This conversation is going nowhere," he said. When he got to the door, he turned back. "Come on, I'm taking you back to your room. And promise me you'll never do something like this again."

For a moment, I stood my ground, not wanting to leave. I didn't feel like this was really over. There was still so much more I wanted to say.

I took one long look around at all of the unreadable books, wondering where the answers were if not here. Then, I gave in and followed Jackson silently back to my room, the distance between us greater than ever.

NEVER GIVE UP

Emotions scattered through me in all directions.

I was angry at Jackson for not being open with me from the start about what he knew and what he'd been working on. I was ashamed for getting caught doing something I was never supposed to do. Disappointed didn't even begin to describe how I felt about the fact that none of the hunter's spell books contained the spell I was looking for. And now, on top of everything, there was a hunter stalking the portal entrance.

I flopped down on my bed and let all those conflicting emotions roll through me like a wave. Or a tsunami, really.

Where did I even go from here?

Jackson had made me promise I wouldn't go back to the training grounds. I knew I couldn't risk going back into the library. Besides, what good would that do if the books I needed didn't even exist? I had come to a wall. A barrier so thick, I could see no way around it.

And as far as Jackson was concerned, I knew there was still

so much unsaid between us. He was hiding something from me, I could tell. Why could he never just be open with me? Why couldn't he just tell me everything and trust that I was ready to hear it? He said I didn't understand his reasons, but how was I supposed to understand when he wouldn't just talk to me?

Would things between us ever change?

I sat up and leaned my back against the wall, trying to make sense of everything that had happened since we got to this world. When I killed the tiger twin, I swear I hadn't done it on purpose. Yes, I wanted to hurt her for what she'd done to Mary Anne, but I don't know where that dark power came from. It was as if I'd stepped out of my own body and some other force had taken control.

Then, during my practices here, sometimes I felt a shimmer of that power creeping in. A darkness, shadowy and elusive. It scared me.

But there was no denying the power that came from me in those moments. It was strong and all-consuming. If I could learn to understand it and use it, maybe I could accomplish amazing things as a witch. Maybe I would have a chance to defeat the Order.

I closed my eyes. The Order.

Jackson said a hunter had followed my power here. I imagined her lurking above the ring of black roses, desperate to find a way inside. Jackson assured me that there was absolutely no way for the hunter to get inside without being let in by someone on the council, so there was nothing to fear. Still, had I put everyone's lives at risk by practicing my magic? What if the hunter somehow did find a way inside? How many would die because of me?

My problems circled me like vultures, waiting for me to give up for good so they could pounce on the flesh of my spirit. But I would never give up. I would keep searching for a new plan, a new way, a new possibility.

I would never give up.

THE GREEN BROUGHT OUT HIS EYES

There was a part of me that hoped Jackson would be around a lot more after our last conversation. He managed to come into the suite more often to check up on me, but he rarely stayed to talk. A couple of times I heard him come in and ask Mary Anne if I was in my room. When she said yes, I expected him to come knock on the door, but instead, he just left.

I spent a lot of time in my room, those next few days, trying to come up with anything I could work on or set my mind to. With the library as a dead end and the training completely off-limits due to the hunter's presence, I was out of good ideas.

I tried to just relax and hang out with Mary Anne and Essex, but my mind was always wandering off. I knew I wasn't being the best of company, but they didn't seem to mind too much.

The three of us were sitting by the coffee table in the main room playing a type of card game Essex wanted to teach us when someone knocked. My stomach flipped. I could feel

Jackson's presence on the other side of the door. He must have come to check up on me. I straightened and stayed put, not bothering to go open the door. He always knocked first, but he had a crystal key to the suite and could get in on his own.

I trained my eyes on the cards in front of me, concentrating on the strange demon symbols and refusing to look at him as he entered. Which of course lasted about six seconds.

My eyes completely betrayed me, flicking toward the door quickly, then back to my cards. But what I saw in that split second made my heart stop in my chest. I suddenly felt like I couldn't breathe. My face grew hot and the space around me felt like it was closing in. All plans to act like I didn't care and that I wasn't thinking about him flew right out the window.

I stared up at him, not understanding.

Jackson stood just inside the door to the suite; dressed from head to toe in a fancy black suit tailored perfectly to his muscular body. Under the suit jacket he wore a dark green button-up shirt with the top two buttons left undone. The green brought out his eyes, which were now looking straight at me.

My hands shook, so I laid the cards down on the table and put them in my lap, so no one would see. For a split second, I let hope lift my heart up into the air about seven feet above my body. Had he come to apologize to me? Maybe ask me to a nice dinner so he could explain everything? I believed it so much that I almost stood and walked to him, dying for that conversation. But before I could stand or make a move, the door at the back of the suite swung open, the sound of high heels clicking on the tiled floor.

I turned my head to look, completely unprepared for what I would see.

Lea walked into the room, her hands up to her ear still adjusting an unruly earring. She was dressed in a floor-length gown adorned with sparkling silver beads.

"Are you ready to go?" she asked Jackson. "Why they insisted on this dinner is beyond me, but I'll be glad when it's over."

My mouth hung open, and I had to force myself to breathe. My eyes saw what was going on, but my brain was two steps behind, not wanting to understand.

Under the table, Mary Anne's hand sought mine. She squeezed hard, and I swear it was the only thing that kept me from screaming.

"You guys have a dinner tonight?" Mary Anne asked.

"Yes," Lea said, rolling her eyes. "Something the council insisted on throwing for me. If they really wanted to honor their possible future Queen, they would have let me wear my own clothes to this stupid thing."

"You look nice," Jackson said. It was the first thing he'd said since he walked in the door, and I wished I could shove the words back down his throat.

Was this a date? He was obviously here to pick her up and walk with her to this dinner. Did that mean they were actually going there together? And flaunting it right in my face.

Jackson's eyes met mine again, and I put all those questions and all the hurt I was feeling into my eyes. His jaw tensed and there was sadness and regret in his eyes, but I had no idea what to make of it. Was he sorry he was hurting me? Or sorry I caught him dating another woman?

My breath came in short bursts like machine gun fire.

"Have fun," Mary Anne said.

Jackson shoved his hands in his pockets. "It's no big deal," he said, lying through his teeth. "Hopefully it won't last too long."

"Amen to that," Lea said. She finally got her earring in. She put her arm through Jackson's and motioned toward the door. "Let's get this over with."

Jackson peeled his gaze from mine, then turned and escorted Lea from the room.

When the door closed, the suite was dead silent except for the sound of my heart pounding out of my chest.

What the hell had just happened? He'd always insisted there was nothing romantic between him and Lea, but that didn't look like nothing to me.

"Harper, your turn is next," Essex said, pushing my cards toward me.

I ignored him, knowing the game was over for me now.

"I think Harper needs a second," Mary Anne said. She turned toward me, concern etched on her pale face. "I'm sure that wasn't what it looked like, you know? I mean, Lea didn't even sound like she wanted to go."

All I could do was shake my head and stare at the door.

"Am I not understanding something?" Essex asked.

Mary Anne sighed. "It's complicated," she said.

For the first time since we'd been underground, the lack of fresh air really bothered me. When did this room get so small and stuffy? I felt a trickle of sweat on the back of my neck. I needed to breathe. I needed to feel wind in my hair and on my face. I couldn't just sit here letting the walls close in on me.

I stood up, not even knowing where I was going to go.

"Wait," Mary Anne said, following close behind me. "What are you doing?"

As soon as the question was voiced, I knew the answer.

"I'm going to follow them."

"No, this is a bad idea," Mary Anne said, tugging on my arm. "What if he sees you?"

"I'll be discreet," I said, not letting her slow me down.

I opened the door and peered outside. They were no longer in view down the corridor. I needed to get moving or I would lose them.

"Harper, don't do this," she said.

"Listen, if there's really nothing to it, then I'll go, I'll be bored for an hour, I'll come back. But if there's more..."

What then? I didn't even know myself. The thought of watching him kiss her or hold her close made me feel dizzy and sick to my stomach.

"You'll just get hurt," she said. "It's not worth it. Just wait until he gets home and talk to him about it."

I laughed, but the sound was hollow and joyless. "Yeah, because that's worked so well up to this point," I said. "Jackson's such an open book."

Mary Anne had no argument there. She knew it was true.

She also knew she wasn't going to be able to stop me from going. "Be careful," she said. "Please."

"I will," I said, summoning my power and disappearing down the hallway.

PAINFUL AWAKENING

I caught up with them in the marketplace. They were headed up the stairs to a hallway I'd never been down before.

I followed from a good distance, hoping Jackson wouldn't be able to feel me if I stayed far enough back. Lea's arm was still entwined with his and every time he smiled at something she said, I felt a dagger twist in my side.

We traveled past rooms that looked like standard housing before we came to a large archway. I was careful to stay behind other couples or just around doorways, so he wouldn't see me. Unlike a lot of the demons here, I knew Jackson could see through glamours if he wanted to. Several dressed-up couples turned and walked through the arched doorway, but from where I stood behind an attractive couple in matching red outfits, I couldn't see anything. Still, this seemed to be the place. Jackson and Lea disappeared into the room.

I let out a silent sigh of relief. No secret doors or strange obstacles.

Unfortunately, I almost missed the red couple stopping mid-stride to adjust the man's collar. I nearly ran right into them, which would have been disastrous. I narrowly missed them, running into the wall instead. I bit my tongue to keep from crying out. It hurt, but all I could think about was the pain I was feeling on the inside.

I needed to know one way or the other.

Behind me, a decent line had started to form. Demons all dressed up and waiting to get into the event of the season, no doubt. A party for the future Queen of the Northern Kingdom. I'm sure everyone in the Underground hadn't been invited. There were too many people. This crowd must just be the council and the more prominent members of the community. Essex certainly hadn't been invited.

I did remember hearing a woman ask him to make a dress for her for a party. She'd said it was a very important event and that she needed an original creation. She must have really wanted to make an impression on Princess Lazalea. Well, she'd be in for a rude awakening when she learned that Lea preferred leather to sequins.

When the line died down a little, I finally made my way into the room, my eyes searching for Jackson in the crowd. I could feel his presence somewhere toward the front of the room where a large oval emerald served as a stage. Round tables had been set up to surround an area that seemed to be cleared for dancing. To me, it looked like a typical arrangement for someone's wedding or party. I hid in the back of the room behind a glass sculpture.

When I spotted Jackson and Lea in the crowd, they had parted ways and were talking to different groups. Relief lessened a tiny bit of the fear pressing on my heart, but I knew it wasn't a definitive answer. Not yet.

I watched him talking to various groups of demons for about half an hour before most of the guests had found their way to their tables. When Andros took the stage, the talking died down and everyone's eyes turned to the front of the room.

His beautiful wife, Ourelia, stood by his side dressed in a tight-fitting white gown that glittered in the light. Jackson and Lea took their seats at the front of the room. They sat close, but as far as I could see from here, they weren't touching.

I hated the speed of my heartbeat. Had I really turned into this jealous person who was willing to sneak into a party just to watch her somewhat ex with another woman? This wasn't who I wanted to be. But I couldn't force myself to leave. If there was something going on between them, I needed to know. Ever since he'd first introduced her to me, I had felt there was so much more between them than he was telling me. I knew in my heart I was about to find out what that was.

Something strange was definitely going on with him lately. He wasn't acting like himself around me.

I had that feeling in my legs like I wanted to be ready to run at any second. As if my body understood that I was standing in the middle of a very dangerous situation.

At first, I hardly heard a word Andros said. He was talking about how he knew Lea, but for me, the words went in one ear and out the other.

I struggled to hold on to my invisibility. My emotions were all over the place, and concentration took more effort than it should have. I stared out at all of the smiling faces of these strangers and wondered how my life had brought me to this moment. I didn't belong here. But did Jackson? Was this really where he'd belonged the whole time? He certainly didn't belong in Peachville.

And where did that leave us?

"I can't tell you how proud I am to be here tonight honoring Princess Lazalea, the rightful heir of the Northern Kingdom and our future Queen."

Lea and Jackson stood as the crowd clapped. All of her earlier annoyance was gone from her face and instead she looked exactly as you would expect a princess to look at this type of affair. But why was Jackson standing with her?

"Our struggle against the Order of Shadows has been a difficult one, but no two citizens have gone as far in the fight as these two standing before us here tonight," Andros continued. "While most of us were still too afraid to speak out against what was happening to our people, Denaer refused to accept that his brother was gone. Even when his own father was too scared and defeated to go after Aerden or even beg the King for help, Denaer was relentless in his search for his twin brother, finally going so far as to travel across worlds. We've missed you dear friend, and I for one am so glad you are home.

"The war, as we know, is far from over, but we can all take inspiration from these two who both were willing to risk everything for their kingdom and their people. Your parents may have made some mistakes in their existence but promising you to each other was one of the best decisions they ever made. Here's to Princess Lazalea and her chosen mate, the future King and Queen of the Northern Kingdom."

The demons rose to their feet, clapping, but the sound was muffled. In my own ears all I could hear was the sound of those four words. *Future King and Queen.*

I felt the breath knocked out of me.

Jackson and Lea were promised to each other. They were to be married. Jackson was her future king. The truth of it tumbled over me like a rock rolling down a steep hill.

It all made sense now. Why he had to break up with me before we got down here. Why he couldn't be seen kissing me or even getting too close or showing too much interest. As far as these demons knew, he was meant for their princess.

And wasn't he?

I certainly didn't hear him denying it. In fact, he stood there at the front of the room with her now, smiling and playing his part. He was never planning to be with me long term. Once his brother was saved, he was always going to come back here, wasn't he? And why not? Who wouldn't want to marry a beautiful woman and lead a kingdom?

My heart shattered in my chest. When he first told me we couldn't be together down here, I think I always assumed it was a temporary situation. Even if he planned to stay down here, I knew I wouldn't stay. And in my heart, I felt that when I left, he would follow me. We would be back to our old relationship eventually. We just needed some time to get through this, right?

But, Jackson had come back here knowing he was taking up his old place as Lea's betrothed. Her future husband.

Just thinking it made my chest tight. I saw my hand flicker in front of me, visible for a split second.

I clasped my hand over my mouth to keep from crying out. I was scared to even take a step, afraid I would collapse then and there. And when Jackson took Lea in his arms and kissed her forehead the way he'd kissed mine countless times, I felt my knees begin to buckle.

The demons in the room took their seats again, waiting for

Lea to address her people. For one moment as the crowd adjusted and settled, Jackson's gaze moved to the back of the room. He looked straight at me, his eyes widening. We stared at each other through the crowded space, the moment becoming a breaking. A shattering. A painful awakening. A goodbye to all we'd known together.

I don't know how I found the ability to walk, but I knew I had to get out of there.

I broke away from the wall and took it one painful step at a time. By the time Lea's voice sounded in the room, I was halfway down the hall, finally finding the strength to run.

WE CAN NEVER BE TOGETHER

I couldn't stay.

Whatever safety the Underground had provided was gone now. There was nothing left for me here. No knowledge to gain, no protection from hurt.

I burst through the door to the suite and ran straight to my room. I picked up the backpack Essex had given me and began stuffing it with clothes and anything I could think of that I might need. Surprisingly, there were no tears, just the knowledge that I had to go.

Mary Anne stepped through the doorway to my room.

"What happened?" she asked. "What are you doing?"

"I'm leaving," I said, testing the words on my tongue. I disappeared into the bathroom to collect my toothbrush and other toiletries that would fit into my bag.

Mary Anne followed me. "Leaving? You mean the Underground? No, you can't leave. Where will you go?"

"I don't know yet," I said, storming back into the bedroom. I didn't even want to stand still in any one place for more than a few seconds, scared that if I stopped moving, I would have to face what had just happened.

"Is it really that bad?" she asked, her face twisted with worry.

"It's worse," I said. "He's going to marry her."

Mary Anne gasped, her hand flying to her mouth. "That can't be true."

"I heard it with my own ears," I said, a slight tremble in my voice that only made me angry. "He's apparently been promised to her since they were born."

I shoved the last of my things into the backpack and zipped it up, having to squish it down to get it to close.

"You would think he might have mentioned that at some point before he told me he loved me," I said. "I love you, but oh by the way, here's yet another reason we can never be together."

I picked up one of my notebooks and tore a page from the back, then carried my backpack out to the living room and set it on the table.

"I don't think you should go," Mary Anne said. "You're not thinking clearly. It's not safe out there."

I thought of the hunter who was waiting for me. She was absolutely right; I was not going to be safe out there. But I wasn't safe in here either. At least out there, I knew who my enemies were.

I sat down at the table and did my best to steady my hand as I wrote. I didn't get any farther than his name before I paused and felt the hot tears bubbling toward the surface. What could I possibly say to him in a note that would let him feel even a tenth of what I was feeling inside?

"I'll come with you," Mary Anne said. "Just give me some time to get my things together."

I grabbed her arm before she had a chance to walk away.

"No way," I said. "You can't come. You can't even cast right now, and who knows how long before your injuries totally heal. Plus, you can't leave Essex."

"Maybe he could come with us," she said. "We'll stop by the marketplace before we go. He had to head back to the shop to help his mom with something."

I shook my head. "You know as well as I do that you can't come with me. It's way too dangerous."

Mary Anne slumped into the chair beside me, tears in her eyes. "I don't want you to go either."

"I can't stay," I said.

My hand trembled as I turned back to the blank page. I wanted to say that I hated him for what he'd done to me. I wanted to say that I never wanted to see him again. But in my heart neither of those things was true. The truth was that I loved him, and he had broken my heart with his lies.

So, in the end, that's all I wrote.

TRYING TO MAKE SENSE OF
THE SCENE

I'd heard Lea once mention that she kept a spare crystal to Jackson's room in her drawer. Thinking of it now made me feel disgusted and sad, but I walked straight to the drawer of her desk and reached in for the small stone that opened his room.

I wanted him to come back from his date with Lea and find my note on his bed.

And I needed to hurry. He'd seen me there despite the crowd of demons in the room. I knew he wouldn't be able to get away from the party, but as soon as he had a chance, he would probably come looking for me. He'd probably have some explanation as to why he hadn't told me yet, but nothing he could say could change the truth of it.

I wanted to be gone by the time he came looking for me.

I hugged Mary Anne and promised her that I would find a way to contact her when I got settled somewhere. To be honest, I had no idea how I would get word to her or where I would go, but if I managed to survive the hunter at the gate, I knew I would find my way somehow.

The hallway was deserted when I left the suite, and I ignored the fact that a shiver of disappointment jabbed through me. So what if he hadn't rushed away from Lea's side to come find me? This was how it was now, and I needed to find a way to understand it.

I walked to the door of his small apartment and pressed the stone into the symbol on the wall. The door clicked open.

I'd never been inside his room before. As far as I knew, he didn't spend a lot of time here except to sleep at night. I expected to see a smaller, simpler version of our own rooms with maybe a few of his clothes strewn about or something. I flipped on the light and froze.

What I never expected in a million years was to come face to face with myself.

Covering every inch of every wall in the entire one-room apartment were drawings of me. Confused, I let my bag fall to the floor. I stepped to the nearest wall and put my hand on one of the pages. The scene was gruesome, yet beautiful. He'd put so much time and detail into my face, I might as well have been looking in a mirror.

I pulled several from the wall, only to realize that underneath were more of the same. He'd drawn the scene from every possible angle, from every distance. Some in pencil, but most in horrifying color.

Each drawing was some version of the same story. Me, lying in a sea of white snow, bright red blood splattered in random patterns against the white. My blonde hair was sprawled out against the snow, my eyes closed as if I might just be sleeping. The white strip of the ritual dress clung to my wrist, but there was fresh blood staining it now.

Slowly, I walked around the apartment, pulling several of the drawings from the wall to study them. In one, he'd drawn a close-up of my hand, my fist closed around something I couldn't quite make out. In another, he'd pulled back from the scene as if he were hovering above me. There was so much blood, much of it seeming to pour from a wound in my back as I lay against the pure white snow.

Overwhelmed, I fell to the floor, spreading the drawings out before me in a circle, trying to make sense of the scene.

He must have seen this over and over in his visions to have recreated it each time in such excruciating detail. In some, I could almost count the number of eyelashes on my eyes. What had he been looking for? Some clue he could use to protect me from this fate?

Hadn't he learned anything in all the many years of his immortal life?

Nothing he drew could be changed or prevented.

My eyes filled with tears, blurring the pictures before me into one unavoidable mass.

When the door to the apartment swung open a few minutes later, I looked up, a single tear escaping down my cheek. Jackson stood in the doorway and as our eyes met, all the walls we'd been holding up since we'd come here crumbled swiftly to the ground.

I'D ALMOST FORGOTTEN

"Why didn't you tell me?" My voice cracked with tears. I motioned to all of the hundreds of drawings spread around the room.

Jackson moved to me, the door closing behind him. He fell to the floor in front of me, the papers crackling beneath the weight of his knees. "I wanted to find a way to make it change," he said. "I won't let this be your end."

I shook my head. "You know better."

He grabbed several papers and crumbled them into a ball. "No," he said the green of his eyes stormy and dark and wet. "I can change it. I just have to find the secret, the weak spot. There's no way it ends like this. I can keep you safe here until I find a way."

I placed my hand on his knee, touching him for the first time in so long I'd almost forgotten his warmth. "There's no escaping these things once you've seen them," I said. "And you know it just as well as I do. Trying to protect me from it is only going to pull us further apart. And I never wanted to feel this apart from you."

He looked away, not meeting my eyes.

"I don't know what's been going on with you since we got to the shadow world," I said, all the things I'd been holding back rushing to the surface. "I don't understand what's going on with you and Lea, but I thought you knew by now that keeping secrets from people you care about only leads to sorrow and loneliness. Why can't you just be honest with me?"

He looked down. "So, you really were there tonight?"

I nodded. "I had to know."

He threw the balled-up papers across the room. "I never wanted you to know about that," he said.

I laughed, then felt the sting of tears in my nose. "Didn't you know I would eventually find out? What was your plan? To see if I would help you free Aerden, then let me just watch all of you disappear back through the portal, never to be seen again? Were you just going to marry her and take your place by her side on the throne and never tell me?"

Jackson studied my face, his eyebrows drawn together. "How could you say that?" he asked. "How could you even think that?"

"What am I supposed to think, Jackson? You've done nothing but lock me out of your life for the past how many weeks?" I said, standing. I walked toward the back of the apartment. "You lied to me."

"I didn't lie," he said. He stood and moved a few steps behind me. "I just didn't tell you everything."

"You did lie," I said, turning to face him. "I've asked you before if there was more to your relationship with Lea than just friendship and you said no."

"That's the truth," he said.

"The truth?" I shook my head, furious. "Then how do you explain what I just saw back there? How do you explain the fact that everyone down here believes you to be her future king?"

Jackson ran a shaky hand through his hair and turned around, pacing. "Yes, when I was born, I was promised to Lea," he said. He paused as if trying to figure out what he wanted to say. "My father is the king's most trusted adviser. He sits at the head of the king's council, and apart from the king himself, he's the most powerful man in the Northern Kingdom. My brother and I were born before the king and his mate had any children. Twins are extremely rare among my people, so when the king's daughter was born, as a sign of loyalty, my father offered to give one of his twins as husband to the princess."

"Why you?" I asked, my heart beating so hard in my chest.

"Because, technically, I was first-born," he said. "I had absolutely no choice in the matter. I was promised to her before I even understood what that meant."

I sat down on the edge of his bed, taking it all in. "You never tried to get out of it?"

"I never had a reason to try," he said. "I understood it as my duty to the kingdom, and I didn't question it. But when Aerden disappeared, I expected my father and the king to go after him. To do something about it."

"But they didn't," I said.

He shook his head. "No, my parents mourned his loss, but they accepted it. The kingdom is so full of fear when it comes to the Order of Shadows; they would rather try to outlive the Order and accept the sacrifices than fight them directly. The king believes that if we wait another few hundred years, the Order will die out on its own, without violence."

I frowned. "But demons go missing nearly every day; don't they even care about what's happening over in my world?"

Jackson's jaw tensed, and he continued to pace. "A small price to pay in the long run, they say. The king believes many more demons will lose their lives if we fight," he said. "I couldn't just sit back and let my brother's memory fade away. I didn't know exactly what they were doing to Aerden over there, but I knew it was some form of torture. I couldn't live like that."

He sat down next to me, so close our legs almost touched. I felt his closeness like an ache in the pit of my stomach. I had no idea if I was losing him forever or finally understanding him for the first time.

"Lea, she tried to talk me out of it, at first," he said. "She cared for Aerden, but she did everything she could to convince me that it would be better for me to wait until we became rulers. She said that when we took over the kingdom, we could build our own army."

"She was in love with you, wasn't she?" My voice trembled.

Jackson paused. "She's always loved me," he said. "She was terrified that if I went after Aerden, she would lose me forever. So when I finally did cross over, she followed me. Once she got over there and saw what was happening to the shadow demons, she was ready to join me and fight back, but by then anything there was between us was dead."

Silence filled the room as I let his words wash over me.

I stared up at the drawings of my death and wondered where that left us. He brought me here to protect me but had also stepped right back into his role as Lea's future king. Had he traded his own future for my safety?

Jackson shifted on the bed, turning to me with eyes so clear and focused, it took my breath away. "I have never loved her. Harper, I swear, you are the only one I have ever loved."

His words hit me with the weight of the weeks I'd spent alone down here, and I was helpless to even respond. Did he still love me? I wanted to ask, but I was too afraid to know.

"I am not marrying Lea," he said. "She knows that, but the demons down here see us as the future of their kingdom. If I had come down here telling them the truth about you and me, they would have hated you, trusted you even less. They would have seen you as an enemy to their own hopes. I couldn't let that happen."

He took my hands in his.

"But I also knew this was the place where you would be safest," he said. "I'm sorry I couldn't tell you the truth, but I needed you to believe things were over between us. One look or touch at the wrong time would have been disastrous. Harper, I need you to understand that I never stopped loving you."

All the doubt and fear I'd been holding on to was released in that moment. I choked on a sob, unable to stop my emotions from pouring forth.

"Don't go," he said, glancing at my packed bag on the floor. He moved down to his knees in front of me on the floor, clutching tight to my hands. "Not a moment goes by that I don't think of you and long to be with you, kissing you, sharing everything with you. It's been torture being apart from you, but as long as you were safe, I knew I was doing the right thing.

When I sensed your pain at the dinner tonight, it broke my heart."

Tears filled his eyes and I had never seen anything so beautiful in my life. I had thought all hope of his love was gone, but with him on his knees before me now, I knew I'd been so wrong.

"Stay," he said. "I'll find a way to make them understand, I promise. I can't live without you, Harper. Please, stay."

DIVIDED FAR TOO LONG

I searched his clear green eyes, hardly believing this could be real.

My breath came in short gasps, my heart breaking and mending in the same moment. Relief and wonder flooded through me. I lost my ability to hear. I could only see him there before me. This whole time, he'd still loved me. Wanted to be with me. At night as I lay in bed, missing him with every fiber of my being, he had been just steps away, feeling the same loneliness and pain.

I pulled my hands from his and placed them on either side of his face, our souls locked in a gaze. No more words between us. Only love.

He lifted his mouth to mine, softly at first, the taste of our tears mingled on our quivering lips. His hands reached up to grab hold of me, his fingers tightening around my forearms. I opened my mouth slightly, speaking to him with my kiss, telling him that if he wanted me, I would never leave.

I slid from the edge of the bed, my body pressing tight

against his as his arms circled around me. Our kiss became a conversation, a confession, a collision of two souls left divided far too long.

I poured myself into him, deeper and stronger with each touch of our lips. My hands ran through his hair, down his back, my fingers fumbling with each button on his shirt, wanting nothing but to know the warmth of his skin and rippling strength of his muscles.

Jackson slowed his kiss, then pulled back to stare at me. The expression of love on his face was so pure and true, I became lost in it. He lifted his hand to my cheek, a single finger trailing through the path of my tears. My arms broke out in shivering goose bumps and my breath came in quick, shallow bursts. He ran his fingertips from my face to my neck and down to my collarbone. With aching slowness, he slid the straps of my tank top off my shoulders, exploring my skin in a way no one ever had before.

I responded with the tips of my fingers on his chest, then down his side, running my hand along the scar that marked the only spot of imperfection on his entire form.

I gasped as I touched the scar, pulling my hand away as if I'd been burned by it.

"What?" he whispered.

A flash of battle ran through my mind. "She did this to you?" I asked. "The tiger I killed when we first came through the portal?"

Jackson nodded. "How did you know?"

"I saw her when I touched you," I said, wondering if her death somehow connected us. Hesitating, I touched the scar again, feeling a piece of the pain he'd experienced when it happened. How long ago must that have been? I'd first seen the scar back in Peachville months ago. "There's so much I still don't know about you."

His stomach quivered at my soft touch and his chest rose and fell with each jagged breath.

"You've never completely let down your walls around me," I said.

"I've only ever wanted to protect you," he said.

"Your secrets hurt me," I said. I touched his face and he placed his hand over mine so lovingly, regret in his eyes. "Promise me that you won't ever keep anything from me, again. If you want to be with me, then I have to be your partner. Your equal. Not some fragile little girl you're afraid to break. I'm stronger than you think I am, Jackson"

His eyes searched mine and a smile tugged at the corner of his lips. "I think I'm finally understanding that."

He leaned in for another kiss, but before our lips met, a loud knock brought us both our feet.

The sound was frantic. Pounding.

Worry stabbed at my heart. Something terrible had happened. I felt it with absolute certainty in my heart.

Jackson rushed to the door and flung it open to find Essex standing there, out of breath, eyes wild with fear.

"What is it?" he said.

Essex leaned against the door frame, catching his breath. "A hunter," he said. Then, he looked up at me. "A hunter has gotten inside the Underground."

NO MATTER THE DANGER

J ackson turned to me, panic in his eyes. "We have to get you out of here," he said. He grabbed his shirt from where it had fallen on the floor.

Essex looked from Jackson to me, then back again. I was guessing a lot of things were starting to make sense to him all of a sudden.

"I'm not going anywhere," I said. "I can't let innocent shadow demons die when the hunter is obviously here for me."

"Many have already been killed," Essex said, his hands shaking. "The hunter has also taken a hostage."

"Who?" Jackson said.

"The daughter of Andros and Ourelia."

I cried out, cut to the core at this news. "Sasha?"

Essex nodded. "The hunter is saying she will execute the child if Andros does not hand you over to the Order."

I grabbed Jackson's arm. "We have to do something," I said. "We can't let this happen."

Jackson kicked the wall with startling force. "Dammit," he yelled. "Where are all the soldiers? The entire Resistance army should be able to handle one lousy hunter."

Essex sucked in a ragged breath. "No," he said. "The Resistance is locked inside the training room. A special practice was called for the evening and somehow the doors to the training area were sealed shut. No one can go in or out."

"How the hell did a hunter get inside anyway? I thought Andros said there was no way."

My mouth went dry. "No, he said the only way was if someone on the council let the hunter in," I said, dizziness washing over me. "Who would do this?"

Essex and Jackson stared at me looking confused.

"I can't believe that," Jackson said. "No one on the council would do this."

"Well, the hunter got in somehow," I said. "But that's not important now. What matters is that demons have died tonight because of me. I won't let Sasha die too."

I pushed past Essex, headed toward the Grand Hall.

Jackson reached for me, pulling me back to him. "You can't," he said. "It's too dangerous."

I gestured to all of the drawings on his wall. "I don't die today," I said. "Not here. Not like this. I'll be okay."

He shook his head, not loosening his grip on my arm.

"If you really want to prove that you believe in me and you see my strength, then you'll let me go," I said, standing up straighter. "You'll stand by my side and support me, no matter the danger."

Jackson let his hand slide down my arm, taking my hand and squeezing it tight.

"It's the right thing to do," I said. "We can save her."

He nodded and together we walked toward the marketplace where the hunter was waiting.

SHE COMES

The feel of evil engulfed me the moment I stepped into the marketplace. It oozed throughout the room like the smell of something badly burned. I didn't even have to ask where I could find the thing. A darkness circled the front staircase.

"Go back to the suite," I told Essex. "You don't need to be here for this. Is Mary Anne there?"

He nodded. "Yes. She wanted to come to your aid, but I talked her into staying inside the room for safety."

"Good," I said. "Go back in there and lock the door. Hide and don't come out until you're sure the hunter is gone."

"I will do this," he said. "I will keep her safe for you."

I gave him a sad smile, then turned my attention toward the cries and commotion in the front of the hall. Jackson's hand was still clasped to mine. "Well, it's possible I'm going to get a chance to show you some of what I learned in the training sessions," I said with a nervous laugh.

He didn't find it funny at all. He kissed my forehead, his lips lingering for a long moment.

"Come on," I said.

My first few steps were weak with nerves. Did I really know what I was getting myself into here? I'd never faced a hunter before. How could I be so sure I could handle her? One thing I had on my side was that I knew the hunter hadn't come here to kill me. The Order would never have wanted that. They still had a ritual to complete, and they needed me alive in Peachville to pull that off.

Still, I wasn't looking forward to whatever pain and torture this hunter would be allowed to dish out.

I just had to make sure she didn't have a chance to capture me.

I set my jaw and lifted my chin higher in the air. I could do this. I was strong. I was ready.

Slowly, my steps became more and more confident. By the time we reached the hunter, I had given myself the pep talk of all pep talks, and I was prepared for whatever she was going to throw at me.

But when we turned the corner and the evil being came into view, I choked back a scream. She was a thing of nightmares. A horror of a human being. While her body took the basic form of a woman, her skin had grown transparent and ghostlike, a grayish green haze surrounding her. Cold radiated from her like a blizzard. She wore a long black gown, the bottom of which rose several feet off the ground. She must have sensed my presence, because her head snapped toward me. Her eyes were completely black, even where the whites of her eyes should have been showing.

She smiled at me, her lips curling up around rotten, pointed teeth. "She comes."

The small crowd of demons that had gathered followed her gaze and the tension grew even thicker. I let my eyes pass across the spectators, settling on the worried faces of Andros and his wife. Andros turned, his eyes meeting mine. He took several long strides to reach me.

"I don't know what happened," he explained, his words directed at Jackson. "One minute we were at the party and the next we heard this awful screaming."

"Is anyone working to release the soldiers?" Jackson asked. "I heard they were locked inside the training room."

Andros wrung his hands and nodded. "I have Jericho working on it, but he can't seem to figure out what's holding it closed."

Jackson looked around as if trying to find a way out of this mess.

"Where's Sasha?" I asked.

Andros seemed to really see me for the first time. He studied me, his eyes lingering on my hand entwined with Jackson's. "She's... she's behind that thing," he stuttered.

"She's going to be okay," I said. I knew it wasn't something I had any right to promise, but somehow, I knew it in my heart.

He studied my face but didn't seem to believe me. "What are we going to do?"

Again, he addressed Jackson. Everyone always took me for granted, believing I was powerless and weak. Maybe it was time I showed them a different side to myself.

I just hoped that in the end I looked brave instead of stupid. Or dead.

I pulled my hand from Jackson's grip and stepped forward,

so close to the hunter I could smell the stench of decay dripping from her every pore.

"I'm the one you've come for," I said. "Release the girl and I'll offer you a deal."

The hunter's head fell back, and she cackled, high and piercing and so loud the ground beneath me shook. "Who are you to think you can offer me a deal?" she asked. Her voice had a strange echo to it, as if several voices were crammed into her body. "All you have to offer me is your life, and I could take that at any moment without your permission."

It was my turn to laugh. I was relieved that my voice sounded much more confident than I felt inside. "You may not need my permission, but that doesn't mean you are allowed to kill me," I said. "Let's not lie to each other. We both know who you work for."

The decaying witch narrowed her black eyes at me and she flew toward me, her face coming so close to mine I almost gagged on the stench. Behind her, I caught a glimpse of the child. She was caught in some type of dark netting. Tears ran down her tiny cheeks. My stomach twisted. I swallowed and pulled my shit together.

"So what about that deal?" I asked, angry at the small quiver that crept into my tone.

"You think I cannot sense your fear?" the witch asked.

Up close, her face was even more terrifying. Holes littered her rotting skin, the greenish smoke moving in and out of them like worms slithering through flesh. It took everything I had to stand my ground.

"I may fear you, but believe me, if you harm that little girl, you will never see another day in this world."

The hunter flew back to her place near the girl. "So cute

that you have such confidence," she said. "I can't wait to break you down to the lowest, groveling version of yourself."

Behind me, I heard Jackson step forward. I threw my hand up and shook my head. There was nothing he could do here except get in the way.

"Let the girl go and you'll have your chance," I said, raising an eyebrow in challenge.

The hunter studied me, then looked down at the child. "What is it that you're offering to me?"

I drew in a breath, locking my knees to keep from collapsing. My hands were sweaty and numb, but I kept my chin raised and my eyes open. "A trade," I said. "You let the girl go, and I agree to come with you."

The crowd around us gasped, whispers rising up. Jackson moved to me, his mouth close to my ear.

"What are you doing?" he said, his words short and angry. "You can't do this. I won't let you."

"I know what I'm doing," I said.

But did I? I was working on pure instinct and adrenaline.

The hunter laughed again. She crouched low beside Sasha. "You would give your life for this demon?"

"If that's what it takes," I said. "Let her go and I'll come with you, on one condition."

"Condition?" The evil witch flew high into the air, her voice low and fearsome. "You dare to place a condition on someone as powerful as me? I could snatch you from this place so fast you would forget your own name."

I shook my head. "No. If you could do that, you would have already done it," I said. "Your years of life have made you wise, and you know that if you take me, you'll have a serious fight on your hand. The same thing goes for the girl. You kill her or hurt her, and the Resistance will never stop until you're dead."

She was listening now, and I knew I'd hit on the truth, or some version of it.

"You can't risk a fight right now," I said. "What if I was to somehow die in the crossfire? What would Priestess Winter do to you if you screwed this up?"

The hunter's rotting jaw tensed, her teeth gnashed together with a gruesome grinding sound.

"I offer myself up to you willingly," I said, lifting my hands up to show my cooperation. "All you have to do is let the girl go safely. Then, I will agree to a contest. A duel."

"What kind of duel?" the witch asked.

I wondered what kind of power the Order had over such a being. When I mentioned Priestess Winter, the rotting hunter had actually winced, fear flashing in her dead eyes.

"A contest between you and me alone, with no interference from any other being in this place," I said. "But, since you are not allowed to kill me, and I do not have the strength or power to kill you, we duel until one of us either surrenders or is no longer conscious. If you win, I'll go with you and no one in this place will fight for me. But if I win, you become a prisoner of the Resistance."

The witch laughed, a low gurgling sound. "The Priestess told me you were a foolish girl," she said. "I could defeat you with a single flick of my finger."

A cold rope of fear tightened around my throat, making it difficult for me to breathe. I struggled against the paralyzing terror of it.

"Then do it," I said.

The crowd in the marketplace stood in stunned silence. I hoped that anyone who ever doubted my hatred of the Order now understood that I was worthy of trust, not suspicion. Surely the Order wouldn't send a hunter to capture one of their own spies.

I held my breath, waiting for an answer from the hunter.

Finally, she lowered her sharp nails to the netting that held Sasha in place. With a flick of her wrist, the hunter cut the strips of fabric. The net fell from Sasha's body and the child stood, her eyes wide with fear. Ourelia ran forward with a sob, taking her child into her arms and pulling her away from the hunter. Andros kissed his daughter's head and whispered something to his wife.

The woman and child pushed through the crowd. Just before they disappeared down one of the side corridors, I saw Sasha reach out toward me, her eyes locked on mine.

Many in the crowd scattered to the caves, but several stayed to watch, including Andros.

I partly watched these events take place, and partly didn't. Even if this witch couldn't kill me right here, right now, I knew this was still a battle for my life. If she took me from the Underground, I would still meet my death in Peachville. For a split second, I wondered what month it was. It rarely snowed in Georgia, but maybe it was a particularly cold winter back home.

Was that the ending Jackson had seen in his visions? A snowy day in Peachville?

Only time would tell.

One thing was certain. I wasn't going to lie down and just let death come to me. Not this time. I would fight until the very moment my spirit left my body.

"I will make this quick so you won't have to suffer for too long," the witch said with a grinding laugh. "I'll put you out so deep that by the time you wake up, you'll be back at Shadowford and it will all be over."

I didn't answer her. Instead, I spread my legs and planted my feet firmly against the tile floor. I blocked everyone and everything else from my mind, lifting my palms up toward the sky. I knew I had a very limited amount of time to connect to my power and try to find the same level of strength I had found in training.

I breathed deeply, the first few nervous breaths coming jagged and uneven but eventually settling into a good rhythm that calmed my heartbeat. I cleared my mind of all worry. I thought only of my mother's favorite flower. A single white rose in the darkness. I poured all of my focus onto that rose, feeling my power center inside of me, its strength growing with each second.

Before me, the hunter turned in a circle, marking out a

makeshift battleground, the boundaries marked by a hazy green line that hovered just above the ground. She crouched low, then began to spin. Slowly at first, then speeding up until she'd become a tornado. The demons screamed and covered their faces, the wind pushing them backward. The market-place shops on this side of the Grand Hall fell over, tents and their contents flying all over the area.

"There," the witch said as she slowed and finally came to a stop. "That's more like it."

She pushed the boundaries of her green haze out a little more, creating more space for our fight Then, she lifted her hands quickly, the green haze stretching from floor to ceiling and all around us, locking us into a bubble together. All outside sounds disappeared, the cries of the crowd silenced in an instant by the new green arena.

I looked up, taking stock of my new prison. The green barrier extended all around us in a messy circle. I was on my own now.

"We can't have any of your friends jumping into the fight to save you, now can we?" the hunter said. "Don't look so worried. This won't take long."

Knowing the fight was about to begin, I willed my nerves to settle. My heart pounded against my ribs. The evil witch moved toward me then, her pointy claws raised, a scream on her rotting lips. I threw my hands out to my side, fire engulfing them. Quickly, I spread the fire in a straight line in front of me, then lifted my hands high into the air, creating a wall of flame so high the witch ran straight into it. I had no idea if she would be able to pass straight through it or not, so I was relieved when she stopped short of the wall.

She placed her palms together, then slowly opened them,

the fire parting like a curtain in the middle. She smiled at me then, an ugly twisted expression that made my insides shiver. I backed away, my wall of fire dying down to nothing.

The hunter gathered an oozing ball between her hands, its color a kind of electric lime-green. With tense arms, she reared back and threw the ball toward me with perfect aim. I didn't react fast enough, diving out of the way just in time to keep the poisonous ball from hitting me square in the stomach. Instead, it grazed the top of my thigh, burning with a vicious heat.

I cried out, clutching the spot that was now covered with a glowing, sticky fluid that mixed with blood as it burned through my skin. I tore a piece of cloth from my shirt and wiped as much of the liquid off my wound as I could.

The hunter laughed and threw another green poison ball toward me. This time, I knew I wouldn't be able to get out of the way fast enough. On instinct, I threw up a shield to block the spell. Unfortunately, the only kind of shield I knew how to create was the one Zara had taught me back in Peachville. The kind that absorbs a piece of the opposing witch's essence.

The second the poison slammed into the shield, I felt the infinite hollowness of the hunter's existence. An intense sadness filled my heart. Underneath the evil at the surface of her power lay a life stolen just as mine had been. I looked up at this wretched being and realized that at one point, this thing had been a girl, just like me. She'd had hopes and dreams of her own, a life, even people she loved. I couldn't see what it was that had sent her to this world to be turned into this evil creature, but deep down, under the layers of decay and stench, she hated herself.

I listened to the echo of her power in my mind, and a single word came to my mind.

Maria.

Leaving my shield up, I stood and took a step toward her, ignoring the pain in my upper leg. "Maria," I said. "That's your name isn't it?"

The witch's eyes grew wide as saucers, the ghostly cloud around her body moving faster. "Don't you dare say that name to me," she growled.

She gathered an invisible power in her hands and angrily threw it toward me, but her anger had affected her aim. The invisible force slammed against the floor several feet in front of me, rolling slowly toward me, bringing up pieces of tile and rock as it rolled. I jumped easily out of the way.

"I see you," I said, taking a step back, careful not to trip over the debris. "You used to be beautiful with your shiny black curls and bright honey-colored eyes."

The hunter screamed and flew high into the air. With a vengeance, she barreled down toward me, her fingertips raised, ready to claw my flesh to pieces. I took hold of the edge of a broken tile and with all of my strength, I hurled it toward her. The jagged edge ripped into her arm. A greenish black liquid spewed out from her, and as it fell on the marble below, it made a hissing sound as if it were made of pure acid.

The hunter fell to the ground, clutching her shoulder. The cut had weakened her.

While she was distracted, I formed a large fireball between my palms and hurled it at her. She moved out of the way and the fire slammed into a fallen tent behind her. The blue tent burst into flames.

"Maria," I said again, forming another ball of fire in my hands. "What I can't help wonder is just how a pretty girl like you got assigned to the shadow world. How did you get stuck doing the Order's dirty work? You must have done something that really pissed them off, huh?"

She snapped her head toward me, saliva dripping from her blackened teeth. "Shut up," she said. "You don't know me, fool. You don't know the first thing about me."

"That's a lie," I said. I hurled the second fireball toward her, but she flew up into the air, dodging it too easily. A pile of debris on the other side of her caught fire too. With two strong fires blazing, I felt somehow stronger. As if my own power drew force from the flames. "I know exactly who you are. You used to be me. Just a regular girl caught in the Order's web of lies and promises. What did you do to piss them off so badly that they sent you here for all eternity?"

The hunter began to shake, her anger getting the best of her. I stood on my guard, creating more fire in my hands. The hunter flew around the circle, leaving a trail of greyish green fog behind her. As I reared back to throw the fire toward her, the gas reached my nose, making me gag and cough. I threw the fireball, but it landed several feet from my mark, barely lighting a small banner that had fallen from one of the shops.

I fell to my knees, coughing. I couldn't catch my breath. The gas surrounded me. My vision went fuzzy, and I began to fall back. Somewhere in the depths of my mind, I realized this was how she planned to end me. If I lost consciousness now, I might as well surrender my life.

I fought against the effects of the poison gas and reached deep inside to find some ounce of power left within. With it, I created a whirlwind around my body, the air moving slowly, then, as the gas began to clear away, faster and faster.

The rotting witch narrowed her eyes at me. She thought

she'd won already and was obviously annoyed I was still standing. Well, kneeling, really.

I felt the warmth of the flickering flames all around me as
the fire caught and spread around the dueling circle. I drew
strength from that fire, standing despite the pain in my leg and
my lungs. I knew I had to end this soon or I would lose my
ability to fight back. The hunter had more power than I did.
She could wear me down slowly if she wanted to. I had to stop
her fast.

Frantic, I looked around for anything I could use to defeat
or injure her. The broken tile had weakened her when it sliced
into her flesh, but she'd be ready for it if I tried to throw
another one. I looked around, seeing only rocks and broken
tile. I looked up and suddenly felt a wave of hope rush
through me.

The black roses carpeted the ceiling, and I knew that just
above the roses was the fragile soul stone. The rock could hold
a witch's power inside of it. It worked like a buffer between the
Underground and the land above it, absorbing any trace of
magic before it could pass through. Maybe I could use the
stone to draw her power from her body.

The hunter flew around, another green ball of poison
oozing between her fingertips. She was toying with me now,
thinking she had the upper hand.

Carefully, I chose the largest rock I could find from the
rubble of the floor and lifted it into the air with a flick of my
hand. My eyes searched the debris. When I saw another size-
able stone, I lifted that one as well. Then, a third.

The hunter's eyes flickered to the three stones I had raised
into the air. She laughed.

"Do you think you can throw these pitiful rocks at me and

win?" she asked. She threw the green poison at me, but I quickly maneuvered one of the rocks in its path, the two slamming into each other and falling down to the ground, powerless.

I chose another rock from the ground and lifted it into the air.

"No," I said, shaking my head. "These aren't for you."

For good measure, I lifted a fourth stone, then dipped my knees, gathering momentum. With every bit of strength I could find in my magic and my body, I hurled all four rocks straight up toward the ceiling above the hunter.

Above me, the rocks hit their mark with a loud crack. The soul stone shattered like a mirror. Pieces of black roses mixed with thick, jagged pieces of shiny black stone rained down on top of the hunter. I backed away and quickly used magic to pull pieces of broken tile over my head like an umbrella, careful to not get cut. But when I looked up at the screaming hunter, I saw that she had been cut in over a dozen places. Her essence drained from her like acid.

Weakened, she tried to stand, but the soul stone had begun to work its magic, pulling the essence of her power from her body. Her power slid through the stones like water, in and out, the grayish green smoke pouring from her.

I knew I had only a small window, so I turned my attention to the flames burning all around us. I reached deep inside my own soul, extending my power outward to encompass every single flame and flicker in the circle. I fed the flames with my own power, connecting to it in a way that frightened me.

A stream of pure white energy began to flow from the center of my palms, and I felt the same dark power I'd felt at the portal rise up within me. I panicked, wanting to drop the power, so scared of losing control again. But as I watched the hunter writhing under the influence of the broken soul stone, I knew this was my only chance to defeat her.

I embraced the new energy, pouring myself into the flames. The red fire turned a bright, hot shade of pure blue. With one huge push, I commanded the flames to engulf the hunter's body. Blue flashed as the flames raced toward the center of the circle, surrounding the hunter in an ocean of fire.

The hunter screamed, a high-pitched sound that vibrated every inch of my body.

Then, as the flames sucked the oxygen from her tiny prison, she began to cough and sputter. Then, slowly, she fell to the ground like a withering flower, her black eyes finally closing.

THE KIND OF GIRL THAT REBELS
AGAINST THE SYSTEM

I collapsed onto the broken tiles. The hazy boundary that held us in dissipated. Andros and a few demons I didn't recognize ran forward and placed a strange silver contraption over the hunter's hands, feet and mouth. They carried the unconscious witch away quickly, the crowd scattering to keep their distance from her.

Jackson fell at my feet. He ripped a piece of cloth from the bottom of his shirt and wrapped it around my injured leg.

I struggled to keep my eyes open. My leg pulsed and burned from the acid of the hunter's blood. I coughed into my hand, a black oily substance peppering my palm.

"What were you thinking?" Jackson said. He ran his fingers through my hair, letting his thumb brush against my cheek. "You could have gotten killed."

"But I didn't," I said, attempting a smile.

"That was really stupid, Harper." His words were angry, but his face was full of love and gratitude. "But, it was also really brave and strong. It was difficult to see you through the haze of the barrier, but I saw what you did with the stone. How did you know it would affect her that way?"

I shook my head. "I'm not sure," I said. "I just guessed, in a way. I mean, I remembered how it pulled Caroline's power from her body, so I thought maybe it would hurt the hunter too."

Jackson pulled me into his arms. My aching body protested, but I ignored my wounds and hugged him harder.

"I need to find the Shaman," he said. "We've got to get that poison out of your leg before it festers."

I nodded. "Want to carry me back to the room first?"

He smiled. "Of course," he said.

I put my arms around his neck and he lifted me into the air. A small group of shadow demons stood around the area, some of them picking up the broken tiles and fragments of stone. Others simply stared at me, perhaps not believing what they had just seen. Or maybe they were just shocked to see their future king caring for a human girl.

I smiled and tucked my face into the warmth of his neck. Maybe I was just destined to be the kind of girl that rebels against the system. It seemed that no matter where I went, in one world or the next, I was always causing some kind of scandal.

Somehow, I knew my mother would have been so proud.

THIS ISN'T HOW I DIE

I slipped in and out of poisoned dreams, waking up several times throughout the night to see Jackson faithfully by my side. He scooted closer to the bed, running his hand gently through my matted hair.

"How are you feeling?" he asked when I finally woke in the early morning hours.

"Probably better than I look," I said, joking. I coughed again, more of the black soot covering my palm. "Gross."

"I've called for the shaman, but several shadow demons were injured by the hunter, and she has a duty to help them first."

I nodded, understanding.

"Is Sasha okay?"

He smiled. "She's fine," he said. "She's just a little scared, that's all. But Ourelia stopped by earlier when you were sleeping to say thank you. She said the little girl knew you would save her."

I laughed, but my lungs screamed in pain. Whatever poisonous gas I had inhaled had really done a number on me.

A knock on the outer door of the suite sent Jackson straight into the air. He rushed into the outer room. "Thank you so much for coming," he said. "Harper's wound is looking worse."

The shaman walked toward my room, and I could hear the beads in her hair clicking together as she moved. There was something so beautiful about the sound. In her presence, I immediately felt calm.

Without a word, she looked over the poison wound in my thigh, then placed her hand against my chest. A warmth spread through my ribs and down into my lungs.

"You will be fine, child," the shaman said.

"I know," I said. "This isn't how I die."

The shaman tilted her head to look at me, then she broke out in a knowing smile. "No, indeed, it is not."

She rummaged through her medicine bag and pulled out a vial similar to the one she'd used with Mary Anne's tiger wound. Only this time, there was no liquid inside. Instead, the shaman uncorked the vial and laid it at the edge of the wound on my leg. She chanted something low and soft and at her command, the poisonous green ooze dripped into the vial. The burning pain disappeared immediately, leaving only a small burned area on my leg.

She corked the full bottle and placed it into a special pouch of her bag. Then, she placed a compress of cool herbs onto my leg. I sighed at the soothing power of the woman's medicine.

"Thank you," I said, coughing.

She moved her attention to my chest and frowned. She studied me for a moment, then went back into her bag and pulled out a long glass tube that was open at both ends. "This won't be as pleasant," she said apologetically. "Try to just relax."

Nervous, I made an effort to relax my shoulders and let my body sink down into the soft bed. The shaman placed one end of the tube into my mouth. Then, she placed her palm at the other end, closing her eyes. Chanting, she began to pull her hand back from the tube, as if pulling some energy forth. She repeated this motion over and over again until suddenly, I felt my chest constrict.

I couldn't breathe or move, and panic filled me. My eyes sought the shaman's, hoping she would look to reassure me. But her eyes were closed shut. She continued to pull air from the tube, ripping the very breath from my chest. Gradually, the tube filled with a black and grey smoke that rose from my mouth and escaped into the air of the room.

Just when I thought I would pass out from not being able to breathe, she removed the tube. I gasped for air, sitting up and clutching my chest. When I calmed down, I realized I hadn't coughed at all. The smoke in the air dissipated quickly, leaving my lungs healed.

Relieved, I collapsed back onto the bed.

"Thank you," I said between gulps of fresh air. "I feel much better."

"Yes," she said, raising one eyebrow. She touched the spot just over my heart. "And your heart is whole again as well."

I smiled and looked toward Jackson, who was standing at the door talking to Mary Anne and Essex. "Yes," I said, placing my hand over hers.

A shock ran through my hand when I touched her, and I pulled away. In that moment, a scene had flashed before my eyes. A man's face. Someone I didn't recognize. He was tall and round. Much older than I, with a full silver beard and silver eyes.

I sat up, blinking. "Who...?" I started, staring at the shaman. "Who was that?"

She smiled, her eyes teasing me with their sparkle of knowledge. She turned to leave, but I reached out and touched the sleeve of her dress.

"What is it that you see when you look at me?" I asked.

She pressed her lips together, not answering at first. Then, she finally nodded and said, "You will know soon enough. You are a very special girl, Harper. Very unique and very powerful. Keep pushing toward your destiny, child, and you will find your true self."

With that, she turned and left the suite, leaving me with so many unanswered questions.

ANOTHER ONE OF THEIR LIES

Shortly after the shaman left, we had another visitor. A courier for the council, requesting that Jackson and I both attend an emergency meeting of the Underground's council.

I wasn't surprised at the news. All this time I'd been waiting to be included in Jackson and Lea's meetings, and it had finally taken a brush with death to make it happen.

"Wait, where's Lea?" I asked. "I haven't seen her since I saw you together at the party."

Jackson frowned and went to knock on her door. "I hadn't even thought of it," he said. "But it's weird that she wasn't there when the hunter appeared."

"Do you think she was hurt?" Mary Anne asked, her face wrinkled with worry.

"I don't know," I said. "I hope not."

Surprisingly, I meant it. Lea wasn't exactly my favorite person in the world, but now that I knew how she felt about

Jackson, I kind of understood why she'd never been crazy nice to me. Could I blame her?

"We need to get to this meeting," Jackson said. "They'll have answers."

I nodded, throwing on my leather jacket. My leg was still a little sore, but I was able to walk on it just fine. "We'll be back," I said. "Are you two okay here on your own?"

Essex and Mary Anne nodded.

"Now that I know my mother is unharmed, I am much better," Essex said.

Jackson took my hand and led me down the hall so fast, we were practically running.

"Are you worried about Lea?" I asked.

He nodded, distracted. "Yes, but I'm also nervous about this meeting," he said. "It can't be good that they're calling you in when they know you were injured."

"I'm fine," I said, but a shiver of fear ran up my spine. The demons here couldn't be happy about the danger they'd all been put in because of me. Also, Jackson and I were going to have some explaining to do about our relationship.

The secret door to the council's meeting hall opened at Jackson's command and we rushed through. He led me down the hall straight into the library. Just inside, sitting at the large round table, was a group of ten shadow demons. Andros sat in the largest chair straight across from the door. I recognized some of the faces of the other demons, including Marlana, the girl who had first let us into the Underground. Still, there were others I did not know.

When we walked into the room, the conversation halted. Several members of the council looked directly at our clasped hands, open-mouthed. Embarrassed, I slipped my hand from Jackson's grasp and walked up to the table.

"Andros, I'm so sorry about your daughter—"

He held up his hand to stop me. "Please," he said. "Have a seat and let us talk about what has happened here last night."

There were three empty chairs at the table. I took one and Jackson sat beside me. Lea was missing from the council's table. Did they know what had happened to her? Was she okay? I wanted to ask, but Andros was obviously waiting for something. Or someone.

I held my tongue, but my knee bounced up and down under the table.

After a few excruciatingly slow minutes, the door to the library burst open. Everyone turned in unison to see who had entered.

My eyes opened wide at the sight of Lea. She had changed out of her party dress and was back in her typical leather attire. In her hand she carried a chain that extended behind her through the doorway.

"Move, traitor," she snarled, pulling hard on the thick silver chain.

Jericho stumbled through the doorway, then fell to his knees before the council. His hands and neck were bound to the chains. Several members of the group gasped, including Jackson. Andros stood, his eyes searching Lea's.

"No," he said. "This must be some mistake."

"I assure you, this is no mistake," Lea said. She put her leather boot on Jericho's back and pushed his face down to the floor. "This demon, who we all considered a trusted friend, has been working for the Order of Shadows. He's the one who let the hunter into the Underground. And he is the one who

locked our army into the training rooms. This scum is respon-
sible for the death of thirty of our brothers and sisters."

Thirty? Thirty had died because of me. Guilt slithered
through me like a snake.

Andros straightened his shoulders, his jaw tense with
anger. "Is this true, Jericho, son of my father's friend? Explain
yourself to your council."

Jericho lifted his head. His lip was swollen and bloodied
and he moved as if he had aches and pains throughout his
body. I had no doubt all of his injuries were courtesy of Lea's
anger.

"I came to this place, following all of you, believing we
were going to make a difference," he said. He swallowed, took a
pained breath, then continued. "I thought you all had so much
power, so much faith in the future. I came here to fight, not sit
around like a bunch of helpless children."

Andros' shoulders slumped slightly as he understood the
truth. "So, it is the truth," he said, his voice thick with disappointment. "It was you who placed my daughter's life in
danger and the lives of all of the shadow demons under
my care."

"Yes, and I would do it again," Jericho said. He searched
the faces at the table, finally coming to rest on me. "If this
human girl had been captured today, I would have been given
a very special gift."

"What gift?" Jackson asked. "What gift could possibly be
worth all of this?"

Jericho laughed and narrowed his eyes at Jackson. "Don't
you know?" he asked. "The Order would have given me back
my parents. My sister Elisha. My promised mate, Sentira. The
Order promised to separate them from their human slavers and

return them to the shadow world by nightfall if I could hand them this one human girl."

His words sent my heart soaring, despite his betrayal. The Order had promised to separate the demons from the humans? Did that mean they knew how to do it? Or was this just another one of their lies?

He continued to stare at me, questioning. "Never in my immortal lifetime would I have imagined you would have defeated that hunter," he said. A tear rolled down his cheek. "Now my family is lost to me forever, thanks to you."

"It wasn't me who took your family," I said. "Besides, you should have known better than to trust the Order. They would have never helped you even if they knew of a way to separate humans and demons."

"The council understands your sorrow," Andros said, clearing his throat. "All of us here have someone we love on the other side, but to betray us all for your own selfish reasons is something we can never forgive. Jericho, you are hereby sentenced to live out the rest of your immortal life in isolation on the third sub-floor."

Jericho's eyes grew wide and he shook his head frantically. "No," he said. "You cannot put me down there with those things. Please, I'll do anything."

"Would you rather we put you outside the protection of the Underground?" Andros roared. "Where the Order of Shadows would surely come for you? Don't you know what they would do to you once they realized you had failed them? My decision is final."

Out of the shadows of the council room, two tall demons emerged and took hold of Jericho's arms. They dragged him from the room, his screams echoing through the dark hallway.

THE WOMAN HE LOVES

L ea took her place in the remaining empty chair around the council's table.

She nodded to me, a knowing look in her eyes.

"Now that the whole of the council is present, we need to address the issue of Harper's presence in the Underground," Andros said. He looked across the table at me. "I would like to commend you on your bravery today. I am sure I don't have to tell you how grateful I am that you were willing to risk your life to save my daughter."

"I'm just glad she's okay," I said.

"We all know that you could have run when word came that the hunter had entered the Underground," he said. "The fact that you stayed to fight against nearly impossible odds says a lot about your character. I'm sure many of the council members are sorry they misjudged you."

Many of those sitting at the table lowered their heads.

"You have shown enormous power for a human," he continued. "To defeat a hunter is no small feat, as I'm sure you know. Still, we cannot ignore the fact that your presence here puts us all in danger. Were it not for you being here, the hunter never would have had a reason to come."

I bit my lip and rubbed my sweating palms against my pants. I had a feeling I knew what was coming next.

"Before you arrived, the council voted on this matter, and I'm afraid our decision was that you must leave the Underground."

Jackson stood, slapping his hand down on the surface of the table. "You cannot do this," Jackson said. "Harper was willing to sacrifice her life for all of you today. She fought that hunter with everything she had, and she won. She deserves a chance to stay. If you throw her out, you're condemning her to death. Besides, the hunter wouldn't have gotten in at all if there hadn't been a traitor on the council."

Andros folded his hands together and leaned forward. "I understand everything you're saying, old friend. As you know, this is not the first time one of the demons of the Underground has betrayed us. This is why we try to keep the actions of this council and the Resistance secret, but we never dreamed we could have a traitor on our own council. Keeping her is a risk. The Order will never stop trying to corrupt and conquer our people until she is gone. We do appreciate her actions today. However, we cannot continue to put all of our citizens in danger for the life of this one human girl."

"Are you forgetting that this one human girl is also connected to my brother? If she dies, Aerden dies too."

"We understand your concerns," a tall female demon responded. "But our responsibility is to the shadow demons who have entrusted us with their lives down here."

"Bullshit," Jackson said. "You have simply chosen to let

fear rule you. How are you any different than the king? Or my father? Sitting down here in the safety of this cave, doing nothing while the demons of our world suffer."

"We fight for the villages that are attacked by hunters," a gray-haired demon said. "We have saved hundreds of lives through our work."

"You don't even make a dent," Jackson said. "You have the power and the ability to make a real difference, but instead you choose the easy fights. You protect one village while the Order simply moves on to the next and steals twice as many from their beds."

"Enough," Andros said. "The decision has been made, friend. The girl must leave tonight."

Fear shot through me. Tonight? My earlier heartache-fueled determination had left me. I had gotten lucky against one hunter, but, how long before another hunter found me?

"I am going with her," Jackson said.

Ten pairs of eyes stared at him in stunned silence.

"Your duty is here with your future Queen," Andros said, finally finding his voice.

At this, Lea stood. I held my breath, unsure what she was going to say. Would she demand that Jackson stay here with her?

"His duty is both to his brother and to the woman he loves," she said. She paused and looked at Jackson, love and sadness mixed in her expression. "Go, and keep her safe."

A murmur went up among the members of the council.

Jackson took Lea's hand and brought it to his lips in gratitude. "Thank you," he said.

She nodded, then turned away. It was the closest to crying

I had ever seen from her. I felt her sacrifice deep in my heart. She loved him, but she was willing to let him go.

Lea sniffed once, then straightened, all signs of her emotions zipped up again behind her sarcasm and strength. "When you get settled, contact us and let us know where you are."

She placed a small stone in Jackson's hand, and he quickly put it in his pocket.

He touched my arm and motioned for me to stand. I knew it was our cue to leave, but I had something more I wanted to say. Before I could talk myself out of it, I turned to the council.

"The Order of Shadows is a powerful organization, but they aren't gods and they aren't invincible," I said. "I know it's not my place to tell you how to live or fight, but someday, I hope we can build an army of demons and humans who can work together to bring down the Order. In the beginning, when the first of your kind came to my world, the first thing he experienced there was not torture or slavery or sorrow. It was love. The Order may have corrupted that, but that doesn't mean we should hate each other for the sins of one group of greedy women. Not all humans want to see your kind hurt, and not all humans value power over love."

I finished my speech and stared out at the faces of those around the table. I couldn't tell what impact, if any, my words had on them. All I could hope was that somewhere in their hearts, they understood what I was trying to say.

LIFE RARELY IS

Breaking the news to Mary Anne was not easy.

"You've got to be kidding me," she shouted. "You saved all their asses and they're kicking you out? Well, I'm going with you."

She turned toward her room, but I grabbed her arm to stop her.

"We've been through this once already, haven't we?"

She scrunched her face up in barely suppressed anger. "You can't go back out there with those things alone."

"I'm not going to be alone," I said. "Jackson's coming with me."

She shook her head. "Then I'm definitely not staying here," she said. "We came here together. We should leave together."

"I'm sorry, but you have to stay here," I said. "This journey is going to be difficult enough without me worrying about you the whole time. You still aren't completely healed from your injuries. It's too risky."

Her shoulders relaxed slightly, and her bottom lip quivered. "You have to go tonight?" she asked. "They won't even let you stay overnight to get your rest?"

I shook my head. "No, they're afraid more hunters will show up if I stay," I said. I pulled her into my arms for a big hug. "We'll be okay."

"Where will you go?" she asked.

"I don't know," I said. "But we'll figure it out. Maybe we'll go back to the cave or something for a few days? We haven't had a chance to really make a plan yet."

"This isn't fair."

"Life rarely is," I said. "Here or back home."

"How will I know where you are or how to reach you if I need to?" she asked. "Will you come back for me if you decide to go home?"

"You can reach us with this," Jackson said.

I hadn't even heard him come back into the room, but he was packed and ready to go. He handed something to Mary Anne, and when she opened her palm to study it, I saw that it was a tiny clear stone.

"How does it work?" she asked.

"All you have to do is close your palm around the stone and think my name," he said. "I have a matching stone with me, so I will hear you if you call for me. The only drawback is that you can only use it a handful of times before it loses its magic."

"Okay," she said, tucking it into her pocket. "I will only use it in case of an emergency or something really important."

"I've asked Lea to watch out for you," he said. "And Essex is going to take good care of you, too."

Mary Anne nodded, her blue eyes filling with tears. "I love you guys," she said.

The three of us joined in a group hug, and I wondered when, or if, I would ever see my dear friend again.

GUARDED SECRETS

J ackson took my hand and walked with me toward the Grand Hall. We had decided to spend the night in another cave Jackson knew from his childhood.

"Do you think we'll be able to make it there tonight?" I asked. "It's already so late, and I can't stand that stupid Obsidian Forest."

He smiled and squeezed my hand as we walked. "The place where we came through to the Underground is just one of many portals," he said. "There are similar circles of black roses all over the Northern Kingdom. I asked Andros to find us a portal closer to the cave where I want to hide out."

I took in a calming breath and felt the relief flood through me. I was so thankful to have him with me. I couldn't believe I'd almost left on my own.

In the marketplace, a small group of shadow demons waited to say goodbye. I recognized the faces of some of the vendors and cafe owners I'd become friendly with over the past few weeks. Essex and his mother were there. Some of Jackson's friends. As we passed by, they offered us food, water, and weapons. Bowing, we took each present, thanking them. Their gifts touched my heart. That they didn't blame me for the deaths of those thirty shadow demons eased my guilt.

At the top of the main staircase, Andros and his family waited to say goodbye.

Sasha jumped from her mother's grasp and threw her arms around my legs. I crouched down to give her a proper hug. "I told my mother she shouldn't worry, that you would come and save me," she whispered.

I smiled at her and kissed her tiny cheek.

Ourelia hugged me and gave me a sweater. "It might get cold where you're going," she said. "Promise me you'll be careful."

I nodded, knowing that no matter how careful we might be, the future wasn't entirely in our hands.

It was Andros' gift that surprised me more than anything. With serious eyes, he handed me a tightly bundled package.

"What is this?" I asked.

"When you first came here, Jackson told me you'd been looking for a clue about how to break the spell that binds Aerden's soul and power to you," he said. "I told him we had never heard of this spell, but I wasn't entirely honest."

Chills ran up my arms. I clutched the package tight against my chest.

"The book you now hold has the information you've been looking for," he said. Then he turned to grasp Jackson's hand. "Please do not be angry at me for keeping this from you. You must understand that this information is one of our most closely guarded secrets, and down here we still have some trust issues. Someday, we wanted to seek the items needed to break the spell and cross worlds in order to free our brothers and sisters. Harper, I now see that your destiny is tied to this book. It was waiting here for you. For this moment. May the suns and moons carry you to safety through all your days and nights."

For a moment, I couldn't move or speak or breathe.

In my hands, I held the key to my own freedom and the freedom of thousands. It was a priceless gift that filled my heart with hope.

"Thank you," I managed, then threw my arms around him.

Andros laughed and patted my back. "You're welcome," he said. "Do not let this information go to waste."

"We won't," Jackson said.

We finished our goodbyes and Andros walked us down the long hallway to the portal. He searched through a collection of stones, and finally placed a new symbol into a square cubby in the wall. Jackson took my hand and moved us to stand just beneath the portal's opening. With a nod, he signaled that we were ready. Andros nodded back slowly, then placed his hand over the symbol.

A familiar hum coursed through my body from feet to head. Then, I fell upward, my body disassembling and passing through the cool soul stone. I forced myself to stay calm through the sudden darkness. When I reached the other side, the crisp air startled me.

My hair blew back in the wind, lifting from my neck and sending a cool breeze straight through me.

Disoriented, I closed my eyes, enjoying the feel of the wind while the world stopped spinning.

THE RING

Jackson's lips descended on mine, so warm. I leaned against him, enjoying this peaceful moment.

"We should go," he said softly.

I opened my eyes and looked around. We were standing at the top of a moonlit hill, the black roses circling us. Above our heads, the sky boasted three moons—one pink, one blue and one lavender.

"Weren't there only two moons before?" I asked.

Jackson laughed and took my hand. "There are seven moons total," he said. "How many you can see depends on the time of the year. Three moons mean warm weather. Sort of like summer here."

"Summer sounds good to me," I said. "No snow in summer."

We stepped out of the ring of roses and onto dark gritty sand. The sand slipped beneath my feet, and I nearly lost my footing. Jackson held tight to me, keeping me from falling.

Carefully, we made our way down the hill and onto a flat, beach-like surface. In the distance, I could hear the sound of the sea.

The cave took another half-hour to get to, and I spent the entire time looking over our shoulders to make sure we weren't being followed. Once we were inside, I was glad to be out of the sand and out of view. Jackson had picked up bits of driftwood along the way and he immediately set to making a fire. Our no-magic policy was in full effect, hoping not to alert any hunters of our presence.

I was completely exhausted, but right now nothing short of death could keep me from reading the book Andros had given us. As soon as the fire provided enough light for me to see by, I untied the package and lifted an old leather-bound book from the cloth. The leather was soft and worn, the binding badly cracked from age. A blue butterfly was embossed on the front cover. I traced the image with my fingertip, my teeth grinding together as I thought of the one family I knew with an affinity for butterflies.

The Winters.

Zara had told me her ancestors were members of the Order of Shadows for a long time, but until this moment, I hadn't realized she meant they were founding members. Judging from the age of this tome, it was possible someone in the Winter family had been around since the beginning.

The leather cracked as I opened the book. The pages were yellowed and worn, but thankfully, the writing was all in neatly handwritten English. I skimmed each page, searching for the information Andros had been talking about.

The first several seemed to contain basic information about how to feel connected to your power, how to control a flame, how to move an object across the room. It wasn't until after the basics that things started getting interesting.

"Look at this," I said to Jackson. "*A witch may perform many spells on her own power, but with the collaboration of a shadow demon, a witch's power grows exponentially.*"

Jackson sat next to me, taking part of the book into his lap so that it was shared between us.

"I think we're looking at one witch's schoolbook of sorts," I said. "These read like lessons at first, right? I mean, these basic spells look like handwritten notes on how to perform simple things. But as you move further into the book, it becomes more complex, as if the witch was learning more as she advanced through the Order or whatever it was that existed before the Order. This may possibly be her private journal or something."

Jackson flipped through several more of the pages, stopping when he saw a drawing of a ritual room with a portal. "What does it say here?" he asked as he threw another piece of wood on the fire.

I read from the page. "*After Magda's journey into the shadow world, my sisters and I have discovered a way to pull shadow demons through so that their power may be used as a type of fuel for our magic,*" I read. "*The secret is in the gemstones found all over the shadow world. They are as common there as simple rocks, but they absorb magic like no stones we have ever seen. Using these stones, we have built a portal to the other side which can only be controlled by the master of the stone.*"

"The master of the stone?" Jackson said, looking over the page. "That must be the person who controls the stone? What else? Read it out loud."

"*We are unsure how it works exactly, but the first stone we mined from the shadow world was a deep blue sapphire,"* the journal continued. *"We found a location at the edge of town where the stone seemed to vibrate with a special power. There, we placed it into the ground, and here, after much experimenting, we created a spell that opened a gateway to the other side. Eloisa, the eldest, was the first to claim the title of master. After several months of trying different techniques, she finally chipped a small piece from the stone and created a powerful ring. She imbued this ring with a powerful spell designed to control a demon's power.*

"The control spell worked beautifully! Within a week, she had returned home through the portal with a demon under her command. After many months, we developed a special spell that trapped this demon into her body. You wouldn't believe the effect! Eloisa is by far the most powerful witch in the history of this town, possibly the world. We now know there is no need to make a demon fall in love with you in order to join with his powers. With this new magic, we can summon the demons and make them into our very own personal energy pool without so much as asking their permission.

"Of course, many of the witches in our town do not approve of these techniques. They call us cruel and evil and say we are using dark magic, but I see it as survival of the fittest. The most powerful deserve the best, and we are by far the most powerful witches in the world. We have decided to call ourselves The Order of Shadows since we now control these shadow demons, and soon, we will have each created our very own demon gate. I, for one, am looking forward to feeling the rush of power Eloisa brags about ever since her demon entered her."

I stopped there, my hands shaking. In my hands I was holding one of the first accounts of the formation of the Order of Shadows. I wasn't familiar with the names Eloisa and Magda, and I was unsure exactly how many witches had been involved at the start of the Order, but none of that was as important as understanding the origins of the demon gates and the purpose of the gemstones.

I turned the page and froze. More drawings of familiar items. A dagger with a stone embedded in its hilt. A chalice. A gemstone necklace. The fourth item was a ring.

"Have you ever seen this ring?" I asked.

Jackson shook his head. "The rest of these things we're obviously intimately familiar with," he said. "But the ring is new to me. Does it say anything else about it here?"

I shook my head. There were no notes on this page, only drawings.

It was on the next to last page that we finally found what we were looking for. "Here," I said excitedly. "This is it, Jackson, oh, my god."

"What?" he asked, gripping the side of the book.

I pointed to the text at the top of the page. *"The magic that binds a Prima to the first demon is one of the strongest binding spells I have ever performed. To reverse this magic, you must perform the original initiation spell backwards, using all of the same original items that were used in the creation of the Prima's bond."*

"Harper, this is exactly what we've been looking for," Jackson said. He took the book into his lap and read the sentences again. Then, he backed up a few pages. "Do we have the steps of the original initiation spell in here?"

"Yes," I said, feeling giddy, my exhaustion forgotten. "It's a few pages back, closer to the drawings."

I flipped back and pointed when we reached the ritual.

"What does it say were the items used?" I asked. "That's what we'll need to reverse the spell."

"The original portal stone," he said. "Which is easy since it's in the ritual room. The master's stone."

"Wait, isn't that the same thing?" I asked, peering over his shoulder.

"I don't know," he said. "I would assume so. Whoever wrote this book called the person in charge of the gate the master of the stone, so I would imagine the master's stone is the portal."

"Makes sense to me," I said. "What else?"

"The ritual dagger."

"That's usually kept at Lydia Ashworth's house," I said. "I saw it there the night of the Homecoming dance. When Morgyn died. I doubt it's still there, though. Not after what happened with Mrs. Ashworth."

I thought of how Priestess Winter's underlings had carried Lydia Ashworth away for her betrayal. If I had to guess, I would imagine all of those items had been given to Brooke's mother, Mrs. Harris. She's the one the Order wanted as their new Prima, so it only made sense.

"The necklace," Jackson said next. "What happened to it?"

I reached up to my bare neck. "They took it from me for the ritual," I said. "They placed it inside the chalice."

"That's the next item," Jackson said. "Who keeps the cup?"

"I don't know," I said. "I always assumed Mrs. Ashworth had that as well. Now, it's either Mrs. Harris who has it or Priestess Winter."

"We'll hope for Mrs. Harris," he said. He traced his finger along the words, his lips moving as he read. "The only other item mentioned here is the ring."

I leaned back against the wall of the cave. The ring. Neither of us had ever seen this item before. I was certain none of the other witches in Peachville had ever worn it. I would have noticed the stone. From the drawing, the stone was large and oval, definitely something that would draw attention.

"Is there any other information there about the ring?" I asked. "It's the only unknown item."

He flipped carefully through each page, then shook his head. "Nothing that I can see here," he said.

I let my head fall into my hands. We were so close, but without the ring, the information was useless.

"It's late," he said, closing the book. "Tomorrow we need to come up with a plan of where to go and how to stay safe out here on our own. You need to get some rest so you're fresh for whatever comes our way. For now, we should be safe here since we haven't cast any magic or left any kind of trail, but we can't stay in one place forever. It's too dangerous."

I nodded. He was right. Without the safety of the Underground, we would have to be on our guard at all times. "What about you?" I asked.

"I can survive with a lot less sleep than you can," he said. He pulled a blanket from his backpack and threw it over me. "I'll be your pillow."

I smiled and snuggled into the space between his arm and his chest. After all the excitement, I wasn't sure I'd be able to sleep, but after a few minutes of listening to the crackle of the fire and the soothing sound of the waves crashing on the shore outside the cave, my eyes began to droop.

"I love you," I said sleepily. Despite the possible dangers that lay ahead, I felt as if I'd never been happier.

Jackson kissed my forehead.

"I love you, too."

PLACES OF GREAT POWER

"Harper, wake up."

The urgency in Jackson's tone scared the crap out of me. I bolted up, ready to run or fight. "What happened?"

He sat near the fire holding the witch's journal, his green eyes bright with excitement. "I think I found something," he said.

I released a huge breath and waited for my shoulders to un-tense. "I thought we were being attacked or something."

He smiled. "Not yet," he said.

I cringed. He said it like it was only a matter of time.

"Come here, I want to show you something."

I looked through the mouth of the cave and saw that it was very early morning. The suns were just coming up on the horizon. "Have you been reading all night?"

"Yes," he said. "I didn't sleep. I wanted to stay up and make sure no one had followed us here."

I nodded. "So, what did you find?"

He shifted his weight and held the book out toward me. I sat down next to him and tilted my head to look at the open page.

"It's just one little section here," he said.

He pointed to a passage near the middle of the book. The witch wrote about how the hunters were created and sent to the shadow world to choose demons and bring them through the portal. I skimmed it, not seeing what it was he was so excited about.

"Here," he said. He pulled the book back toward him and read. *"Eloisa was reluctant to give up her favorite bauble, afraid it would be lost forever, but in order to create more demon gates from the blue stone, we needed the ring to stay in the shadow world as a sort of anchor."*

"The ring," I said. "It's here?"

"It has to be," Jackson said. "From reading, here's what I learned. Originally, there was only one demon gate per sister, and one gate per gemstone. One blue; that was the first. Red, Yellow, Green, Purple, and Diamond followed."

I listened, my body humming with excitement.

"But after the Order had created those original gates, they got greedy. They wanted to expand," he said. "They started looking for ways to open more gates of each corresponding stone. But at first, they failed. None of the new gates would stay open. Then, they discovered that the ring was the key. Somehow, the power of the ring is that it acts as an anchor, connecting all of the blue gates together and so on."

I tried to put it all together in my mind. Peachville was a blue gate, but it definitely wasn't the first one. There had to be at least fifty or more blue gates in the human world by now. The same was probably true of all the other stones as well.

"Does that mean if we find the ring, we can close all of the portals?" I asked.

"I'm not sure," he said. "I think the demon gates themselves will still exist, but the portals there won't open anymore if the ring is brought back to the human world."

"This is huge," I said. "We could cripple the Order and keep them from pulling any demons through. Does it say where the ring is in the shadow world?"

"No," he said. "Not exactly. It only says that the rings were hidden in places of great power here in the shadow world. Places where each stone would draw power from sister stones. I'm not sure what that means."

We were so close to something big. With the ring, we might not be able to close the gates for good, but we could keep the Order from opening them to bring more demons through. It would be a huge victory.

"What about the other items?" I asked. "Does the journal say how each of those is important to the initiation spell?"

"From what I understand, each demon gate has its own chalice, dagger, necklace and portal stone," he said. "But the rings are rare. Only one exists per colored gemstone."

An excited chill ran through my body.

"We have to find it."

THIS IS WHAT THE ORDER OF
SHADOWS DOES

J ackson caught fresh fish for breakfast and cooked
them on the fire. I had never been one to like fish, but
this was delicious, almost sweet.

"This is the first time you've ever cooked for me," I
teased.

"Not quite as romantic as it could have been, I guess," he
said, holding up a bright green fish head. "But it'll do."

I smiled and shook my head. "I wish we could stay here," I
said. "It's happy here. Like we could just forget the rest of
the world."

He looked out at the sea beyond the cave. "If we make it
through this mess, I promise I'll bring you back here and we
can stay as long as you want."

If we make it through.

"It's a deal," I said. "But what's our plan until then?"

"I remembered this vendor when I was a little boy," he
said. "My father used to take us there when he had business in

the smaller villages. The shop was full of little trinkets. Mostly junk, really, but I remember this guy had a thing for rocks. He had a collection on display and was always looking to trade for rare gemstones or unique rocks."

"Do you think he might know something about the blue stones?"

"It's worth a shot, right?" Jackson finished his fish and threw the scraps into the fire. "This was a long time ago, so I guess it's possible the shop isn't there anymore, but I'd like to try."

"How far away is it?" I asked.

"Maybe a day's journey at the most," he said. "It's very close to the borderlands between the north and south."

"We should get moving, then," I said. I stood and packed my blanket and things back into my bag while Jackson put out the fire.

Within ten minutes, we were back out in the open. The carefree joy I'd felt in the safety of the cave was replaced by tension and worry. We had to keep an eye out for Sentinels, hunters and anyone who might want to harm us. We trudged through sand for about twenty minutes before we finally reached a rough dirt road. For most of the journey, we didn't run into any other demons. The road to the south had stayed pretty deserted since the two kings became such rivals. Now, most of the cities along the borderlands had fallen into poverty.

Somewhere just north of the vendor's city, we came across a small collection of thatched homes.

"Should we find another way around?" I asked.

Jackson stopped and looked around. Off to either side of the road were rough patches of woods or hills. "We'll waste a lot of time going around," he said.

"But what if someone here is affiliated with the Order or has a problem with humans?" I asked. "Are you sure it's safe to just walk through?"

Jackson took my hand. "I doubt anyone here has any love for the Order of Shadows," he said. "Come on, if anyone comes out to ask about you, I'll tell them you're an enemy of the Order. I think it'll be fine."

I hesitated. There were about six houses still standing in what might have once been a flourishing village. It was difficult to say if anyone still lived there at all, but what if they were dangerous? I wasn't in the mood to get into a fight of more than six against two.

I forced my feet to move. I'd faced much uglier fears lately, so I would just have to face whatever came our way here in this little village.

We made it past the first set of little houses without seeing any movement or indication of life left in the village. Then, as we passed the fourth home, I saw a flicker of movement just inside the door. I clutched Jackson's hand tighter and tilted my head toward the house. Jackson kept walking but turned his head to look. I surveyed the remaining houses, my body tense and my hand moving toward the silver dagger hooked to my belt.

"Wait," Jackson whispered. He stopped and turned toward the fourth hut. "Look."

I turned, not knowing what to expect. When my eyes landed on the small child standing in the doorway, I gasped and took my hand off the dagger. The boy was dirty-faced and wild-eyed. He wore no shoes or shirt, only a dirty pair of pants that looked like they hadn't been changed in months. Something about his eyes broke my heart.

I released Jackson's hand and stepped toward the boy. Scared, he ran back into his house. I moved to position myself right in front of the door so he could see me, but I was careful not to get too close.

"I won't hurt you," I said. I got down on my knees and peered into the darkness of his little hut.

I could see that the boy was just inside the door, staring at me and sucking his thumb. He couldn't have been more than four years old in human years. I had no idea how that translated to shadow demon years, but he was just a child, either way.

I shrugged out of my backpack and found a pack of food and a bottle of water. I held them out toward the boy. "Are you hungry?" I asked. "It's okay. We're friends."

The boy looked from me to Jackson and back again. He shuffled forward, stepping into the sunlight.

"Are you all alone here?" Jackson said.

The boy stared up at Jackson, then nodded slowly.

I looked around again, wondering why such a small child would be alone in a place like this. What had happened here?

I set the food down on the ground and backed away. Slowly, the boy walked forward and snatched it up, then hurried back toward the safety of his house.

"How does something like this happen?" I asked Jackson.

His expression grew dark. "This is what the Order of Shadows does to my world."

WE SHOULD GO SOUTH

We spent nearly an hour trying to coax the boy from his hiding place, but nothing we could do would make him trust a human. In the end, we left him a stack of food and water and moved on toward the vendor's city near the border.

We finally arrived just before nightfall... Jackson shook his head.

"This is the place," he said. "But it looks nothing like I remember from my childhood."

The village was much bigger than any other place we'd come across that day, but it was every bit as rundown. All of the buildings were in disrepair and the people who walked the streets wore tattered clothes. It reminded me of a ghost town from the old west.

"How does a place get like this when there is so much magic in this world?" I asked. "I mean, can't they just create new clothes and fix their houses with their magic?"

"It's not that easy," Jackson said. "Magic may come from

within, but it isn't free. Not really. Performing magic is always a trade-off. You know that from getting sick when you were first learning to cast. Here in the shadow world, the more these demons use their magic, the more attractive they become to the hunters. Once a town builds up and becomes successful and powerful, the Order comes knocking, wanting to take advantage of the most powerful demons in the area. The only places safe from this are the Underground and the king's city. Places where there are guards and safety nets."

I looked around, feeling nothing but sadness for these shadow demons.

"Is it safe for me to come in here with you?" I asked. "I don't want my presence to make anyone nervous or upset."

"I'm not about to leave you somewhere alone," he said. "Just stay by my side. It'll be fine."

We left the road and entered through the center of town. Thankfully it was almost nightfall and most of the town's residents had already gone home or retired for the evening. I could only hope the vendor we needed was still open. Otherwise we'd have to find someplace nearby to camp for the night.

The few demons milling about stared at me with cautious, curious looks, but no one spoke or threatened us. Jackson led us past a muddy fountain and a few closed carts, down a side alley and finally, to the door of a light grey building.

"This is it," he said. "Fingers crossed this guy is still here."

He knocked on the door and waited.

I bit my lip, so nervous. So far, this was our only lead. We needed for this guy to tell us something useful.

Footsteps sounded on the other side of the door and when it flew open, a beautiful woman with amber hair and chocolatey brown eyes opened the door.

"Yes?" she asked. Her smile faded when she looked at me, and I noticed a slight tremble in her hands. She backed away and called out to her father.

Jackson and I exchanged hopeful looks.

An older man came to the door, but Jackson's shoulders slumped in disappointment.

"May I help you?" the man said. "We don't want any trouble here."

"Please excuse me," Jackson said. "I know it's getting late, but my friend and I are looking for a shop-owner who used to have a store here in this house. He collected rocks."

The man studied Jackson's face, trying to decide whether to trust him. "What do you want with this shop-owner?"

"My father used to bring me and my twin brother here when I was younger," Jackson said. "I remembered the gemstone and rock collection and had a few questions about it. Please, if you know where I can find this man, it's very important that I speak with him. We simply come for information."

The young woman stepped closer to the door, then whispered something in her father's ear. The old man nodded and opened the door wider, inviting us in.

Jackson thanked him and stepped inside. The four of us sat down at a large harvest table in the corner of the room.

"The man you speak of was my father," the man said. "He moved on many years ago when my mate and I decided to have a child. I remember you and your brother. Children of the king's adviser. My father had great respect for your dad. I still have his collection of rocks and will help you however I can."

Jackson bowed his head in gratitude. "Thank you," he said. "May I see the gemstones your father collected?"

The man nodded toward his daughter and she stepped

away from the table, returning a few moments later with a large box. She laid it on the table between us.

"This is a complete collection of the best quality of every colored gemstone that exists in the shadow world," the man said. He opened the top of the box and presented its contents one at a time, laying them out on the table.

Blue, red, green, white, orange, purple and yellow. Seven distinct stones.

But the witch's journal had only mentioned six. I wondered why the Order never used the orange stones.

"Are some of these rarer than others?" I asked. I picked up the blue stone. It was exactly the same color as the stone in my mother's necklace. Almost sapphire, but not quite as dark. Almost topaz, but not as light. Somewhere in between.

"Oh yes," the man said. "Like the one you're holding in your hand. You can find them here in the Northern Kingdom if you're lucky, but most of the blue stones come from the south. Of course, trade between the borders is forbidden, so you don't see many of the blue stones here on this side."

I sucked in a shaky breath. The blue stones were in the south.

"How much do you know about the magical properties of these stones?" Jackson asked.

The man picked up the purple stone and stared at it as if the stone had the answer he was looking for. "Gemstones absorb magic easily, holding on to specific types of energy. That's why we use them so often for sources of light or communication."

"What if I wanted to take one of these stones to the place where it would be at its most powerful?" Jackson asked. "Is there a place where they would have extra power?"

I held my breath, hoping this man had an answer.

The man thought for a moment, scratching the side of his temple. "My father used to speak of a mine," he said. "A quarry in a way. A collection of same-colored stones where each one's power amplified the rest. That might be the kind of place you're talking about."

Jackson's eyes met mine for a split second, and I could see the excitement burning there.

"Do you know where we could find a place like that?" I asked. "A quarry?"

The man shook his head and shrugged. "I'm not certain," he said. "Supposedly there's one for each gemstone somewhere in the world."

"What about the blue stones in particular?" Jackson asked.

"If such a place exists, it would be in the Southern King-dom," the man said. He rose from his seat, holding up his finger as if he'd just remembered something. He came back with an old ledger. He opened it and ran his finger down the page until he found the entry he'd been searching for. "Ah," he said. "Here. Back in the days before the borders closed, my father used to have a friend on the other side who knew a lot about these stones. They used to trade back and forth, comparing color and clarity. I have no idea if this friend is still alive or if you'd be able to find him, but it's better than nothing. Still, I don't recommend trying to cross through the borderlands."

"Why not?" I asked.

"The borderlands are extremely dangerous," the man said. "No magic can be cast there and there are tales of giant monsters that guard the path to the south. Besides, if the

Southern King discovers a northerner on his land, he will show no mercy."

Outside it had begun to rain. I could hear it pounding against the roof of the small house. I had so many questions about how this rivalry between the demons of the north and south had gotten started, but it was late, and we'd already asked so much of this man and his daughter.

"Thank you for all your help," I said. "We sincerely appreciate it."

The daughter turned to me, her eyes full of questions. "Tell me, what is a young human girl like you doing here in our world? It's very rare for us to see a human here."

"I'm here looking for answers," I said.

"About what?" she asked.

I paused. I didn't want to get into a discussion about the Order. Andros had said we should be careful to put our trust in anyone. "Answers about who I am," I said instead. "About how to become something different."

The girl seemed to accept my answer. She nodded and placed the stones back into the box. When she stood, we all stood with her. I gathered my things and strapped my backpack onto my back.

"No," the old man said. "Please stay with us for the night. We don't have more to offer than a couple of blankets and a hard floor, but it's better than being out in the elements on a night like this."

"Thank you," Jackson said. "We would appreciate a place to sleep, and we'll be out of your way first thing in the morning."

"No bother," the man said.

After he and his daughter had moved into the back rooms

to sleep, Jackson and I fixed our beds on the floor of the main room. In hushed whispers, we discussed what the man had said about the stones.

"What do you think we should do?" Jackson asked, his eyes meeting mine in the darkness.

"We should go south," I said.

He nodded, kissed my cheek, then turned over to sleep. I cuddled up next to him but kept my eyes wide open. We were already in danger. Was going to the Southern Kingdom really the best idea? And yet I hadn't hesitated when he asked me what we should do. It was really the only logical choice. We'd come too far and risked too much to stop now.

Hours later, sleep finally found me, bringing dreams of borderland monsters and rival demons.

THE GLASS FOREST

We woke up just before dawn, left a note to say thank you, and stole out of town before most of the residents were awake. It took us a couple of hours before we reached the edge of the borderlands. A thick forest spread out in front of us. The trees here were strange, almost as if they were made of a dark crystal. Their branches were free of leaves and twisted around in knots and points.

Jackson stopped to pull his sword from his pack.

"What kind of monsters do you think we might face?" I asked.

"I'm not sure," Jackson said. "Ever since I was young, I've heard stories of demons who got too close to the border's edge and were never heard from again."

His face drained of color. He was truly spooked by this. I suddenly felt a lot less confident about my decision to come this way.

My heart pounded, but I knew we had to press on. The forest looked dark, but it was nothing like the Obsidian Forest we'd had to pass through on our way to the Underground. I hated to think about what monsters we might find lurking in the shadows, but we had no choice but to face it.

"You ready?" Jackson asked.

I nodded. "Just keep your eyes open. You'll be able to see a lot better than I will in there."

We stepped into the shadows under the canopy of trees, taking our steps slowly and deliberately. Every muscle in my body tensed, ready to fight if something pounced on us from the darkness.

Every strange noise or whisper of movement sent my heart into cardiac arrest. I could swear I heard someone walking behind us, but when I turned, there were only shadows.

Above us, strange birds with long black feathers cawed and screeched. I expected one of them to descend on us and try to peck our eyes out at any moment.

Something slithered on the ground in front of my feet. I let out a terrified scream that echoed off the glass-like trees, but when Jackson came running, he reassured me that the snake wasn't poisonous in any way.

"This place has me totally creeped out," I said.

"Let's just keep moving," he said. "Stay close."

We walked, taking each step with care. Our senses were on high alert, our legs ready to run if we came upon trouble. And when we emerged from the glass forest hours later, I nearly fell to the ground with relief. Somehow, we'd safely made it to the other side.

THE SCARIEST THING OUT HERE

The forest lay at our backs and grassy swamplands stretched out before us. In the far distance the sun reflected off a wall of silver metal that marked the official entrance to the Southern Kingdom.

"Be careful where you step," Jackson said. "Try to stay on the solid patches."

I let him lead the way through the maze of swamp. I tried my best to keep to the grass, but the pathways were extremely narrow and squishy. I felt like a tight-rope walker.

A noise off to the right surprised me, causing me to lose my balance. I tried to reach out for Jackson's arm, but he was too far ahead. I lost my footing and fell into the dark green water of the swamp. Immediately, I felt some kind of strong undercurrent pulling me under. I sank like a stone, flailing around to find something, anything I could hold on to.

Jackson's hand found mine and he lifted me with ease, depositing me on a narrow strip of grassy land.

"Are you alright?"

I breathed in and out, trying to slow my racing heartbeat. "I'm fine," I said. "But something under there was pulling me down."

So far, we hadn't seen any real monsters, but now more than ever, I was wound as tight as a spring.

I walked more slowly through the swamp, holding on to Jackson's hand and never taking my eyes off my feet.

A splash behind us nearly sent me off-balance again, but Jackson reached out to steady me just in time.

"What was that?" he asked.

"I don't know," I said. "But I've had this feeling all day that we were being followed."

"What? Why didn't you say something?" he asked.

I shrugged. "I don't know, I thought I was being overly-dramatic."

In the water just a few feet away, something pushed itself frantically toward the surface, yelling out in fear. Jackson left me where I stood and ran to see what had fallen into the swamp water.

"Oh my god," he said.

"What is it?" I asked.

He didn't answer. Instead, he crouched down and reached deep into the water, pulling something out with all of his strength. I carefully made my way toward him, fear gripping my chest.

I gasped as the figure in the water came into view. The little boy from the abandoned village!

Jackson set him onto the grass and the boy scrambled close and held tight to his legs, as if his life depended on it. And in a place like this, it just might have.

When the child caught his breath and had stopped shaking, I leaned down and caught his eye. "Have you been following us all this way?"

The boy lowered his head, then nodded slowly.

I closed my eyes and let out a sigh of relief. "I thought you were a hunter or something," I said.

The boy shook his head violently, and I laughed. "I know you're not, now," I said. "But you shouldn't sneak up on people like that. You scared me to death."

Jackson laughed, some of the tension of the day's journey relaxing his shoulders. "I can't believe this," he said. "My whole life people have warned me of the extreme dangers of the borderlands. And look, the scariest thing out here is a child."

I smiled. He had a point.

I lifted my hand to shield my eyes from the sun. I turned around and looked out over the swamp. Other than the water itself, there didn't seem to be any other dangers here. No monsters or poisonous gases. No soldiers waiting to take us to the dungeons. How had everyone in the north been so wrong about this place?

It made me wonder what other lies had been told about the Southern Kingdom.

I HOPE I NEVER DO

"The part about the wall was true, at least," he said after the three of us had safely crossed over the swamp. "Of course, to hear most people tell it, the wall is guarded by a thousand demons."

"What is this made out of, anyway?" I asked, staring up at the bright silver metal.

"Remember the rare type of silver the Order used to create the ritual daggers?" Jackson said.

"The kind that's strong enough to kill shadow demons?" I asked.

"That's the one."

"That's what this is made of?" I asked.

"Yes," he said. "It's mined here in the Southern Kingdom and is one of the strongest, most indestructible types of metal there is."

"How do we get around it?"

"Normally, we would just fly over the top," he said. "But I really don't want to use my magic, not even for a second."

I understood his fear. We had no idea just who or what might be tracking us. Hunters. Witches. The king's guards. We needed to stay as under the radar as possible.

Jackson pulled a drawing from his pocket. "Last night, the old man drew this map for us," he said. "He said he remembered his father talking about the gem dealer being located in a medium-sized city just past the Eastern gate."

He looked down the length of the stone wall and pointed to his left. "If we walk a couple miles this way, we should get to the East gate pretty easily."

"You don't think it will be guarded?" I asked.

"I'm not sure," he said. "I guess we'll find out soon enough."

The walk to the gate only took us an hour. Jackson carried the boy on his shoulders most of the way. To be careful, we stayed back from the gate and watched for a while, making sure there were no patrolling guards or anyone there to keep northerners out. After another hour with no activity in sight, we decided to risk it and walk straight through the gate.

Excitement created butterflies in my stomach. We were so close now to another clue. If we could somehow locate the gem dealer, he would surely know where to find the concentration of blue stones.

But when we passed through the gate, my eyes widened as I looked out at the ruins of what must have once been a flourishing city.

I stood speechless. There was so little that was really known about the Southern Kingdom, but from the looks of it, they were having just as rough a time with the Order here as the north.

We wandered through the debris, stepping over burned wood, crushed stone walls, toys and ruined furniture. Unlike the small villages we'd passed on the road, this had been a real city. From the sheer size of the destroyed area, I would have guessed at least ten thousand demons must have lived here at one point.

"This can't be it," I said. "Can I see the map?"

Jackson handed me the paper, but I immediately saw that this was exactly where the old man remembered the gem dealer to have lived.

I kicked at a charred chair. "This can't be it," I said again. "There's no way we'll ever find the dealer now. No one could have survived this."

Suddenly, I felt the events of the past few days begin to take their toll. I'd been living on adrenaline and hope, but this was a blow to everything I'd been feeling. My body was completely wrecked and exhausted. My leg was better, but the spot where the hunter had wounded me still ached. After two straight days of nonstop walking, it screamed in pain. Somehow, I'd forced myself not to feel it. Everything else had been going so well, I didn't want to admit the desperate situation we were really in here.

I sat down on a heavy stone and put my head in my hands.

"Don't give up," Jackson said. "Maybe there's another city just down the road or something. Or maybe if we look around we could still find the gem shop and find a clue there."

I shook my head and looked out over the ruins. "How would we possibly find a gem shop in all this rubble? Besides, what would we find there? Gems? How is that going to help us?"

"Then let's just sit here and whine about it," he said. "That'll help."

Angry, I stared at him through squinted eyes. "Oh, excuse

me for expressing some disappointment," I said. "It's not like we've been through much in the past few months. Hell, all told this has been such a happy, positive year for me."

Jackson sighed and set the boy down on the ground. "Look, I don't want to argue with you, okay?"

I closed my eyes and took a deep breath. "I know," I said. "I don't want to argue either. It's just that I feel like we have no idea what we're really doing, you know? It feels like we're doing something that's impossible and crazy and probably really stupid. I was really getting my hopes up, but now this. When I saw all this, it was like the weight of the past few days just came crashing down on me."

Jackson pulled me into a hug and I leaned into him, loving the feel of his chin as it rested on the top of my head.

"We're going to figure it out," he said. "We just have to keep trying. As long as we never stop looking, we'll find it, okay?"

I nodded.

Footsteps sounded behind us, and I flipped around, my heart racing.

A man stood at the edge of the rubble, near the road. He froze as we turned, throwing up his hands as if surrendering.

"Sorry to disturb," he said. "Just was kinda going through the ruins looking for something that used to belong to my mate."

Surprisingly, he didn't seem the least bit interested in the fact that I was human. He didn't give me that fearful look so many of the demons in the north had given me.

"You used to live here?" Jackson asked.

"Oh, yeah," the man said, squinting and looking out over the expanse of the rubble. "It's a shame isn't it?"

"I wouldn't have thought anyone could survive destruction like this," I said. "You must feel very lucky."

The man looked at me like I'd gone insane. "Well, by the time this happened, no one was living here anymore," he said. "The king's centralization project and all."

I raised an eyebrow. This guy seemed to not even realize we were from the north. For someone who was walking right along the border between north and south, he didn't seem afraid or scared or even the slightest bit nervous. What was going on here?

"We were looking for a man who used to live here," Jackson said. "A gemstone dealer?"

The man rubbed his chin and thought for a minute. "You must mean Sorian," he said. "Older demon with a passion for rocks?"

Jackson nodded.

"He passed into the next world some time ago," the man said. "Is that what you guys are doing so far out from the Center? Lookin' for rocks?"

"Yeah, something like that," I said. "What we were really hoping to find was a kind of quarry of blue stones. A place where they were sort of concentrated. Have you ever seen such a place?"

The man eyed me suspiciously. "You know those gem deposits are pretty rare, right? Only one per stone," he said. "Plus, they're dangerous. Hunters like to hang out there. I don't recommend it."

"We know," Jackson said. "So, does that mean you know where it is? Could point us in the right direction?"

The man shook his head. "I shouldn't even be out this far, but you know how mates can be. Mine is dying to get hold of her mother's favorite cooking pot. She keeps sending me out here to find it in the ruins, but I know that pot's long gone by now," he said. "There's no way I'd wander as far outside as the blue stones."

It was the first sign of fear the man had shown since we met him.

"Where are you two from anyway? One of the villages still on the outskirts or something?"

I shook my head. "We're from somewhere even farther than that," I said. "But we aren't looking for any trouble. We just need to find those stones if we can. Please, if there's any information you can give us, we'd really appreciate it."

The man shrugged. "It's your lives you're risking if you go out there." He looked off into the far distance, holding a hand up to his eyes to shade them from the sun. "If you keep walking that way for about a day or two, you'll come upon the blue stone quarry you're talking about. Still, I would highly recommend against it. There are some patrols that still guard those lands, but you're much safer near the Center these days. You wouldn't want to run into a hunter."

"No, we wouldn't," I said.

The man shuddered. "I've never actually seen one myself, and I hope I never do."

He leaned over and grabbed something metal from underneath a broken wall. He held it up, shook his head, then threw it back into the pile.

"Wish you two the best of luck," he said. With that, the man disappeared into a fog of pure white smoke.

I stared at the white fog, confused. "Why is his power white?" I asked.

Jackson shook his head and shrugged. "I don't know,

maybe it's a southern-demon thing?" he said. "We should get moving."

I realized the boy wasn't with us, and for a moment I panicked. Then, I saw him crouching low in the rubble. "What are you doing over here?" I asked.

He looked up at me and smiled. He held his closed hand out to me as if he had found something for me. I opened my hand and he placed a pure blue stone in my palm.

ENJOY THESE MOMENTS

Much of the day was already gone, but we decided to push on toward the blue stones. We didn't have a road to follow, so we just made sure to keep heading southeast. The best we could do was hope the demon in the ruined city had given us good directions.

Along the way, we ran into a lot of animals, but no demons. Every village in between was completely deserted or ruined. The wildlife out here flourished. The deer-like creatures here were much smaller with black-spotted pelts and dark black antlers. Wolves with pure white coats roamed around the tree-line of a forest in the distance. Tiny green and white flowers grew all around us and every once in a while, I spotted tiny blue and red jumping things in the grass.

When I originally pictured the demon world, I don't know why I'd imagined a drastically different terrain or set of living creatures. Now that I'd had some time to explore it a little more, I realized it wasn't all that different from earth. There was a lot more nature here than I was used to with all the trees and grass and such, and there was no need for cars or things like that, but overall, I was comfortable here. In fact, the Southern Kingdom was growing on me. Somehow it felt like home.

"I think we should make camp before it gets too dark," Jackson said after we'd been walking for a couple of hours.

Relief flowed through me. As much as I enjoyed the scenery, my feet were freaking killing me. "I second that," I said. "I could use a rest and some food."

He looked around, surveying the space around us. He pointed toward the tree-line. "I think we should get closer to those trees over there so we're less out in the open. Let's see if we can find a good spot that's a little hidden."

It didn't take long to set up our camp since all we had were a few blankets in our packs. Jackson started a fire to keep us warm, and we snacked on mushrooms and berries we gathered from the nearby woods.

The boy never said a word. He wouldn't even tell us his name. But he was sweet, and he seemed happy to have company. He fell asleep in my lap soon after dinner.

Spending time with Jackson like this was amazing. It was hard to believe that we had been acting like complete strangers just a few days ago. Despite all that had happened in the past year, it never ceased to amaze me how fast things could change. I wanted to enjoy these moments together while I could. I never knew when it all might be taken away again.

"Do you ever think about what you'll do if we actually manage to free Aerden?" I said. I figured I was opening a can of worms with this conversation, but he had promised to be more open with me, and I wanted to know. "Will you come back here?"

Jackson propped his back against a tall red-barked tree and I leaned back to stare up at the three moons and a sky full of stars.

"I won't be coming back to marry Lea, if that's what you mean," he teased.

I reached up to smack his arm and laughed. "You better not."

"I honestly don't know what will happen," he said. "You'll be free too, you know. You could come back here with me if you wanted. I mean, if that's what we decided to do."

I liked the sound of the word 'we'.

"I won't live nearly as long as you will," I said. "I'll grow old and wrinkly before you even look like you've aged at all."

He ran his fingers through my hair, nearly putting me to sleep with the gentle rhythm of it.

"We'll figure it out when the time comes," he said. "I think we've got enough to think about right now without trying to decide on the rest of our lives."

I nodded and closed my eyes, wondering just how long the rest of our lives might last.

TOO LATE

I tossed and turned under the stars that night.

A man's face kept invading my dreams. His silver eyes looked so familiar, but I couldn't place him. Where did I know him from? I slipped in and out of my dreams, confused and anxious. When I awoke the following morning, I finally understood where I'd seen his face before.

The shaman. When the Underground's shaman had come to heal me after my fight with the hunter, I had seen a vision of this man, his silver beard and eyes so unique and kind and strangely familiar.

Jackson and I resumed our walk toward the blue stones, but I couldn't shake the feeling that I should know this man. It left me feeling a little disoriented.

"Is everything okay?" Jackson asked after we'd walked a little ways. "You've barely said two words today."

"I'm fine," I said, trying to just shake off the feeling from the dream. "Have you ever met a man with silver eyes? Was there someone in Peachville like that?"

Jackson shook his head. "Not that I've ever heard about. Why?"

"I don't know." I hiked my backpack higher to take some of the weight off my lower back. "It's nothing. Just a dream I had."

"I never really sleep well out in the open like that," he said. "Too many noises and things to wake me up throughout the night. You probably just didn't get any good sleep."

I nodded. Yeah, that's all it was.

The boy rode on Jackson's shoulders most of the way, smiling and taking in the scenery.

The rest of the day passed without event. We got to see some beautiful countryside, but we still had yet to meet up with any of the other Southern Kingdom demons. It was weird, really. Had their population really been so drained by the Order? From the looks of it, they'd been hit really hard down here.

It wasn't until about dinner time that I started to feel it.

At first, it was a small buzzing feeling in my hands and feet. I thought it was probably some effect of all the walking we'd been doing. I was just tired, and my body was exhausted.

But after another mile, I started to feel it everywhere, like energy coursing through me with growing strength. I stopped and just let it flow through me for a second. Jackson stopped with me and raised his eyebrows.

"What's going on?" he asked. "Do you need to take a break?"

I shook my head and just continued to feel. I had never felt it so strongly before, but it was sort of like the way I felt every time I connected to my inner power. A warmth and a constant current. Only now it was amplified. Instead of a small stream, this was beginning to feel like a full-on river.

"I'm feeling something." How to put words to it? "Different."

"Different how?" he asked.

"Let's keep walking," I said. "I think we might be getting close."

Jackson walked close by my side, watching my expression as we moved forward.

"Stop staring at me," I said with laugh. "You're making me self-conscious."

He gave me that sexy half-smile I'd missed so much when we were apart. "I'm just getting excited," he said. "Let me know if anything changes, okay?"

Not even half a mile later, I stopped again. The humming feeling was now a strong charge throughout my body. I felt like I'd been connected to some kind of super battery.

"We're so close," I said. "I can feel the power of the stones. I don't know how or why, but my body is having a very strong reaction to it. It's like a flood of power."

Something in my pocket buzzed. I reached my hand in and found the small blue stone the boy had given me. "Look," I said.

The stone seemed to glow from within.

"Follow it," he said. "Maybe you can lead us there."

I closed my eyes for a minute and allowed myself to really connect to the feeling. When I opened my eyes, I could see very clearly where I needed to go. The force of the stones pulled me like a magnet. A hill up ahead blocked the way, but in my heart, I knew what we would find on the other side of that ridge.

Too excited to walk, I threw my backpack to the ground

and broke out in a run. As I crested, the hill, tears sprang to my eyes and I pressed my hands hard against my face. We'd found it. The valley below us was filled with perfect blue stones, the suns shining off of them to create an almost diamond-like effect. Jackson ran up behind me and threw his arms around me. The boy laughed and cheered, even though I knew he didn't understand our excitement.

For a moment, we both just stood there in awe. This is the place where all of Peachville's stones had come from. This place of power might have been where my troubled past originated, but right now all I could see was hope for the future. Breaking loose, I ran down the hill, placing each step carefully so as not to trip. Jackson ran even faster, hitting the bottom before me. The boy sat at the top of the hill, looking down on us as he played with a small flower.

Together, Jackson and I searched the large area for any sign of the ring.

"It's going to be here somewhere," I said. "This is really going to be it. We just have to find it."

I crouched low and studied every crevice, searching for any place a ring might be hidden among the stones. I lifted the loose stones from the ground and looked underneath. I studied the area from different angles, even going back up the hill to look at it from a new perspective. But the ring wasn't here.

With each passing minute, I grew more and more frantic.

We couldn't have come this far for nothing. Please. I had been so certain it would be here. I stood with my hands on my hips, staring out at the quarry. Wasn't there something here that looked out of place? Some rock that could be moved to reveal a secret hiding place? Something.

Jackson joined me, shaking his head.

"We've been looking for over an hour," he said. "What if it's not here?"

His words tore through me like a hot arrow. Even though I'd been thinking it myself, I wasn't ready to hear it said out loud. I refused to accept it.

"It has to be," I said, a quiver in my voice.

I went back down the hill and started over, checking each section of rock again.

When I got to the center of the stones, I saw something on the ground I hadn't noticed before. A very small faceted stone. My heart jumped in my chest. All of the other stones here were raw and uncut. They had no polish or shape to them. But this stone was different. It was shaped and buffed and shined.

I reached down to touch it and suddenly, a stone sculpture appeared in front of me. My eyes nearly popped out of my head. I turned to Jackson and screamed for him to come to me.

He rushed my way, out of breath. "What is it? Did you find it?"

"I don't know," I said. "But look. What do you think it is?"

He drew his eyebrows together and looked all around. "What are you talking about?"

I pointed to the square stone sculpture. "This statue-thing," I said. "You're telling me you can't see it?"

He shook his head. "I don't see anything."

I stepped closer and put my hands on the surface of it, trying to figure out if there was a way to get inside. When my hand touched the stone, an electric shock went through my entire body. I tried to let go, but it held on to me. Then, the top slowly began to open from the middle, two parts sliding out to reveal a special compartment just inside.

I peered in, my heart beating so fast I could barely breathe.

On the inside of the statue was a small pedestal with a hole in the top, perfectly made to hold a ring. Only, there was no ring inside. It was empty.

I slumped forward, a dull pain spreading across my chest.

"It's gone," I said, unable to hold back my tears.

"What do you mean?" he asked. "I can't see whatever it is you're seeing Harper."

I tried to breathe, but I felt like my breath was coming in through a thin straw. My head was spinning, and I knew I couldn't keep standing or I would pass out. This couldn't be happening. Not now.

"There's a statue here that's made to hold the ring," I said. "We were right. This is where they keep it. But it's gone. They must have gotten to it first. It's gone. It's empty."

I turned around and slid down the side of the sculpture. I sat on the edge of a bright blue stone, unable to believe we'd come this far only to have lost our chance.

A dam broke inside me.

I wanted to fight. I wanted to be strong. But I also wanted to let go. I wanted all of this to be over. A year ago, I was just a girl who hated foster homes. I knew I had a different life, but I still had dreams of getting out on my own. Going to college. Having a life of my own.

Going to Shadowford was just a bump in the road. Something I had to get through in order to come out the other side.

Only, it turned out to be so much more than that. I was grateful for the friends I'd made and for the relationship I had now with Jackson, but the weight of everything else I'd been through came crashing down on me. It wasn't fair that I had been thrown into this life, and as much as I wanted to be everyone's hero, I felt so weak and defeated.

My tears burst forth, growing more desperate with each passing second. The exhaustion and fear and anger of the past couple of months finally broke through me like a tidal wave, refusing to be contained for another moment.

Jackson put his arms around me and held me as sobs shook my body.

I cried for my mother and for her horrible death. I cried for the demons who had lost their freedom. I cried for Brooke and every other girl whose life had been stolen from her before she could even question it.

A cold chill ran through me as I realized that it had begun to rain. I looked up, letting the drops land on my cheeks and mix with my salty tears.

Jackson stood and held his hands out to catch the rain. Then, with a worried panic on his face, he turned to me. "Harper, you have to stop crying," he said. "This isn't natural rain."

I choked back a sob and shook my head. "What do you mean?"

He crouched beside me and grabbed my shoulders. "It's your magic," he said. "Your emotions are so strong they're affecting the weather."

I breathed in slow gasps, holding on to him so I could stand. "Are you sure?"

"Yes," he said. "I know it's difficult, but you have to stop crying. They'll be tracking your magic."

I closed my eyes and willed my emotions to settle. Fear gripped my soul. Had I just put us in serious danger? I took a deep breath and as I calmed down, the rain slowed to a light drizzle.

But it was too late.

When I opened my eyes, I could feel their presence like a cold nothingness surrounding us. I looked toward the hill and froze.

The hunters had found us.

TO KNOW MY FEAR

I stared up at them, my flesh crawling.

Three hunters hovered at the top of the hill, and I couldn't so much as find the strength to run or move or even scream.

The air around us turned icy and the drizzling rain quickly turned to snow.

Jackson took my arm. Maybe he was thinking of trying to run. I knew he could move fast, but where did we have to go? There was no safe haven to run to. No Underground. Not even a single city where we knew we could get help. And I knew the hunters would not stop until they had me in their clutches.

White flakes stuck to my hair and face. My entire body shivered, but I felt a sudden clarity. A knowing.

I planted my feet firmly on the blue stones at my feet and plugged in to the buzz of power it sent through me. If we were going to have to fight them, this was the place to do it. At least here, I had an advantage.

I looked toward where the boy had been sitting, but he was gone. I closed my eyes and prayed he had seen the hunters in time and had found a safe place to hide. We should have never brought him with us. What were we thinking?

But the time for regrets had passed. We had to stand in this moment and face it as it was.

I locked eyes with Jackson, and I knew he saw my decision in my eyes. His face had turned so white, but he nodded, accepting our fate.

"Okay," he said. "I trust you."

Those three words resonated through my being, filling me with a sense of love and pride and confidence. For the first time since we'd met, he truly believed in me. He'd stopped trying to protect me like I was a little child and was letting me be my own person. A fighter.

I lifted my chin and waited.

Taking their sweet time, the three hunters floated down toward us, circling us. Their collective stench overwhelmed my nostrils. Two of the witches looked very similar to the one I'd faced in the Underground, but the third hunter was different. She was older, her decay more complete and gruesome.

She was obviously the leader of the group, her purplish-black eyes never leaving my face.

I stood tense and ready, waiting for them to make their move.

The lead hunter finally slowed and settled in a spot just in front of me. "Isn't this a pretty twist of fate," she croaked. Her voice grated on my nerves, so dry it sounded like she hadn't had a drop of moisture in years. "Our hunting expedition had nothing to do with a lost Prima, but won't the Priestess be pleased?"

She moved closer to me and reached out a gnarled finger. Her blackened fingernail ran down the edge of my cheek, but I stood my ground, not even flinching. Not wanting her to know my fear.

"Such a beauty," she said. "Too bad you couldn't see the right path. It's always a shame to lose one like you."

"I won't come with you," I said. "You'll have to kill me."

The hunter clucked her tongue and shook her head. "No, no, you know we have to bring you alive," she said. "But you'll be dead soon enough, right sisters?"

The other two hunters laughed. The sound made my stomach lurch.

"Of course, your boyfriend here can die now," she said, circling Jackson like a buzzard.

"Don't touch him," I said, grinding my teeth together.

"Or what?" she said with a cackle. "You'll send me to bed without any supper?"

I didn't answer her. She was just like the other one. Toying with me. The life of a hunter must be pretty boring for them to like to play with their catch. I didn't have the patience for this.

The ancient hunter moved to grab my arm, but I stepped back, avoiding her.

Anger flashed across her rotten face. "The more you resist us, the more you will suffer," she said.

A flutter of anticipation moved through my veins. Before I had time to doubt myself, I reached inside and grabbed hold of my power. With one swift movement, I lifted my palms in front of my chest and pushed back.

The three hunters went flying backward in separate directions, screams echoing against the blue stones.

Jackson jumped to action, shifting into his demon form

and flashing to the side of the younger hunter on the right. Before she had time to recover from her shock, Jackson had woven a cage of ice around her entire body, locking her in.

Making the most of the dwindled numbers, I turned my attention to the other weaker hunter. I pushed the force of my power down toward the ground, breaking up the stones into large boulders. Without hesitation, I lifted several stones into the air and sent them hurtling toward the hunter's body.

She easily dodged two of them, but one of the smaller stones hit her squarely in the neck, the jagged edge slicing her open. With a screech, she fell to the ground, greenish black liquid flowing through her fingertips as she lifted both hands, desperate to close the wound.

With the other two temporarily disabled, we turned our attention to the ancient hunter.

Rage in her eyes, she flew toward me, claws out. I tried to throw up a shield, but she moved too fast. Her nails sliced into my arm with searing pain. She opened her mouth and breathed on my wound, a poisonous cloud seeping into my open cuts. I screamed and fell back against the stone sculpture. The scratches burned so badly, the pain seemed to seep into my brain.

Jackson formed a ball of ice between his hands and threw it at the ancient hunter, sending her flying off to the side. He moved to try to heal my wound, but I pushed him away. We didn't have time to nurse injuries right now. I forced the pain from my mind and took stock of the situation.

The witch in the ice was thawing herself with fire, but she was obviously not very good at it. Fire must not have been her strongest energy. The hunter I'd hurt with the stone was on her feet again, her wound still leaking. The ancient hunter had disappeared behind the hill for now, but her absence made me nervous. What was she doing up there?

"Behind you," I said to Jackson.

He turned just in time to see one of the younger hunters descending on him with a net in her hands. She barely missed him, which threw her slightly off balance. Jackson took advantage of the moment and created a large block of ice that he used to bash the thing's head. She fell to her knees, disoriented.

I summoned a pile of blue rocks and quickly moved them toward her with great force, burying her beneath them. Working perfectly with my plan, Jackson encased the blue stones in a layer of ice, freezing the hunter inside.

An enormous sense of pride swelled through me. We were winning against the most fearsome creatures the Order could send after us. We were outnumbered, yet still alive.

But my celebration was premature. Without warning, the ancient hunter flew out from her hiding place behind the hill, some kind of dome-like glass structure in her hands. I rolled out of the way, but Jackson hadn't seen her fast enough. She brought the glass dome down on top of him, sealing him inside. He pounded against it, yelling something, but I couldn't hear him. I scrambled backward, stunned at how fast the tables had turned.

I watched as he tried several attempts to break the glass, but nothing would shatter it. He was trapped and helpless.

I quickly lifted the largest rock I could find and sent it flying toward the glass, figuring he might get cut a little, but at least he would be free. But the rock merely bounced off the structure, leaving it completely unharmed.

My heart sank, and panic rose in my throat.

I was on my own.

THIS UNKNOWN POWER

I needed a new word for fear.

My body tensed, and my vision blurred. I stumbled backward, searching my mind for anything that could get me out of this moment. There was no escaping it. Above us, dark clouds gathered. Thunder rumbled, echoing the fear in my heart.

The hunter Jackson first encased in ice was free now. She flew to her older sister's side, hatred rolling off of her like a haze.

"There's no use fighting us," the ancient one said. She wiped greenish fluid from her forehead from where Jackson's orb of ice had sliced her. "You may be stronger than we expected, but you will never have the strength to beat us."

My eyes flicked to where Jackson stood, still pounding on the dome. His eyes were dark with panic.

Terror ran through me like lava, leaving a hot flush on my cheeks.

I straightened up and lifted my palms, summoning a strong flame.

The ancient witch narrowed her eyes at me. "You will regret this, girl."

"I told you I would not go with you," I said through gritted teeth. "You can break me down all you want, but I'll never go willingly."

The witches moved toward me. Not knowing what else to do, I created a circle of fire around myself, trying to block them from reaching me.

A tidal wave of icy cold water descended on me, dousing the entire fire and leaving me shivering and wet. I drew in a freezing breath, shocked and so incredibly cold.

"I'm tired of playing with you," the ancient hunter said. "This ends here."

She raised her gnarled hands and lifted me into the air. She threw me as hard as she could. I lost all control of my body, flying through the air, over the top of the hill on the opposite side. I lost sight of Jackson and the blue stones. The ground rushed toward me with unthinkable speed. A field of pure white. I braced myself for the impact.

Pain shot through me as I hit the ground. Something sharp stabbed through my skin in the back, just below my shoulder. The blood that poured from me was warm and sticky against my cold skin. My breath was knocked from my body, and I gasped desperately for air. My head hit the ground hard and my ears throbbed.

I turned my head, trying to see if the hunters were coming after me. Time moved in painful, slow ticks. Out of the corner of my eye, all I could see was white.

My heart stopped beating as the scene became clear.

A light snow fell from the sky above me, falling onto my face and melting into tears that slid down my cheeks. I knew that if I could see myself, I would be the perfect replica of the scene from Jackson's nightmares.

Horror seized me, and I drew in a sharp, painful breath.

This was it. This was the moment. I closed my eyes as the blood slowly left my body.

A shadow fell over me. I blinked and saw that both hunters were hovering over my body, smiles twisting their horrid faces. How had it come to this? How could I let my life end like this?

My head fell to the side, not wanting their ruined bodies to be the last thing I saw in this world.

I braced myself for the cold snow against my cheek, but instead of cold, something soft and silky caressed my skin.

I blinked, not sure whether to believe what I was seeing. I reached out, my fingers brushing against the soft petals of a white rose. My mother's favorites.

I plucked a petal from the rose and held it tight in my hand.

Jackson had drawn it wrong. It wasn't snow that cradled my wounded body. It was a bed of white roses. Hundreds of them all around me, telling me not to quit. Not to give up until the last breath had been ripped from my body.

In the distance, I saw the small boy. He emerged from his rocky hiding place, staring at me with tears in his eyes. I had a feeling he'd seen this horror before in his young life. I wanted to shout out and tell him to run. To hide.

But before I could do anything to help him, the ancient hunter followed my gaze, spotting the child.

I cried out as she sent a ball of poison toward him. The

green splashed against his side and he fell helpless to the ground.

Anger took control of my body, and I could feel the dark power inside of me rise up.

Control it, I told myself. *Use it.*

I blocked all noise and worry and doubt from my mind and went inward. Deep down to the root of my power. There, I found a flowing river of untapped essence, something more when all else seemed lost. I dove into the source, feeling only a moment of panic as a strange darkness seeped into my being.

The hunters descended on me, their hands reaching out to take their prize.

I took a deep breath, then let go. I surrendered to this unknown power, trusting it as a part of my own foundation, my core. Just as their hands reached me, my body split into a million pieces, turning into pure white smoke.

I AM THE THING THAT ENDS YOU

My body was gone. I was air. Smoke. Wind.

I moved in a flash, feeling suddenly strong despite my injuries. I took form again behind the hunters, and it happened so fast, they were still standing there trying to figure out where I had gone.

I let this new power stream from my hands, the white smoke thick like a rope. I wound it around the younger hunter's chest, neck and mouth, squeezing so tight I could feel the breath leaving her shriveled body.

The ancient hunter sliced through the flow of my energy, but I quickly recreated it. She moved back, confusion contorting her wretched face.

"What are you?" she screeched. Fear shone in her eyes.

"I am the thing that ends you," I said.

I reached deep into the ground with my mind, the tendrils of white smoke disappearing down in the earth surrounding the ancient witch. I bent my knees and pulled up with great force, pulling the ground upward in large slabs of rock and dirt.

I created a stone prison around the hunter that muffled her terrified screeches.

I held the structure up for a moment, then with all of my strength, I slammed it down on top of her, crushing her body into nothingness.

The remaining witch lay on the ground, gasping for air. She trembled in fear as I turned my eyes toward her. I lifted my hands to end her but realized all fight had left her. She was defeated already. Killing her out of hatred didn't seem right. She was no longer any threat to me.

That's when I noticed something gleaming on her finger.

I looked closer, my hope rising as I recognized the ring. I held my hand out to her. "Give me the ring," I said.

She looked down at the ring on her finger, as if just now remembering she had it on. "I can't," she said. "The Order will destroy me."

"I'll destroy you," I said. "Give it to me."

Shaking, she removed the ring and placed it in my hand. I closed my fist around it, tears of joy stinging my eyes. The hunter seized the moment and fled off into the distance. I didn't bother following her.

Instead, I slipped the ring on my finger and rushed over to where the little boy had dropped in the field. He lay still, but his eyes were open, and he was breathing. Carefully, I picked him up and carried him over the hill to where I'd last seen Jackson. His domed prison was gone, no doubt destroyed when I'd killed the hunter who created it. I set the boy down near him, then touched his face with my hand.

Jackson opened his eyes, blinking against the sun that now shined down on us. "Are we alive?" he asked. His question brought a smile to my face. Hadn't I asked nearly the same question just a few months ago when he brought me to this world?

"Yes," I said. "We're alive."

"How?" he asked, his voice cracking.

I still didn't understand it myself. Somehow, I had tapped into some unknown power. But where had it come from? Had I connected to Aerden's power somehow? I couldn't figure it out. All I knew was that I had survived.

Jackson struggled to sit up, then as his eyes looked around, a new panic seized him.

My stomach turned. I followed his gaze, expecting to see a new group of hunters waiting for us.

Instead, the entire hill above us was lined with uniformed soldiers. They stared down at us with no expression. The glint of silver at the waist betrayed their weapons, and I had a feeling their magical skills were nothing to laugh at.

I was almost numb to the sight. There had to be at least two dozen of them. I wasn't sure I had the strength left to face them all.

But I promised I would never give up.

I struggled to my feet and lifted my palms, ready to fight.

To my surprise, a tall demon stepped forward from the small army. His laughter boomed throughout the quarry.

Confused, I stared at him, not dropping my stance.

He walked down the side of the hill toward me, a crooked smile on his face. He shook his head. "It's uncanny," he said. "You're just like your father."

WELCOME HOME

I struggled to stay on my feet.

"I don't know what you're talking about," I said.

"My name is Gregory," he said. He held his hand out to me, but I was so disoriented and confused, I didn't know whether to trust him or fight him.

"What are you doing here?" I asked, looking up at the soldiers.

"My men and I patrol the lands on the outskirts of the Center," he said. "We'd been tracking this group of hunters when they suddenly disappeared. It took us a while to find them again and believe me, we were shocked to see that they'd been taken care of."

Gregory leaned down to examine the block of ice and rocks that still encased the third hunter.

"Do you think she's dead?" I asked.

"I doubt it," he said. "These things are extremely difficult to kill. Especially when it's three against two. You're lucky to be alive."

"We know," Jackson said. "Too bad you guys didn't come along a little sooner."

"We only caught the tail end of the fight," Gregory said, looking at me with one raised eyebrow.

I ducked my head, wondering if he'd seen what happened to me. I still didn't understand it myself.

"What did you mean about my father?" I asked. "How could you possibly know who my father is?"

Gregory smiled. "Your father is a dear friend of mine," he said. "I can take you to him if you'd like to meet him. I know he'll be very happy to see you."

For the second time in ten minutes, I felt the breath knocked from my chest. How could this be? My father was here? In the shadow world? What was he doing here? Had he been here my whole life?

"Does he know I'm here?" I asked, not sure what else to say.

"I sent a runner back to the Center," he said. "I imagine by now everyone knows you're here. Word spreads fast in the city."

Jackson took my hand. "Do you think he could be telling the truth?" he whispered in my ear. "Could your father really be here?"

"I don't know," I said. My mind was spinning. I turned back to Gregory. "How do we know we won't be in any danger in your city?"

He smiled and laughed, shaking his head. "I promise, Harper."

My mouth opened in surprise. "How do you know my name?"

"A lot of demons in this area know your name," he said. "You're kind of famous around here, actually."

None of this made sense. I wondered just how hard I had hit my head back there.

"I promise, once you get to the city, your wounds will be looked after," he said. "As will the wounds of your small friend there. He needs immediate medical attention. You'll be completely free to come and go, and I can assure you, you'll be much safer there than you will be out here alone. Especially now that the hunters can track your magic to this spot."

Jackson nodded. "I think we should go," he said.

I had no idea if this soldier really knew who my father was, but after wondering about my father for my whole life, I had to know one way or the other. And I needed to get the boy to safety.

"Okay," I said. "We'll come with you. How far is it to the Center?"

"We can get there almost instantly," Gregory said. "Just take my hand."

I hesitated. Jackson picked up the child, took one of my hands and nodded. I reached out and grabbed Gregory's hand. The feeling of falling and rushing forward at the same time took over. We shifted into smoke and flew through the air at amazing speeds. Before I had even gotten used to the feeling of being light and fast, we came to a halt just outside an arched gate made of pure silver.

It took a moment for me to get my breath, but once I did, I gasped at the beauty of this place. We stood on the outskirts of a gigantic domed city. I took a step back, trying to take it all in. I turned and saw that behind us was the same beautiful scenery we'd been walking through for two days. The domed city seemed out of place here.

A soldier stepped forward and took the boy from Jackson's arms. "We'll get him to our shamans right away," the soldier said.

"You'll find us when he's better?" I asked.

The soldier nodded, then disappeared inside the dome.

"What is this place?" Jackson asked.

"This is the one remaining city in the Southern Kingdom," Gregory explained. "Years ago, the King of the South started an initiative to move all citizens into one central location where everyone could be guarded and safe. Over time, the entire country moved into the safety of what we call the Center."

"And the dome?" I asked. "What's that for?"

"The dome is a special kind of barrier that keeps anyone inside from casting human magic," he said. "Pure demon magic still works, but human magic simply doesn't work. If a hunter were to enter through this archway, they would be completely powerless."

"Amazing," Jackson said.

I was actually grateful for the conversation. The thought of possibly meeting my father after all these years scared me to death. It had already been one of the most emotional weeks of my entire life. How much more could my heart take at this point?

"We'd better get inside," Gregory said. He motioned for us to go ahead.

Jackson and I passed through the archway and into the streets of the Center. The city sat on a long hillside with a large, ornate castle at the very top of the hill.

Gregory led us up through the main path and as we walked, a crowd began to gather on both sides of the street. Everyone stared at me, whispering. Had word about my battle with the hunters spread this far already?

"What's going on here?" I whispered to Jackson.

"I'm not sure," he said. "But Harper, there are both humans and demons living here. I know everyone looks the same to you, but it's amazing. I've never seen this kind of community before. The Southern Kingdom is nothing like we thought."

We continued up the hill, the streets becoming more and more crowded. Several people bowed their heads down low as I passed. Confused, I nodded to them, unsure what exactly was going on. "How much farther?" I asked.

Gregory looked up toward the castle. "Not much farther now," he said.

In minutes, we had reached the steps of the castle. With shaky legs, I walked to the top. Gregory led us through an enormous entryway, then straight up a beautiful crystal staircase to the second floor. We followed him down a long corridor, my heart beating so fast in my chest.

As we approached a set of tall double doors, servants on either side opened them to reveal a large open room. With tentative steps, I walked inside, my eyes fixing on the golden throne at the far end. I turned back to question Gregory, but he had bowed down, his knees touching the ground.

Confused, I glanced back to the throne room. Then I saw him. There, standing in a strip of sunlight, his back turned, was the King of the South.

I took a step toward him, feeling strangely drawn in his direction.

When he heard my footsteps, he turned slowly, his silver eyes lighting from within.

I gasped. I recognized this man from my dream. From the vision I had when I touched the shaman. His cheerful face broke out in a wide smile and he opened his arms to me.

"Welcome home, daughter."

ONLY THE BEGINNING

I stood frozen in the moment.

I stared at this familiar yet foreign face and instantly knew he was telling the truth. I didn't know how or when, but I knew in that instant that this demon, this king, was my father.

He moved toward me, tears shimmering in his eyes despite his smile. My feet broke free of the floor's hold on them, and I ran forward to meet him, letting his arms wrap around me.

"Oh, Harper," he said, his tears falling like diamonds into my hair. "You have no idea how long I have longed for this moment. Let me look at you."

He held me at arm's length and studied my face. He picked up one of my curls and his smile grew sad. "You look so much like your mother."

"I have so many questions," I said, not knowing where to begin. It was as if a whole new life had just opened up to me. I thought of the strange white smoke. "Am I a demon?"

The king laughed. "Half," he said. "Actually, a little more than half, but we'll get to all that in time, I promise."

Jackson joined us, and I reached out to take his hand.

"And this must be Jackson," the king said. He extended a hand and the two shook.

"It's an honor to meet you, sir," he said, putting his arm around me. "It sounds like you know a lot more about us than we know about you. I think we all have a lot to talk about."

"Yes, yes," the king said, wiping the tears from his bearded face. "There will be plenty of time for your questions. But come. Harper, the people of the kingdom have waited so long to meet you. I'm sure they've all heard of your victory today, too. Your inner strength never ceases to amaze me. I have never felt so proud in my life."

Hot tears filled my eyes. My father was proud of me. Those were words I never thought I'd hear in my life. In all my years, I had never met a single soul who belonged to me. I had never known anyone who could truly be called family.

Until now.

At his urging, I stepped out onto the large stone balcony. Cheers rang out as the crowds below came into view. Fireworks soared into the air and burst into various colors. I stared out; not believing this could be real.

Someone down below shouted out, "Welcome home, Princess Harper."

I gasped, my hand flying to my chest. Princess? Me? Now I knew I must be dreaming.

"Can this be real?" I asked.

Jackson took my hand and gave it a hard squeeze.

On my other side, my father put his arm around me, then

thrust his other fist high into the air. A roaring cheer went up from the people below, filling my ears with sounds of joyful celebration.

"It's real," my father said, hugging me tight. "And I promise you, it's only the beginning."

ABOUT THE AUTHOR

Sarra Cannon is the author of several series featuring young adult and college-aged characters, including the bestselling Shadow Demons Saga. Her novels often stem from her own experiences growing up in the small town of Hawkinsville, Georgia, where she learned that being popular always comes at a price and relationships are rarely as simple as they seem.

Sarra recently celebrated seven years in indie publishing

and has sold over half a million copies of her books. She currently lives in Charleston, South Carolina with her programmer husband and adorable redheaded son.

Love Sarra's books? Join Sarra's Mailing List to be notified of new releases and giveaways!

Also, please come hang out with me in my Facebook Fan Group: Sarra Cannon's Coven. We have a lot of fun in there, and I often share exclusive short stories and teasers in the group. Join now.

Want more? Get insider information on my writing process, inspiration, and what it's like to be an author with weekly videos on my YouTube channel.

Connect With Sarra Online:

www.sarracannon.com

Made in the USA
Middletown, DE
24 September 2020